Praise for MONSTER MYSTERI

Amazon #1 Bestseller in Marine Biology (non-fiction)
　　　　　　　　　　　　–**Amazon Kindle Books**

Amazon #1 New Release in Paleontology (non-fiction)
　　　　　　　　　　　　–**Amazon Kindle Books**

Amazon #1 New Release in Marine Biology (non-fiction)
　　　　　　　　　　　　–**Amazon Kindle Books**

Praise for KRONOS RISING: KRAKEN (vol. 3)

"A great finale to a brilliant series. Gripping from the word go and breathtaking all the way to the jaw-dropping climax. Max Hawthorne does it again, as only he can!"
　　　　–**Peter Tonkin, bestselling author of 45 novels, including *Killer***

"Max Hawthorne's climactic finish to his award-winning Kraken trilogy latches onto you with all the power and ferocity of its legendary namesake and doesn't let go. A truly heart-pounding and well-crafted conclusion."
　　　　–**G. Michael Hopf, bestselling author of *The End***

"The Kronos Rising: Kraken series requires a finale as big and bad as its name — and Hawthorne delivers. Fast and edgy, Kraken 3 pits strong protagonists against their most nefarious nemeses, with plenty of nail-biting action to keep you flipping pages."
　　–**Kurt Anderson, author of *Devour* and *Resurrection Pass***

Praise for I WANT A TYRANNOSAURUS FOR CHRISTMAS

"One of the cutest books to come on the market for children. This book is perfect to snuggle up and share with a child, as the beautiful illustrations really capture a child's attention."
–Dr. Melissa Caudle, bestselling author of A Day at the Zoo

"Perfect read for young dinosaur fans who have always wanted a dinosaur of their own . . . told with amusing illustrations and filled with messages of kindness, giving and friendship!"
–Jason Zucker, Walt Disney artist

"A fun, sentimental, and beautifully illustrated romp for any kid who loves dinosaurs--which is all of them! I wish I'd had this book when I was a budding 6-year-old paleontologist. I would've read it to pieces."
–Martin Powell, Golden Moonbeam Award Winner

Praise for KRONOS RISING: KRAKEN (vol. 2)

". . . it takes some of the lessons nobody ever learned in Jurassic Park and ups the voltage exponentially . . .the ultimate aquatic smackdown, and it's gonzo good action fun."
–The Horror Fiction Review

"Kronos Rising: Kraken (vol. 2): 2018 Gold Medal winner" (action/adventure category)
–AUTHORSdb

"Master of Marine Terror, Max Hawthorne pens the perfectly crafted blockbuster, taking his readers on the thrill ride of their lives! To say that 'Kronos Rising: Kraken (Volume 2) is a 'page turner' is an understatement! Equally rivaling the likes of Crichton's 'Jurassic World', Benchley's 'Jaws' and Alten's 'MEG' book and movie franchises, 'Kraken V2' truly earns its proverbial place on the shelf! Hawthorne's 'Kraken V2' reads like a bullet train thrill ride from the first gripping page and takes you hostage until the explosive end! Hawthorne's original characters possess the dimension and sparkle, deserving of a cast of Hollywood's top A-list stars to bring them to life on the big screen! It's brilliant storytelling and THE way a story should be told! Now, that's entertainment!!!"

–Kevin Sasaki, Media Representative

". . . unrelenting suspense, incredible action sequences, vividly realized characters, and unexpected plot twists that nail you to the page. Get this book immediately if you love a great sea monster story!"

–Monster X Radio

Praise for KRONOS RISING: PLAGUE

KRONOS RISING: PLAGUE: 2016 Gold Medal Winner (horror category)

–AUTHORSdb

"The entire horror universe now has a new writer . . . a delightful edge-of-your-seater, guaranteed to leave readers wanting to keep the lights on."

–YeahStub.com

"Max spins another harrowing, action-packed monster tale, painstakingly researched, and rich in scenic and historic detail, while delivering the same true-to-form, page-turning intensity as always."

–The Crypto Crew

Praise for KRONOS RISING: DIABLO

"*Kronos Rising: Diablo*, one of 2016's Top Ten Books!"

–AUTHORSdb

"... the story retains Max Hawthorne's uncanny ability to make his monsters feel like characters in their own right, as well as his innate aptitude when it comes to invoking a sense of awe and wonder in the reader."

–Geek Ireland

"A riveting offshoot of the wonderful Max Hawthorne books, *Kronos Rising* and *Kraken*! Keeps the excitement and momentum of those stories going strong! More, more, more!!"

–Kevin Sasaki, Media Representative

Praise for KRONOS RISING: KRAKEN (vol. 1)

"It's *Jurassic World* on steroids . . . a fun, fast read even if you have to take the kids to the ball game and mow the lawn."

–From My Shelf Books

"KRONOS RISING: KRAKEN (vol. 1): 2016's People's Choice Award Winner & Book of the Year!"

–Geek Ireland

"Hawthorne's writing evokes a sense of awe and terror, tapping into a deeply-rooted and primal fear of the unknown. The Kraken possesses an otherworldly aura which is hard to describe, but it really makes your skin crawl."

–Sean Markey, DinoGuy

"While most authors would have played it safe and stuck to a formula emulating the successful elements of the first novel (think the "Meg" series), Hawthorne's vision is cast on a larger canvas. KRAKEN jumps ahead 30 years into the future, depicting a worldwide ecological shift in earth's oceans as a consequence of the events in the first novel. Hawthorne certainly knows how to tell and pace a fine adventure tale, in the tradition of Robert E. Howard."

–Cryptomundo

Praise for KRONOS RISING

". . . a master class in the suspension of disbelief. Kronos Rising is reminiscent of the work of Michael Crichton (Jurassic Park, Congo) in that it weaves together an exciting and gripping yarn which, despite depicting fantastical subject matter, doesn't insult the reader's intelligence by appealing to the lowest common denominator."

–Krank.ie

"*KRONOS RISING* by Max Hathorne; 2014's PIX Book of the Year!"

–Prehistoric Times Magazine

"Batten down the hatches and brace yourself . . . Hawthorne delivers suspense at a breakneck pace in his terrifying debut."
–Ryan Lockwood, Author of *Below*

"A word to the wise: if you bite your nails, you'd better wear oven mitts when reading *Kronos Rising*. It will drag you down to the depths of fear and take you back for a breath of air as fast as you can turn the pages. Readers beware: a new Master of Marine terror is in your bookstore, and his name is Max Hawthorne!"
**–Stan Pottinger,
NY Times Bestselling author of *THE BOSS***

"*Kronos Rising* takes readers on a roller coaster ride of gigantic scale. We're talking prehistoric big."
–Toledo Free Press

". . . a great addition to this genre, worthy of sitting on the shelf next to Peter Benchley's *Jaws*."
–Publisher's Weekly/Book Life

". . . a fabulous debut by Max Hawthorne. Simply put, it's got teeth. Big ones!"
–Chris Parker, screenwriter (*Vampire in Brooklyn, Battle of the Year, Heaven is for Real*)

"What a ride! An adrenaline pumping, non-stop descent into terror, *Kronos Rising* will do for this generation what "JAWS" did for the last one. Forget going *into* the water; I'm not going *near* it!"
–Mara Corday, sci-fi classic star of *Tarantula, The Black Scorpion,* and *The Giant Claw*

Praise for MEMOIRS OF A GYM RAT

"Max Hawthorne's raunchy, revealing memoir is certain to induce bouts of calorie-burning laughter, embarrassed grins, and reconsiderations of one's gym membership. A smutty and enjoyable exposé of life behind health club doors, *Memoirs of a Gym Rat* is both a scandalizing and edifying read."

–Foreword Clarion Reviews

THE SLEIGH

A NOVEL

Max Hawthorne

FAR FROM THE TREE PRESS

The Sleigh is a work of fiction. Names, characters, places, and incidents are either the products of the author's imagination or are used fictitiously. Any resemblance to actual persons, living or dead, events or locales, is entirely coincidental.

Copyright: ©2021 by Max Hawthorne & *Far From The Tree Press, LLC*
Copyright ©2017 (script) by Max Hawthorne & *Far From The Tree Press, LLC*

ISBN-Hardcover: 9781732378582
ISBN-Paperback: 9781732378599

All rights reserved. No part of this book may be copied, scanned, used or reproduced in any manner whatsoever without written permission, except in the case of brief quotations embodied in critical articles or reviews. For more information contact: *Far From the Tree Press, LLC.*

Published in the United States by: *Far From the Tree Press, LLC.*

Visit *Far From the Tree Press, LLC* online at: www.farfromthetreepress.com

Manufactured in the United States of America

First Edition

Sale of this book without a front cover may be unauthorized. If this book is coverless, it may have been reported to the publisher as "lost and destroyed" and neither the author nor the publisher may have received payment for it.

*For my daughter Ava, and for all the other children of the world.
One day, someone will tell you that Santa Claus isn't real.
What they really mean is, he's not real for them.
Remember that.*

"Fear grows in darkness; if you think there's a bogeyman around, turn on the light."

- Dorothy Thompson

ACKNOWLEDGMENTS

It is with great humility and pride that I acknowledge the following individuals for their support and/or contributions to this book.

First and foremost, I'd like to give a big shout-out to the following radio/podcast personalities whose shows I've been privileged to appear on. That includes Hadley Thorne, Morgana Calder, Henry Tully, Cecile Fletcher, and Steven Hill over at *Wyrd Realities,* Mark Eddy at *Night-Light,* D.A. Roberts at *Ex Machina,* Kat Hobson at *Fate Mag Radio,* Matthew Bennett at *Introspection,* Michael W. Hall and Dave Scott at *Spaced Out Sundays,* and Richard Syrett over at *Coast to Coast AM* and *Conspiracy Unlimited.* Also, respect to Solaris Blueraven from *Hyperspace,* Tim Weisberg over at *Midnight FM,* and Craig Ansell, Chris Harmon, and Austin Burke at *3 Beards Podcast.* Two thumbs up for Kelly Steffen from the *Sky Door Network;* I'm looking forward to the podcast version of *Max Hawthorne's Monsters and Marine Mysteries* finally surfacing.

I'd be remiss if I didn't express my gratitude to artist extraordinaire Nancy Afroditae for completing an amazing cover art painting for *The Sleigh.* I'm a real tyrant – I mean *perfectionist* – when it comes to getting book covers the way I want. In addition to talent, Nancy exhibited poise, patience, and wholeheartedly shared my vision. Very well done. Also, props to graphics artist Lana B. for implementing the perfect fonts that helped bring *The Sleigh*'s cover to life.

As always, a nod to my invaluable Grammar-Nazi-slaying editor, Willis Beyer, for taking the time to review the book. Also, special thanks to retired agent Michael Larsen (of Larsen-Pomada Literary Agency fame) for giving me some terrific feedback on my opening scene.

Of course, hugs and back scratches to my (really my daughter's) two gorgeous Siberian Forest cats, Mace and Olaf. Thank you for surrounding me with love, laughter, and oodles of cat hair, and for keeping me company when I write.

Last, but certainly not least, to my always supportive family, in particular my beloved daughter Ava (AKA my raison d'etre), my everlasting devotion. And to my readers, including the eternally enthusiastic (but oft impatient) *"LEGIONS OF KRONOS,"* thank you for continuing to tolerate me and my monsters.

As always, there's plenty more where that came from.

– Max Hawthorne
"Prince of Paleofiction"

CHAPTER 1

The sun was a midnight memory when the cry rang out. It was high-pitched and breathless, and in its aftermath came a tinny grating sound, like metallic crepitus.

No sooner had the noise faded, when a dark and foreboding shadow filled the bedroom doorway. It wavered but a moment before starting forward, a phantom invading the little girl's room, weaving its way around an assortment of toys and other obstacles. Its behavior suggested both experience and precision, and the shade's owner took full advantage of the plush carpeting to pad its approach.

Unaware of the intruder, the girl slept on, sheltered within her cocoon of soft blankets and fuzzy pajamas. Emboldened, the shadow crept closer, only to freeze as she shifted unexpectedly. It hesitated, waiting for her to relax. The moment she did it resumed its approach, drawing ever nearer until, finally, its towering form loomed over the innocent child.

It studied her intently. Her cherubic face was hard to make out, illuminated as it was by little more than a butterfly-shaped night-lite and the lone shaft of moonlight that struggled to pierce her room's tightly-drawn blinds.

The shadow inhaled sharply as the girl, perhaps detecting its proximity, began to flail. Eyes closed but arms extended beseechingly, she cried out once, twice, then sank back once more into her dreams. Oblivious to everything around her, she failed to detect the hand above her as it started to descend.

Down it came, its fingers outstretched. It moved purposefully, passing first her, then her mattress, then her mahogany bed frame. All the way to the floor it went, until it reached its target.

Her unicorn-colored teddy bear.

Strong-yet-supple fingers latched onto the lost treasure, hoisting it aloft. Then the hand began to rise. Its partner joined in and, through their combined efforts, the bear was placed gently against the little girl's chest. She sensed its presence immediately; her delicate arms wrapped around it and she hugged it tightly, smiling and sighing blissfully as she descended into a deeper and less troubled slumber.

Stepping carefully back as he retreated toward the doorway, Doctor Donald McKinley smiled lovingly down at his sleeping daughter. "Goodnight, Amy," he whispered, before softly closing her bedroom door.

Whew, that was a close one, Don thought, one hand patting his heart while the other brushed a lock from his sweat-dampened brow. *No Mr. Sparkles? We almost had a nightmare on our hands!*

Grinning now, the relieved dad moved silently through his family's residence. He noticed that his wife Amanda was absent from her usual perch on the sofa, then remembered her mentioning she was going to take a shower. That was a few minutes before Amy called out.

Don hesitated outside the doors to his study, his forehead creasing up. He considered going back in to review his notes for tomorrow's procedures one more time, but a glance at the hallway's aged grandfather clock quickly changed his mind. Losing any more sleep would be a moronic move on his part. It was late and he had a full day ahead of him.

He paused to roll out aching shoulders, then cricked his stiff neck from side to side.

No worries. I could do those breast augmentations in my sleep. Well, except for the poor Reiner girl's, he conceded. *Fixing the disaster left behind by that Pakistani butcher she went to won't be easy – the dislodged implants is one thing, but the scarring left by the infections he caused is the worst I've ever seen. Still, I made her and her mom a promise and I intend to keep it.*

Don exhaled through his nostrils as he carefully closed the doors to his study. He glanced up as his assorted degrees on a nearby wall and gave himself a barely perceptible nod of self-acknowledgment. At age forty-four, he was one of the East Coast's most sought-after cosmetic surgeons. It was a reputation he'd earned with syringe and scalpel, and hands that many of his clients claimed possessed actual magic.

He didn't know about the "magic" part, but getting to that point had been no mean feat. Coming as he had from an impoverished background had made things particularly challenging, especially back in college when he'd discovered that, based on his ethnicity, getting a medical school scholarship was nothing but a pipe dream. Undeterred, he'd gritted his teeth and seen things through. All the hard work, sleepless nights, and a veritable mountain of student loan debt had eventually paid off. He was at the top of his game now and pulling in almost twice as much as a President of the United States.

Well, an honest President, at least.

Don took pride in his hard-won success, but he made it a point to keep things in perspective. He'd learned early on that money had a way of changing people, and usually not for the better. He accepted that as a matter of course. But unlike many of his peers, he'd managed to avoid falling victim to the "cash cow apathy" that accompanied their high-paying careers.

He'd watched, time and time again, as they began to see their clients as dollar signs instead of people.

He, on the other hand, always tried to focus on what drew him to his chosen field in the first place – using his God-given talents to improve the quality of his patients' lives. Inevitably, that brought to mind the one thing that never failed to infuriate him; the seemingly endless parade of cowboys that popped up, hawking their wares while proclaiming themselves "board certified plastic surgeons", and taking advantage of people's trust.

Often, with disastrous results.

Plastic . . .

Don shook his head in disgust. The word was sadly apropos. There were times when, while wading through the aftermath of their incompetence, he found himself wondering if half of those charlatans had honed their so-called skills by practicing on actual Barbie dolls.

It was no wonder his malpractice premiums were so exorbitant.

His face flushed, and he found himself wondering if he was being a tad hypocritical. After all, a large chunk of his business came from salvaging what others had ruined. Granted, it felt good making things right. But it was difficult looking into the distraught and distrusting eyes of people whose noses, chins, or chests ended up looking like they'd spent their formative years skinny dipping in the waters around Fukushima.

Of course, rebuilding and reshaping the human body was where he shined. To hear his parents tell it, it was in his DNA. And always had been.

Don paused outside the living room, running his fingers contemplatively along a section of their home's ornate crown molding and relishing the intricacies of its smooth-shorn edges.

He remembered how, as a child, his room had always been littered with blocks of clay and worked and reworked tubs of Play-Doh.

He'd always had a passion for creating. He loved making and shaping faces and figures – everything from his parents and pets to his favorite superheroes and anime characters. He'd fantasized that, one day, he'd become a renowned sculptor like Michelangelo. Ironically, he had. Except that, instead of working with lifeless marble or bronze, he was carving people: their outsides and, to hear them say it, in some instances, their souls.

He couldn't understand what was wrong with so many of his colleagues. His work was something he could never become apathetic about. He found it more than just rewarding. He reveled in it.

And why shouldn't he? He was in the business of changing lives.

When it came to his or anyone else's face or form, Don had a simple philosophy: everyone had what he considered to be a sacred duty to take care of themselves. That included not just engaging in proper nutrition and exercise, but also making sure to avoid pitfalls such as tobacco and recreational drugs like the plague.

It was only natural. As he told his clients, *'Our bodies are the vehicles that carry us through life. In fact, they are the only thing that we really, truly own. Short of killing us, they are the one thing no one can take from us. What we see when we look in the mirror each day has a direct impact on how we feel about ourselves, and how the world responds to us. Therefore, we owe it to ourselves, our spouses, and our children and grandchildren to always be the best we can be, both physically and spiritually.'*

Chuckling as he realized he was giving himself the same lecture he gave his patients; Don entered their spacious living room. He looked around and smiled. Christmas Eve was just a few days away. As usual, their residence was adorned in full holiday regalia. The illuminated garlands, faux-fur-trimmed, oversized stockings, and a bedazzled nine-foot blue spruce, topped with a blazing five-point star . . . it was like a scene from a holiday picture postcard. As Amy put it, Christmas was when, for a few weeks each year, their "boring old house" got to look like Santa's workshop.

She was right.

Don looked up, taking in the living room's soaring ceiling and the huge blackwood beams that supported it like buttresses in a cathedral. He let slip a sigh of contentment that rivaled his daughter's. He had to admit, the way things were going, he and his family must be blessed.

There was no other explanation for it.

In just eight years, they'd gone from a modest two-bedroom apartment in Rutherford, New Jersey to an upper-class Manhattan residence that looked like a magazine spread shot in oldtown Prague; a huge, loft-style apartment with hand-wrought, suspended light fixtures, elegantly framed floor-to-ceiling windows, and polished sandalwood floors that both looked and smelled divine. The white walls, coupled with an abundance of sunlight, offset the dark ceiling timbers and kept the place feeling light and airy. Combined with its tasteful décor, it literally *oozed* comfort and style. Everyone who'd visited their home went gaga – something his wife never tired of.

True, buying a place like that – on Central Park South, no less – was a major investment. In fact, it represented a substantial portion of the family's combined savings. When Don had first heard the price, he'd balked. He felt it was simply too much too soon. That was, until they'd toured the property, took in the views, and, of course, laid eyes on the fireplace.

Amanda fell in love with the outsized ingle the moment she saw it. After an initial inspection, Don couldn't blame her. At a full six feet in width and nearly as high, the antique French Rococo statuary fireplace had been flawlessly crafted from a single block of ivory marble. Its ornate paneled frieze and bracketed jambs were adorned with woven trails of flowers and vines, and offset a spectacular serpentine-shaped opening trimmed with exquisite beading. Topping all of that was a custom-shaped shelf with inlaid egg molding. The antique hearth was clearly the result of hundreds of hours of toiling by a master craftsman – a labor of love the talented surgeon could truly relate to.

After that, acquiring the property was a foregone conclusion. Of course, the fireplace had to be upgraded from wood to gas – Don loved a traditional fire, but had no time for such things. Once the work was complete, it was the perfect centerpiece for their home. Not to mention, the ideal location for the pricey flatscreen that hung directly above it.

Don's expression grew grim as his eyes lifted from the fireplace's comforting flames to the muted TV. There was a news broadcast on, discussing the previous night's Manhattan murder spree. The victims – a well-to-do family – had been found butchered in their beds. The culprits were a gang of maniacal cultists, and a member of the victims' immediate family was apparently one of them. At least, that's what the media was claiming.

Of course, with those guys you never knew.

Don glanced back toward their high windows, out at the darkness beyond. His incisors started worrying his lower lip. Then his stubborn streak kicked in and he tamped down on his burgeoning paranoia. He was being illogical; there was nothing to be concerned about. They were in a private building, protected by armed guards, and warded by more security cameras than most banks.

Not to mention, there was no fire escape and they were five stories up.

Don scoffed as he clicked off the set and returned the remote to its tray. There was nothing to worry about. Of course, they'd be fine. He knew that.

Still, the uneasiness remained.

He frowned at his inability to shake the feeling and headed into the master bedroom to get ready for bed. He could hear the shower still running in the master bath and rapped his knuckles hard against the door.

"Honey, can I come in?"

To his surprise, the door was slightly ajar and opened a few inches from the force of his knock.

"Hon, are you in here?"

When no reply was forthcoming, Don opened the door enough that he could peek in.

"Babe, are you—"

His words morphed into a startled gasp and he flung the door the rest of the way open. The glass door to their shower was wide open and water was spraying out onto the bathroom's tiled floor.

Far more concerning, however, was what was *on* the floor.

Don nearly took a header on the wet tiles as he rushed into the steamy room. Steadying himself, he dropped down onto one knee and reached down to confirm that his eyes weren't playing tricks on him.

They weren't. There was a discolored towel on the floor. It had a series of foot-long rents in it and was stained with blood.

A lot of blood.

"Amanda!"

Head snapping up, Don lunged for the doorhandles of his and his wife's matching toilet rooms. Yanking both open, his head whipped from side to side like a windshield wiper. He expected to find her inside one room or the other; perhaps struggling with the sudden onset of an unusually heavy menstrual flow, which could explain the bleeding. Or, God forbid, she might be having a miscarriage.

Of course, Don conceded, there was nothing in their history together that suggested either of those circumstances was at all likely. But they were the only "safe" possibilities his science-minded brain could come up with.

He was wrong. Both rooms were empty. His wife wasn't there. All he had was an abandoned shower and a ruined towel. And blood. Not just on the towel, either, he realized. It was all over the floor, too. He hadn't noticed it at first because the steam and spray had diluted it. In fact, upon closer inspection he discovered there was—

A trail of it . . .

Don's eyes turned to hen's eggs as he espied the pinkish footprints leading to the bathroom door. They were Amanda's. From the look of things, there had been a struggle, after which she'd been dragged or, perhaps, carried out. He looked closer and swore silently.

There was another track mixed in with hers. It was a partial heel print of some kind.

A big one.

Don ground his molars in an effort to clamp down on the fear that sought to unnerve him. They had an intruder. There was someone in the house and, whoever it was, he had Amanda.

His heart pounding, he rushed back into the master bedroom and made a beeline for their tiny wall safe. It took him three tries with fumbling fingers to enter the four-digit security code, after which he extracted a stainless-steel .357 magnum revolver. His hands were trembling so badly he could barely pop open the weighty weapon's cylinder to confirm it was loaded.

It was right after closing it, however, that he heard the thump.

It wasn't the sound of their home's heating system kicking in; he knew that sound like he knew his phone's ringtone. This was reminiscent of something heavy being dropped. It sounded like it had come from within the apartment, somewhere outside the master bedroom.

Feeling more confident with the gun in his hand, Don tiptoed toward the door. A glance at Amy's baby monitor confirmed that she was still in bed, and he was grateful to release the breath he'd been holding. He took hold of the doorknob, gave a few quick pants, cocked the revolver's hammer back, and then yanked it open.

There was nothing.

A disturbing thought came to him, and he decided to uncock the gun and keep the barrel pointed skyward before starting forward. He could feel his heart beating like a hummingbird's and he did his best to slow his breathing. Ten years earlier, he'd had some basic self-defense training, including a required firearms class, but he knew he was no warrior. Nor was he a fool. He realized he was in over his head. The safest thing would've undoubtedly been to call the police, or at least the building's security, but he didn't; his instincts told him there wasn't time.

Whatever had happened was still happening.

He had to protect his family. And he had to do it now.

Swallowing nervously, Don moved through the kitchen. Drops of fresh blood lay every few feet – several badly smeared – and, as he checked his feet, he realized he'd walked over them without noticing. He steeled himself, then followed the trail of gory breadcrumbs into the living room. When he got to their lit-up Christmas tree, he hesitated. He half-expected to find the intruder crouched behind it with a knife to his wife's throat but, as he sprang to the far side, pistol at the ready, he found nothing.

As he approached the imposing fireplace, however, Don spotted something odd. The ornate metal fire screen doors they'd had installed – the ones Amy picked out, shaped like the burning bush on Mt. Sinai – was open. Even stranger, there was ash, actual *ash*, all over the carpet, starting at the hearth's surrounding stonework.

Don's mind spun and he tried making sense of this bizarre development. Theirs was a gas fireplace, so where had the ash come from? Had someone entered the apartment and burned something, perhaps to get rid of some incriminating evidence – evidence of this crime or a previous one? It galled him that someone had gotten into their home to begin with, let alone managed to swing open a pair of heavy-gauge wrought iron fire screens and stand there, messily burning things. How could he not have noticed? And why hadn't the burglar alarm gone off?

He vacillated, his brow furrowing up. There was something strange going on. Maybe he should at least notify the--

The sudden gnashing sound that waylaid the frightened surgeon's thoughts made the hairs on his nape prick up. He had no idea what had caused it, but he had a pretty good idea as to its point of origin.

It was coming from the hallway, just beyond the living room.

"Daddy?"

Jesus Christ!

Amy materializing behind him nearly gave Don an apoplexy. With his eyes bugging out, he wheeled in her direction. He took a calming breath and, with the revolver concealed behind his thigh, dropped into a crouch, shushing her and cautioning her to keep silent. Then, with her following a few yards back, he advanced toward the source of the strange rasping noise. Whatever it was, it was rhythmic; it repeated itself every five seconds or so, and he used that to home in on it.

With its protective screens open, the heat from the fireplace was incredible. As he inched past it, Don could feel the perspiration trickling down his chest and back. He glanced back at Amy and his brows tightened. Then he reached out with his free hand and quietly swung the fire screen doors closed. As he did, a bit of shadowy movement on the mantle drew his eye. He found himself locking gazes with one of Amanda's expensive Santa Claus figurines. He shook his head. In the flickering firelight, its smile looked almost creepy, and he could swear the thing was watching him.

Chiding himself, Don continued on. He could feel still-warm ash crumbling underfoot, but refused to take his eyes off the hallway ahead. Ten yards further, the blood trail came to an abrupt end. Besides the big grandfather clock, there was nothing there except the hallway closet, just a few feet from his study.

He heard the gnashing sound again, and paused to wipe the sheen of sweat from his brow with the back of one forearm. The sound seemed to be emanating from the closet. With his target sighted and Amy a safe distance behind him, he advanced, the heavy revolver extended before him.

He was almost there when the smell hit him.

It was an awful sulfurous stench that made him gag. What the hell *was* that? Had the intruder ruptured a sewer pipe?

No. The smell may have permeated the entire hallway, but it grew noticeably stronger the closer he got to the closet. Whoever had taken Amanda was in there and he had her with him. It was the only possible explanation.

Don drew a breath and held it. He realized it was time to make his move but, for some reason, when he tried he discovered he couldn't. For the first time in his life he didn't know what to do. He'd seen situations like this on TV a hundred times, but he wasn't a police officer or part of a SWAT team.

What if something went wrong?

What if he screwed up?

Oh, God . . . can I actually do this?

A hundred nightmarish scenarios flooded Don's brain, and a moment later, he felt panic's chilling embrace. It wrapped around him like icy tentacles, freezing him into immobility. He tried to fight it, to leap into action and be the hero, but strive as he might he couldn't force his ash-and-sweat-stained feet to take those final, life-altering steps.

In a daze, he felt Amy tugging at his pajama sleeve. "Daddy, someone's in there," she whispered, pointing at the closet.

It was his daughter's tiny voice that finally gave Don the strength to break the chains that bound him. One glance into those big, brown eyes of hers – eyes searching for the strength and security he'd always provided – and his chest swelled with fatherly pride.

What was he afraid of? He could *do* this.

He blew out a huge breath, gave her a reassuring smile, and then gestured for her to take shelter behind the big clock, Then, gun at the ready, he yanked the closet door open and peered inside.

An even fouler stench washed over him, and it took a moment for his eyes to adjust to the darkness. What he saw then turned his blood to ice. There was someone in there, alright.

No, not someone. Some *thing*.

Don couldn't see it clearly – the closet was room-sized and it was crouched in the back – but it was there. It looked like a man, but it was big and dark and had a hunched-over look. It was immobile except for what he assumed was its head, which periodically twisted from side to side, then pulled back. He didn't know what it was doing, but it was definitely the source of the unnerving crunching sounds.

It finally dawned on him that what he was hearing were the sounds of mastication. Whatever it was, it was eating something. But what?

The figure shifted as if reading his thoughts, and something small and pale flopped from its lap into the light. Don stared confusedly down at it, his anxious eyes blinking over and over, as if by doing so he could somehow change or alter what he was looking at.

It was an arm.

Amanda's arm.

It was limp and pale as a piece of paper, and blood was streaming down it in crimson rivulets that spilled onto the floor. It appeared lifeless, yet every so often it would twitch in conjunction with the thing's violent head jerks.

It was eating her. It was eating his wife.

Unable to process the horror of the situation, Don drew in a breath to scream. As he did, the figure opened its eyes. They were red and glittered in the dark, like the eyes of night-hunting lions. He gaped at it in disbelief, then his jaw slowly dropped as it rose up with a crash. It was impossibly tall and twisted, and radiated a malevolence the likes of which he'd never before known.

All of a sudden, its gaze shifted to his daughter, standing terror-stricken behind him. Its beady eyes blinked and it dropped what was left of Amanda.

"Amy, run!" he screamed.

Then he pointed the gun at it and pulled the trigger.

He fired five rounds in rapid succession and watched, wide-eyed, as the .357's hollow point slugs slammed into the intruder like blows from a sledgehammer. It staggered back from the repeated impacts, but it didn't go down. Instead, what passed for its mouth split open and it uttered an unearthly bellow that sent his heart plummeting down into his bowels.

A split second later, it charged.

Vaguely aware of his daughter scrambling to hide, Don had no choice but to stand his ground. Extending the smoking pistol before him like a spear, he aimed for the approaching monstrosity's fang-filled maw.

Just as its jaws enveloped the revolver, and his hand with it, he pulled the trigger one last time.

There was a clap of thunder, then darkness.

CHAPTER 2

Ilsa Dunbar's hazel eyes glittered like a hunting hawk's as she alternately kicked, punched, and shot her way through the custom combat course. Actually, *razed* might have been more apropos. She couldn't help her unbridled enthusiasm. The thirty-by-fifty-foot space that had been the original homeowners' foyer, living, and sitting rooms, and then her parents' home gym, was now fully refitted. Sure, it had been expensive, but it was worth it. The urban-style scenarios allowed her to practice a perfect blend of firearms and close-quarters combat techniques. On top of that, it was a great way to let off steam. She was sure her dad would have approved. After all, a woman in her line of work needed to maintain her edge.

And Ilsa Dunbar was nothing if not well-maintained.

At thirty-four years of age, the veteran homicide detective was at the top of her game. Tough, street-smart, and fearless, she was packing one-hundred-and-forty pounds on her five-foot-eight frame, and was as skilled with her fists and feet as she was with a rifle, pistol, or shotgun.

A brief amateur cage-fighting career, coupled with a stint in the military, had contributed to that, she conceded as she ducked behind cover, just as a plywood "perp" lunged out from behind a corner. She sprang out low, double-tapping the target's painted chest with her laser-tag-style pistol, then holstered her weapon and rushed the man-shaped grappling dummy, five yards to her left. She came at it bobbing and weaving, unloading a stiff jab to the bridge of the free-standing figure's nose, before slipping under its extended left arm and following up with her go-to finishing move: a right hook to the temple that would've rocked any of her old sparring partners.

With her peripherals, Ilsa could see Kareema watching her in the floor-to-ceiling mirrors that lined many of the combat course's outer walls. The teen's youthful eyes went wide as she did a quickdraw and plinked three pop-up bullseye targets in rapid succession, then holstered her pistol once more and made her way toward the one-hundred-twenty-pound Muay Thai heavy bag she had tethered at the end of the course. She loved the seven-foot bag's elongated design. It allowed her to practice full-power kicks with no problem, even to the shins, and the dense padding let her get away with using tactical gloves only, with little fear of injury.

She flew at the bag like a demon and let fly with a spitfire of punches, followed by a series of knee-level roundhouse kicks that sounded like a baseball bat striking leather sofa cushions.

"So, what do you think of the . . . upgraded course?" Ilsa panted after dishing out a few more full-power barrages. She was breathing hard now, but continued to whale away at her towering "opponent".

Kareema eyed her host's sinewy arms with a mixture of apprehension and admiration as she approached. "It's, um . . . pretty cool." She indicated the lit-up control panel on a nearby wall, by the makeshift gym's entrance. "Does it do the same moves every time?"

Ilsa paused to blow a rebellious lock of auburn from in front of her face, then wiped the sweat from her brow with the back of a gloved hand. "The bags and dummies are wherever I place them, naturally, but the pop-up targets are on special tracks that randomly decide which side of their respective obstructions they'll emerge from, as well as their height, speed, etcetera."

"So, for an actual situation, that makes it more real?"

"Something like that."

Ilsa checked the wall clock, then decided she'd call it a few minutes early. She'd noticed Kareema had been coming by more often of late. She lived alone, so she didn't mind, but she suspected the teen was there for a reason; something or someone was bothering her.

She was familiar with Kareema's history. Their impromptu friendship had started six months earlier, after she'd issued her a verbal warning for being involved in a scuffle on the street outside her home. She felt bad for her. Like many kids in New York's crime-ridden neighborhoods, Kareema had grown up fatherless. Worse, she had a mother who worked two jobs, and who left her alone most of the time. At age fifteen, it was a potentially perilous stage for a burgeoning young woman.

On a positive note, at least she had no record – juvie or otherwise. If Ilsa had her way, and with a little guidance, things would stay that way.

"So, um, Ilsa. About what you told me the other day . . ."

Ah, the creep again. So, this is why she came by. Okay, time to go into 'big sister' mode.

"Yes?"

"Are you sure he really just wants to do me?"

Ilsa's lips tightened and she made a show of removing her sweat-soaked gloves while she considered the weight of her words. "Sorry, kiddo. I checked on him. Besides being twelve years older than you, he's got a serious rap sheet – a dealer. He's also fathered five kids with four different women, and owes child support to all of them."

Kareema's eyes tailgated the corners of her frown, straight to the studio's padded floor. "But he said I was special, and that my first time should be special..."

Ilsa felt her maternal instincts kick in and she placed a supportive hand on the girl's shoulder. "Hey, you *are* special. But you deserve a boy who touches *this*," she said, pointing at her heart, "not just *that*."

Her finger lowered, indicating somewhere a little further south.

Kareema nodded and exhaled heavily. "Well, that sucks. 'Cause he's really hot."

"I get it," Ilsa said, nodding. "But you've got to learn to master your basal instincts. Justin is eye-candy, nothing more. Trust me, I--"

"Anyone home?" a distinctively male voice called out, giving both of them a start. "Please don't shoot me."

Ilsa smirked at Kareema and cocked an eyebrow. "Speaking of eye-candy..."

After making a mental note to remind Kareema to properly close the front door after she'd been buzzed in, she watched with veiled interest as her newly assigned partner, Detective Andrew "Andy" Alvilda came bounding up the stairs.

Andy was a recent transfer, all the way from the West Coast. Down at the precinct, he stood out like a nudist on Wall Street, and for reasons above and beyond the khakis and python skin cowboy boots that were his stock and trade. Tall, athletic, and disgustingly handsome, with just the right amount of swagger, he looked like he belonged on *The Bachelor* versus working for the NYPD.

For Ilsa, whose admittedly surly disposition offset her innate buxomness, and who hadn't had a date in six months, Andy was an enigma. They'd spoken on several occasions, and she found him to be as charming as he was annoying. Especially with that wry sense of humor of his. He never said anything overt or disrespectful, but he had this subtle cockiness about him that got under her skin, to the point she couldn't decide whether she wanted to slap that chiseled face of his or sit on it.

Actually, either one would shut him up, she thought, smirking.

A grin creased Andy's square jaw, broadening as he took note of Kareema staring at him, doing the deer-in-headlights thing. He placed the two brown paper bags he was carrying onto a nearby counter and walked over, his Nordic-blues flashing, and extended his hand.

"Andy Alvilda," he said, smiling rakishly. "And whom might you be?"

Ilsa could see the poor girl was mesmerized and sprang to the rescue.

"This is my friend Kareema," she interjected.

Andy took her limp hand and shook it gently. "Nice to meet you, Kareema."

"Um . . . uh . . . I . . ."

Ilsa cleared her throat. "It's getting late, kiddo, time you got home."

She put an arm over the teen's shoulder and guided her toward the stairs, ignoring the look on her face as she glanced back over her shoulder at Andy, then turned to her and mouthed the words, *'Oh my God!'*.

As they reached the door, Ilsa snapped her fingers to bring Kareema back to reality. "Get home safe, and remember what I said about Justin."

"W-who?"

"That's my girl."

Ilsa gave her a smile, then closed her front door tightly before hoofing it back upstairs. Her mood darkened as she saw Andy wandering aimlessly around, his tawny head doing the owl thing. Left unattended, he'd probably start wandering through the house, proper. Snorting irritably, she pulled her clammy gloves back on and resumed pummeling the heavy bag.

"You're forty minutes early, detective," she said in between combinations. "That an LA thing? Or did you forget to read your 'how to impress your new partner' manual . . ."

Andy continued his inspection, then nodded approvingly. "Well, I keep hearing about this fancy pad of yours and I had to see it for myself." He ignored the obvious side-eye she was giving him and added, "It *is* impressive."

When he saw Ilsa's eyes narrow, he extended his hands in a placating gesture and hoisted one of the paper bags he'd brought.

"Sorry. For the record, I think it's better to be early than late. And I *did* read the part about bringing breakfast," he said, grinning disarmingly. He reached in the bag, pulling out a foil-wrapped sandwich and a sizable cup. "Egg whites and turkey bacon on an everything bagel. One large coffee, no cream or sugar."

Ilsa's hands went to her hips. "Who told you I take it black?"

"Ramirez. He said you like your coffee 'dark, like your soul'."

Ilsa's brows cranked down over her eyes. "That little candy-ass. Wait till I get my hands on him . . ." She walked over, opened the proffered beverage, and took a sip. *Wow.* She had to admit, it was delicious.

It figures; tall, dark and dorky has good taste.

"Thanks," she said. "And how do you take it?"

"Me? Oh, I like my coffee like I like my women."

"Bitter and cheap?"

Andy held up his pricey cup and winked. "Hot and on the expensive side."

Ilsa grinned and tossed her gloves on the counter. She was halfway to the system's control panel, when Andy resumed his sightseeing. As she watched, he sauntered over to the old brick mantle by the south wall – the only part of the original room she hadn't had covered with sheetrock. Then he zeroed the one thing she didn't want him messing with – an ornately framed photograph of a well-dressed young girl, seated on some department store Santa's lap.

Andy's head cocked to one side. His eyes flitted to Ilsa, then back to the dusty photo. He reached for it, only to jerk his hand back as a burst from Ilsa's laser pistol made it look like it was on fire.

"Don't touch that," she growled.

Andy eyes rounded and he replied in a mock Brooklyn accent, "*Whoa*, my bad." He raised his hands as if he was surrendering. "Take it easy."

She threw him an annoyed look, then headed out the door, tossing him her targeting pistol on the way. "I gotta get cleaned up," she said, then indicated the still humming combat course. "You can--"

She stopped in mid-sentence as Andy's phone uttered a piercing wail. It took a second for it to register, then she chuckled and shook her head. *The whistling ring tone from 'The Good, the Bad, and the Ugly'? How much cornier can this guy get?*

Andy winked as he picked up. "This is Alvilda."

At her current distance, Ilsa couldn't make out what the caller was saying, but whoever it was, he sounded both loud and authoritarian.

"Shit, thanks captain. We're on it!" Andy said, hanging up.

Ilsa felt her jaw go slack. "That was Janus? He called *you*, personally? Why? What happened?"

"You might want to skip that shower, slugger. We got us a crime scene, and we've got one of *them . . . alive.*"

Ilsa inhaled sharply. "A Christmas cannibal? In custody? Are you fucking serious?"

Andy pressed his lips together and nodded.

"Shit!" Ilsa hesitated as a picture of her much-needed shower sprouting wings and flying away soared through her head. "Oh, well. Guess I'm stinking it up tonight."

"Relax, my lips are sealed," Andy said, then took an exaggerated sniff. "Whew! Maybe my nostrils, too!"

"Worry more about your mouth," Ilsa said, smiling and holding up a fist. "You tell any of those ass-cracks down at the precinct, and I'll--"

Andy held up his hands. "Relax, we're partners, right? I watch your back and you watch mine."

"Hmph. I hope so."

* * *

As he waited for his surprisingly testy partner to get changed, Andy busied himself exploring Dunbar's fancy training course. He was eager to get on their case, however, and a moment later sat the pricey target pistol down on a nearby table. He looked up at the room's high ceilings and whistled softly.

Quite a setup, he admitted, admiring all the gear and equipment. He didn't know what the rest of the house looked like, but, even without the automated training course, the place had to cost a fortune. No way someone was paying for all that on a cop's salary.

At least, not an honest one's.

Curiosity tugged at him, and he was tempted to explore what looked like a sizable living room on the other side of the

French doors Dunbar disappeared through, but he thought the better of it. Him merely attempting to touch what he assumed was a photo of her as a child had evoked an unexpectedly hostile response. He was afraid if he trespassed beyond the boundaries of her modified gymnasium he'd get shot for real.

Probably not fatally, of course.

Bored, he walked back to the old brick mantle and studied the photo up close. Yep. Definitely her. But why had she gotten so upset? Was picking up a photo an indictable offense?

Andy took a step, then frowned as he came close to tripping over a dilapidated cardboard box, sitting on the floor by the mantle. It was open and crammed with Christmas cards – unopened ones, from the look of things. He dropped into a crouch and peeked at them. Judging by the postal markings, the top ones were from the previous year, and they aged chronologically, the deeper one went. He imagined those at the bottom were quite old.

Not sure what to make of the box and its contents, he was about to rise when he noticed the stack of cards sitting in a haphazard pile beside the box. He picked one up, checked it, then set it carefully back where he'd gotten it. Those were from this year.

The sounds of booted heels approaching had Andy on his feet lickety-split. He whipped out his phone and pretended he was checking texts.

"Okay, LA, let's roll," Ilsa said as she appeared in the living room doorway.

Andy's eyebrows elevated as he glanced up from his phone. She had her bob cut tied back, exposing her diamond-shaped face, and wore jeans and a red turtleneck sweater that, even with her bulletproof vest's help, failed to disguise the woman underneath. Her detective's shield was clipped to her belt, and draped over one forearm she carried a stylish Maven black leather jacket that was both well-insulated and would conceal her shoulder holster.

A true B&B, he thought. *A beauty and a badass.* He felt a smirk coming on, then remembered he had no time for such things. He headed for the door instead.

Ilsa slipped on her coat as she fell in beside him. "Are you driving, or am I?"

Andy feigned aghastness. "Are you kidding? I took the train here."

She wore a "that figures" look as she sighed and locked her front door. "The train? Why, you too much of a pussy to drive in the city?"

"What?" Andy scoffed, then incorporated an even heavier Goombah accent. "Fuhgeddaboudit!"

CHAPTER 3

The traffic lights all seemed to favor Ilsa as she and Andy made their way toward the crime scene – a luxury apartment building situated on Central Park South. It was mid-week and, at this hour, traffic in Manhattan was as good as it would ever be. She was thankful it hadn't snowed the last few days, but the roads were still slick with a mixture of black ice and salt. Cautious by nature, she took it slow, her hazelnut eyes glued to the road.

"Not exactly the kind of holiday lights one hopes for," Andy remarked from the passenger seat.

A hundred yards ahead, the strobes from a veritable fleet of police and emergency vehicles overpowered a lone string of Christmas lights, entwined around a nearby lamp post. Ilsa glanced up and frowned. She hated this time of year, and for good reason; still, it saddened her to see her city so dark and depressed.

Then again, she conceded, a seemingly unstoppable cult of marauding serial killers could do that to you.

With no parking spots in sight, and even the bus stop occupied by a pair of ambulances, she pulled her Subaru next to an available hydrant and threw it in park. She paused contemplatively, before leaning over and reaching past a straight-faced Andy. Their eyes locked as she opened the glove box by feel and retrieved her detective's placard.

"Ready?" she asked as she leaned back and positioned it on the dash.

Andy eyed the near-zero temperature reading on her console, then zipped up his coat and donned his gloves. "Ready and able, ma'am."

"You know, that's actually really nice," she noted, admiring the deep-pile shearling collar and cuffs of his dark-brown leather B-3 cockpit bomber jacket. "Is that a Schott?"

"Nah, Cabela's," he replied, then winked as she turned off the ignition.

"I must say, you have an eclectic fashion sense."

Andy shrugged. "Well, not all of us can afford five-point-four-million-dollar brownstones. Although I'm a bit confused as to your choice of transport." He ran his leather-covered fingers over the dash. "Don't get me wrong, the Forester is a great vehicle. Top safety marks, reliable, not to mention the adaptive headlights, plus blind spot and driver distraction monitoring systems. I just expected someone with your means to drive something a little less . . . modest."

Ilsa pulled a face as she got out. "I see. And how is it that you happen to know what my home is worth? You some gold digger, stalking me?"

"You *wish*," Andy chuckled. "I got bored standing in front of your place, so I Zillowed it. All the property details are there; anyone can see."

"Hmph. Unfortunately. Wait . . . bored? How long were you *out* there?"

"Oh, around twenty minutes."

"Oh, my God. Why the hell were you so early?"

"Hey, it's not my fault the trains in this town run on time. I didn't want to be late on my first day."

Ilsa slowed as they approached the police barricade. She felt the wind's bite as she opened her jacket and gritted her teeth. "So, you stood out there in near-zero temps for *twenty minutes* before you decided to make your presence known?"

"Actually, no. Then I hoofed it over to that little coffee shop. Nice place. Very friendly staff."

"What are you, a moron?"

"Only on alternate Tuesdays," Andy said, grinning. He held up an index finger. "Wait, is today Tuesday?"

Ilsa ended up mumbling to herself as she moved through the crowd of bystanders. Despite the late hour, a group of two dozen individuals watched, enthralled, as a bloodied individual was wheeled out of the building's front doors, toward a waiting ambulance. She flashed her badge to the nearest uniform.

"Dunbar and Alvilda," she said, zipping her coat back up. She stepped past the barricades with Andy in tow and indicated the man on the gurney. "What've we got?"

The mustached cop wiped away the sheen of sweat that had formed on his brow, despite the freezing temperatures. "Shit, we've got the first 'Christmas Cannibal' taken alive, that's what we got. Fucking psycho." He grimaced, then spat on the frozen ground. "My wife's afraid to put up our tree. My kid's terrified. Maybe you dicks can finally solve this thing, huh?"

The expression on Ilsa's face mirrored Andy's as they approached the two EMTs prepping their prospective quarry. The suspect was a Caucasian male, late-thirties to early forties, from the look of things, and in halfway decent shape. *Not a bad-looking guy, either*, she observed.

Well, except for his eyes, she amended as she watched him gaze ferally about.

The perp's eyes reminded her of that poor bobcat she'd managed to free from a jaw trap last spring, while hiking. They had that same, fear-crazed look.

As she watched, the man pulled hard against his restraints. He seemed to realize the futility of doing so, however, and stopped. But then he spotted her and her partner and began thrashing wildly, struggling to free himself.

"Help me, please!" he shouted. "Father Giordano . . . he needs to know! He-he killed my wife. I-I-I couldn't stop him!"

Ilsa cocked an eyebrow as she turned to the nearest EMT. "*This* is our suspect?" She wore a dubious look. "Okay, who am I looking at?"

The bald-headed technician wore an apathetic expression as he read from a clipboard. "Doctor Donald McKinley, an obviously well-to-do cosmetic surgeon. Wife, Amanda. Daughter, Amy."

Ilsa leaned forward, studying the surgeon's flushed face. "Is the good doctor *on* something?"

"Not that I can tell."

Suddenly, McKinley began to buck to and fro, heaving against his bonds. "Listen, Goddamnit! I'm telling you, it's still *here!* Y-you gotta protect my little girl. *Please!* I-I . . ."

In mid-sentence, his eyes unexpectedly glazed over and he went limp.

Ilsa felt a spike of alarm and spun around. "Where's his daughter? Is she okay?"

"Relax, she's alive," The bald EMT replied. He gave Andy an appraising look. Judging by his expression, she figured he was envying the LA cop's impressive coiffure. His lips tightened and he focused on checking his patient's restraints. "They've got her isolated upstairs, waiting for Child Protective Services."

Ilsa exhaled heavily. "And the wife? Is she--"

The second EMT walked over. He was a thickset fellow with Coke bottle glasses, who made a show of donning a fresh pair of vinyl gloves. "Oh, *she's* dead. And let me tell you, it ain't pretty." He indicated the building behind them. "Upstairs . . ."

Ilsa nodded, then noticed Andy eying McKinley's unconscious form. His tanned face cocked to one side and he signaled to her, before leaning over the man. With his gloved hands, he peeled aside a bloodsoaked section of the surgeon's torn pajama shirt, exposing a trio of nasty lacerations. He frowned, then glanced down, noting the antique rosary that, despite his being unconscious, McKinley had managed to keep a tight grip on.

'We got some pretty deep knife wounds here," Andy announced, peering closer. "Any idea what kind?"

The first EMT looked up from scribbling notes. "Most likely a large, curved blade, like the kind you use for gutting deer." He shook his head in disgust. "Sick people, those fuckers."

As if he'd heard him, McKinley's eyes flew open and he lashed out, one gnarled hand seizing Andy by the throat.

"Son of a--"

Ilsa's eyes popped, then she was in motion. Andy was a lean and muscular six-foot-three, but she could tell even he was having a tough time breaking the surgeon's adrenalized grip.

"A little help here, fellas!" she grunted as she pushed and pulled with all her might, struggling to keep McKinley immobilized. For a doctor, he was frighteningly strong. It was all she could do to keep his other arm in check, while her partner continued to fight to free himself.

With a muttered expletive, the bald-headed EMT joined the bizarre struggle. Behind him, his partner hastily prepared a syringe of what was undoubtedly a sedative of some kind.

"You, fools!" McKinley hissed at them. "Find Giordano, before it's too late! It's coming back . . . coming for *all* of—uh-ack-ack!"

The spasms that wracked the surgeon's body were so powerful, it was like he was being electrocuted. His grip on Andy became a memory, and foamy drool spewed from his nose and mouth.

A moment later, McKinley went limp.

The bald EMT sprang forward and started checking his vitals. "Shit, we're losing him, man!" he shouted to his partner. "Come on, we gotta go! NOW!"

Stashing his syringe behind one ear, the chunky EMT grabbed hold and together they rolled, then hoisted, the gurney into the back of the ambulance. Once it was inside and secured, they both hopped in and thumped loudly on the vehicle's inner walls.

"Let's go! Hit it!" one of them shouted as the ambulance's rear doors closed with a thump.

Her chest still heaving, Ilsa stood beside Andy and watched in bemusement as the ambulance sped off, it's lights and sirens blasting. She felt a glimmer of concern as she turned and noticed him absentmindedly rubbing his bruised throat. It was only when he looked at her that she realized the apprehension and confusion she felt was reflected in his eyes.

* * *

The first thing Andy's eye fell on, as he and Dunbar approached the crime scene, was the damage to the apartment's front door. It was a big, heavy door, and had obviously been forced open. The deadbolt was shattered, the opposing frame and strike plate ruptured; even the security chain had been snapped. He assumed Dunbar noticed this as well, but she flashed her badge at the uniform standing guard and breezed by without stopping.

Andy gave the guy a friendly nod and followed her. Normally, he'd have insisted on going first – something the feisty New Yorker would have undoubtedly railed against – but in this case, there was no need; the crime scene was secure.

The tall Californian's eyes twinkled with amusement. Sooner or later, it would happen. But there was no point in facing down *that* particular demon until there was no avoiding it.

He inhaled slowly as he took in the ruined apartment. It was huge and opulent – did *everyone* in New York except him have money? – and, under normal circumstances, must've been a sight to behold. Now, however, it looked like a landfill. The living room's towering Christmas tree had been knocked over and snapped in mid-trunk, paintings and artwork were torn from the walls, and most of the furniture was broken. Any pieces that weren't were scattered and upended, and there appeared to be quite a bit of blood spatter, along with a black, powdery substance trekked around that smelled like sulfur.

Or maybe *ass*.

Adding to the disarray, word of a murder taking place in such an affluent neighborhood had resulted in a flurry of law enforcement activity. Normal crime scene procedures appeared to have been shelved in favor of an all-out feeding frenzy. Everywhere you looked, investigators and lab technicians weaved around one another or crawled on the floor as they collected and bagged potential trace evidence, and there were so many photographers' flashbulbs going off you'd have thought there was a passing thunderstorm. The master bedroom had been taped off and Andy moved cautiously forward, trying not to bump into anyone or step on anything important, and trying even harder to not appreciate how enticing

Dunbar's impressive rear looked in those form-fitting jeans of hers.

His admittedly well-developed ego notwithstanding, he couldn't help wondering if she'd worn them for his benefit. Or more likely his discomfiture.

Andy's private thoughts were waylaid by a sudden squeaking sound, followed by his partner raising her front foot. Her boot had come down hard on a foot-tall Santa figurine – something that had previously decorated the mantle topping the marble fireplace to their left.

When Dunbar did nothing but stare at it, Andy shook his head. Stepping forward, he bent at the waist and picked up the antique figurine. It had been dusted with talcum powder for prints and, courtesy of his partner's gunboats, had a crack running through its smile that, in the fire's glow, gave it a Joker-esque look. He sighed, dusting it off as best he could, and placed it back on the mantle.

"You got no respect for Santa," he muttered.

"The feeling's mutual."

Andy gave her a look before following her, past a pair of particularly talkative uniforms, down a hallway at the rear of the apartment. Judging by the funerary expressions on the faces of the trio of cops standing outside an open closet, Dunbar must have deduced the victim was inside.

He concurred. If he'd had any doubts, they evaporated the moment a young forensic photographer emerged from said closet, his camera tightly gripped in both hands. His youthful face was a shade of olive green, and he barely made it past the closet's fallen door before vomiting all over the place.

That doesn't bode well.

"Jesus, what a mess," he heard Dunbar say as she entered the walk-in closet.

Mess was an understatement. The scene inside was like something from a horror movie, complemented by the awful stench of blood, mixed with urine and feces.

The closet itself was largely intact, with most of its coats and raincoats still suspended from their respective hangers. The ceiling light fixture, about two feet over Andy's head, had been dislodged from the drywall, its bulbs broken, and a halogen dual work light atop a six-foot tripod had been brought in to compensate.

He grimaced. Some things were better off seen in shades of black and white.

Dunbar's chin dropped and she cleared her throat. "How much is . . ."

"Left?" the forensicologist inside commented, barely looking up from his laptop. He was seated next to the corpse, in what was probably the only intact chair in the place. He wore wire-framed glasses and had a thin face topped by thinner hair, with pale skin that had an almost cadaverous look to it. "Cranium and entire cervical column are missing, as are thoracic vertebrae one through four." He paused, his blinky eyes taking in Dunbar, then he noticed Andy hovering and droned on.

"Clavicles are broken, uppermost ribs and sternum are gone, along with the surrounding muscles." He leaned forward in his seat, wielding a ballpoint pen like a pointer. "However, most of the internal organs are still present." He gave the two detectives a meaningful look. "They must've been interrupted."

"Couldn't have been the husband," Dunbar stated as she turned to Andy. "He's way too clean. Not to mention, scared shitless."

"And *alive*." The forensicologist pointed out. He resumed keying in notes. "So far, every family member that's 'partaken' has choked to death on their loved ones' intestines."

Trying hard to breathe through his mouth, Andy exited the closet and moved past a pair of double doors, into a nearby sitting room. He felt the temperature drop to frigid levels the moment he entered, and he inhaled sharply as he saw the reason why.

The room's entire southern wall consisted of a series of floor-to-ceiling windows, of which the central three had been replaced by a gaping eight-foot-high hole. The jagged opening was oval-shaped and, judging by the lack of debris, the entire section appeared to have exploded outward.

Andy's eyes contracted. It wasn't just glass, either. The window frames, drywall, studs . . . even the outer wall of brick and mortar had been annihilated by whatever had been hurled at it.

But what? A sofa, maybe? A refrigerator?

He whistled softly. Whatever the missile had been, it suggested an astonishing feat of strength. In any case, the only thing stopping someone from stepping too close and plunging to their death was a double row of yellow police barricade tape, formed like an "X".

Andy approached the wounded wall of windows with caution, aware of Dunbar approaching from his left. He could hear the wind's icy whistle as it hurtled past, and he was glad he'd decided to keep his bomber on. He peeked out and saw the debris dotting the cordoned-off sidewalk below, then stepped back. He wasn't afraid of heights, per se, but he wasn't a fan, either.

Suddenly, the detective noted a junior forensicologist walking by, and he caught up to him in a few quick strides.

"Do you mind?" he asked, indicating the evidence bag the researcher carried.

Nodding as the youngster handed him the thick Ziplock bag, Andy peered through its transparent walls. It contained a .357 magnum revolver – a stainless-steel Ruger GP100, to be exact. It was a superior weapon: rugged and reliable, but it packed quite a bit of kick. A bit much for a surgeon who relies on his hands, in his opinion.

With Dunbar watching, he opened the bag and took a whiff.

"It's been fired," he said.

"Five of six rounds accounted for," the forensicologist interjected. He held up a second bag containing a handful of spent bullets, then pointed toward the nearby closet. "We pulled one out of the doorjamb, two from the walls, and two were just lying there on the carpet."

Without asking, Dunbar reached for the bagged shells and held them up to the light.

"And number six?"

A simpering smile creased the forensicologist's youthful face. "I imagine someone . . . took it with them?"

Dunbar grinned hugely. "Wounded perps are my favorite kind."

She wore a speculative look as she offered Andy the bag of bullets. He studied them. All were deformed, as if they'd struck hard surfaces, but two especially so. Pancaked, in fact. He handed the evidence bag back to the forensicologist, who spun on his heel and left.

"Looks like one of our cannibals is wearing body armor."

Dunbar's nod of acknowledgment was supplanted by a start as a child's voice rang out from behind them both.

"He wanted me, but daddy fought him."

The two wheeled around to see a little girl standing forlornly in the hallway, a few yards away. She couldn't have been more than six – a tiny thing with brown hair and big eyes, dressed in footed pajamas, and hugging a stuffed animal of some kind. She had a dazed, almost catatonic look to her.

Andy could only imagine what she'd seen.

Actually, no. He didn't want to.

Dunbar gave a startled gasp as she realized the closet containing the little girl's mutilated mother was right behind her. She rushed over to her with Andy in tow and put an arm around her shoulders, shielding her from the sight and guiding her back toward the living room. The horrified social worker who came running stopped short and breathed a sigh of relief.

Dunbar afforded the woman a perfunctory nod, then dropped down on one knee so she and the girl were at eye level.

"Hi, you're Amy, right?"

The girl nodded mechanically.

"I'm Det—I'm Ilsa," she said, showing the girl her badge. "I'm a policeman. I'm here to help you. Did you see the man who did this?"

Amy nodded again, only this time her eyes widened.

"Do you know who it was?"

She shook her head. "It was the boogie man. He ate my mommy. Is he going to eat me too?"

"Oh, God, no!" Dunbar exclaimed, hugging her protectively. "Nobody's gonna hurt you, sweetie. You have my word." She stroked the little girl's hair, trying to reassure her. "Amy, listen . . . do you think you could describe the 'boogie man' to us?"

"He was dark and big. *Real* big."

"How big?" Dunbar asked, then indicated Andy. "Was he as big as Detective Alvilda?"

Amy looked up at Andy and shook her head. "Nope, bigger. Much bigger."

The two detectives exchanged looks, but before Dunbar could say another word, the social worker cleared her throat and stepped anxiously forward. "I'm sorry, officers, but I gotta get her outta here. Her aunt's en route to the hospital to meet us."

As the CPS woman ushered Amy away, Andy followed Dunbar into the living room. He could tell from the set of her shoulders she was tense. He figured it was her maternal instincts kicking in and smiled. She'd make a good mom, one day. Assuming, of course, that the right guy came along.

Dunbar came to a stop a few yards from the apartment's entrance, her eyes fixed on its battered door. She turned to the uniform standing guard, a ginger-haired officer with a pronounced mustache, and indicated the damage.

"Was it like that when PD arrived?"

"No, ma'am," came the reply. "Place was locked up tight as a drum. We had to bust it down."

Andy felt his lips purse. "Now, *that's* interesting."

Dunbar's eyes lifted to find his, then she backtracked through the living room, her gaze sweeping the walls, ceiling, and floor. When she got to the big marble fireplace, she located the controls and carefully reduced its flame until it was little more than artificial embers. Then, she squatted down between the open fire screens, leaned one hand against the top of the antique ingle's serpentine-shaped opening and, despite the oppressive heat, peered intently up at its flue.

"Nobody came through there," Andy stated. "Unless they were wearing asbestos undies."

She gave him an unamused look then shifted position, settling back on her haunches. A confounded expression crept across her countenance, and she remained there, not blinking and grinding her molars. All of a sudden, her head swiveled hard on her shoulders. She rose and, stepping past the fireplace's insulated stone edging, peered intently down at a section of ash-and-blood-stained carpet.

Andy realized what she was focused on and immediately joined her. Someone had carved or burned a symbol deep into the rug, probably with the same knife they'd used on the hapless homeowner – after heating it in the fire. It looked like the number eight, but it was a little hard to discern. Between the cinders and a parade of people having inadvertently stepped on it, it didn't exactly jump out at you; but it was definitely there.

Dunbar reached for her phone and took a photo of the blackened numeral. Then she reached out and snagged the arm of the young forensicologist they'd spoken to as he was passing by.

"Did you document this?" she asked.

He looked down, then back up at her and blinked. "You mean the eight? Sure. One's been gouged into the floor of every home that's been hit."

Dunbar's eyes took on a faraway look as she watched him go. Andy studied her micro-expressions with interest; he could practically see the wheels spinning inside her head.

"You think it's a gang sign?"

"Beats the fuck outta me . . . shit!" Her brows snapped together, then she turned and started walking and talking with Andy rushing to keep up. "The door was secured from the inside, and there's no other way in or out. If the husband's not the killer, then where *is* he? Or *they*?"

Frustrated, she stalked through the hallway at the far end, then turned right into the nearby sitting room. "The only other way out is . . ."

Her voice trailed off as she came to a halt, directly in front of the jagged wound in the room's once-imposing wall of windows. Outside, past the razor-edged opening, the city lights shimmered, the wind howled, and a fusillade of flurries commenced their frenzied final dance.

The night beckoned.

CHAPTER 4

To casual passersby, Ilsa Dunbar was a stone study in recalcitrance. Her jaw was set, booted feet spread, and toned arms folded across her chest. She was in no mood to talk, which included turning a deaf ear to the wind incessantly reminding her she should've worn thermals underneath her jeans.

Of course, she should have; she didn't know why she hadn't.

Was it because she felt they made her look fat? So, what if they did?

Her frustration continued to mount, until she found herself staring irritably back at the crime scene's damaged windows, five stories up.

She shook her head irritably. She knew it wasn't the cold that was getting to her, or the snow continuing to fall, concealing potential clues and dampening her hair. Nor was it the lone beat cop, assigned to guard the cordoned-off impact site, who'd gone on a "bathroom break" thirty minutes ago. It wasn't even Andy's disgustingly chipper attitude as he pored over each and every bit of glass, piece of brick, and section of window frame he could find, airbrushed across a forty-foot section of sidewalk.

It was the fact that nothing about the case jibed.

Ilsa was very good at analyzing crime scenes; she had a sixth sense about such things, and she was rarely wrong. Yet, to her surprise, according to all the first responders, there was nary a weighty projectile to be found at the center of the debris field – no file cabinet, table, or desk. Not even a chair. Nor was there a body, or anything to suggest one had ever been there. All they'd found was the wreckage expelled from the apartment above, which made no sense. The dispersal pattern suggested something had been violently heaved through the windows, and that something had been substantial enough to leave behind an eight-foot hole.

Could it have been their perp? Maybe there was more than one of them?

She reached up and stroked her chin. That could be it; there could've been a falling out. There was little honor among thieves – less among killers. Maybe things got pissy and someone gave their associate the old heave-ho, then disappeared the body and cleaned up afterward.

Her hand closed into a fist. No. There would've been evidence of that.

Not to mention, they wouldn't have had time.

Ilsa's eyes compressed into slits and she glared resentfully up at the windows and their makeshift iris. As if sensing the foulness of her mood, the wind cut into her thighs once more and she hugged herself for warmth.

Enough of this shit.

She was tired of Jack Frost's invasive caresses. She wanted to move on, she wanted her heated and massaging car seat, and she wanted Andy to stop whistling *A Holly Jolly Christmas*.

What a partner they'd saddled her with . . . Only someone hailing from Texas via LA would come across a cordoned-off crime scene and announce that the ring of wooden police barricades reminded him of how, as a kid, he and his friends used to use borrowed laundry hampers and milk crates to "circle the wagons", when they played Cowboys and Indians.

Boys...

An approaching figure caused Ilsa's eyes and ears to prick up. Although the overdue site cop's return signaled her and Andy's imminent departure, the smug look on his face, coupled with the coffee and half-eaten donut he carried, added serious fuel to her fire. With an effort, she clamped down on her ire and nodded.

She decided to focus her attention where it mattered.

On her partner.

"This is ridiculous," she scoffed. "*Nobody* could survive a fall like that. Who the hell are we looking for, 'Spiderman'?"

"Not his style," Andy said over his shoulder. He was in a crouch, a flashlight in one gloved hand, and the other furiously fanning a yard-wide section of sidewalk to whisk away the thin layer of fresh-fallen powder. "Hey, check this out."

Ilsa glanced down, then did a double-take. Beneath the frosted flakes lay a pair of imprints, pressed deep into the compacted snow and ice from last week's storm. The tracks were oval-shaped and a good twelve inches across.

They also looked remarkably like hoofprints.

"She said he was big, right?" Andy said, his eyebrows hiking up. "Well?"

Ilsa's patience ran out. Her eyes rounded, then she brought her hands up to her cheeks and did a mocking version of the classic "Home Alone" pose.

"My God, Andy; you've done it! You've singlehandedly solved a decade-long murder spree and saved Christmas!" Her arms extended out from her sides. "Who would have suspected a carriage driver's horse had turned man-eater?"

Ignoring the cool look she got back, she beamed at the Central Park horse and buggy that just so happened to go clopping by at that exact moment. Talk about timing! She wanted to run over and kiss the driver, or at least give a well-earned sack of oats and a few carrots to the tired old Clydesdale heading back to its stable for the night.

Unable to suppress a shit-eating grin, she turned back to Andy and paused, both for effect and for the carriage driver to get out of earshot. Then she extended one hand at eye level and swept it from left to right, imitating a TV news ticker. "I can see the headline now: *'City Terrorized by Hannibal Heifer'*!"

With a snort, she spun on her heel and stormed off, the dry snow scrunching beneath her boots. Not slowing, she stripped off one glove, then fished out her key fob and remote-started her Forester from fifty yards away – its heated seats included.

Behind her, Andy followed, shaking his head.

"Ya know, I like the sarcasm," he shouted. "But technically, a heifer is a *cow* not a *horse!*"

"Whatever you say, Billy Bob!" she yelled back as she opened her door and climbed in.

Judging by his lopsided grin, Andy handled derision well. He dusted the snow off himself as best he could before climbing in, then sank back into his seat. A moment later, he blew out a breath, reached for his seatbelt, and turned those Nordic blues of his in her direction.

"So, where to now?"

Ilsa wore a steely look as she flipped on her wipers. After a moment's deliberation, she glanced at her mirrors, put the crossover in gear, and pulled smoothly out.

"Some place I don't want to go."

* * *

With the exception of the set of her jaw, Ilsa managed to hide her sulking as she sat back against the fender of her idling Forester, her hands in her pockets. Fifteen yards away, atop the steps of Saint Patrick's cathedral, Andy chatted happily with Father Sean Giordano.

She exhaled heavily, then glanced back over her shoulder and inspected her six. Across Fifth Avenue, Rockefeller Plaza's brightly-lit *International Building* soared 512 feet into the sky. Down in its courtyard, she spotted a familiar figure – the plaza's imposing sculpture of *Atlas*. The forty-five-foot, seven-ton figure stood permanently perched atop a pedestal of marble, with its muscular arms raised overhead to support its celestial burden. It exuded an aura of indefatigable purpose, and it was only upon close inspection that one detected a hint of malevolence, seeping from an otherwise stony countenance.

Ilsa couldn't begrudge the old Titan for being in a bad mood. After all, he'd carried the weight of the world upon his shoulders since 1937.

She could relate.

She faced front again and, when she was sure he wasn't looking, afforded Giordano a surreptitious glance. The aging priest was garbed in mortician monochromatic – basic black from head-to-toe. Only his dusky skin and silvery beard stood out. Behavior-wise, he didn't act like she remembered. His body language suggested he was being guarded, and when he spoke, the minimalized movements of his lips meant he was worried that some passerby might eavesdrop on their conversation.

It was decidedly odd behavior from someone who, suspect-wise, wasn't even a blip on the NYPD's radar.

As the conversation became more animated, Ilsa noted that, despite a concerted effort on his part to appear affable and innocuous, Andy couldn't help towering over the sixty-year-old priest. The intimidation factor was noticeable, and a bit amusing. At five-foot-eight, the man who'd baptized her was the same height she was. Interestingly, she never felt intimidated or threatened when her partner was around her.

Quite the opposite, in fact.

Ilsa's lips quirked up. Of course, her having black belts in both judo and aikido could well be a mitigating factor. That, and the fact that she carried a Glock 9mm semiauto and several spare magazines.

Behind the conversing men, the illuminated outline of Saint Patrick's loomed large. To her, it looked like a kaiju-sized escapee from the old *Hunchback of Notre Dame* movie she'd watched on one of the classic movie channels. Of course, she knew there were vast differences between the two buildings; yet, in her mind, the mid-nineteenth century structure remained remarkably similar to its significantly older French predecessor.

She let slip a heartfelt sigh. *Where's Lon Chaney when you need him?*

With no heroic hunchback in sight – except for her gabby partner, that is – she decided to do a quick refresher on what she knew about the old church. Rising nearly four hundred feet into the air, the richly decorated neo-Gothic cathedral was an architectural landmark, not to mention a seat of power for the Catholic church.

A flicker of movement drew Ilsa's eye, and she spotted what looked like a pair of bats winging past one of Saint Patrick's towering spires. She couldn't tell how big they were, but they may as well have been moths; they seemed so small.

She had to admit, the Tuckahoe marble monstrosity was impressive. Of course, instilling awe in the masses was what it had been designed for, and it definitely did its job. Millions flocked to it every year, to ooh and aah at its rib vaults, buttresses, and pointed arches. She figured when they looked up at it, they saw the power of God and, predictably, a potential stairway to the heaven they'd been promised.

She saw it as something darker.

Andy was in the middle of showing Giordano something on his phone, when Ilsa's downcast eyes fell on the granite steps they stood upon. Despite the dim lighting, she could pinpoint the quartet of decades-old gouges in the stone as easily as if she had caused them. Her pulse began to pound, her pupils dilated, then, before she knew it was happening, time pulled the rug out from under her.

Her body stiffened as she heard the familiar screech of brakes and the car doors, followed by a warning cry and the shriek of automatic weapons fire. Then came the inevitably screams – always on cue, high-pitched and piercing. The sounds riddled her body and she trembled in response.

"Detective Dunbar?" a voice called out from just beyond the scope of her tunnel vision. She blinked rapidly as she fought to focus, and a face emerged into view. "Ilsa, are you okay?"

There was genuine concern clouding Father Giordano's lined features.

She cursed inwardly as she realized he'd seen her zone out, but she played it off by gesturing at the marred steps. "You *still* haven't fixed this shit?"

The old priest hesitated, his bearded face creasing even more deeply. "Some wounds run deep, even in stone."

"Yeah, whatever."

Ignoring the appalled look on Andy's face, Ilsa walked away and climbed back into her SUV. Once inside, she belted herself in and sat back, her focus on the series of calming breaths she was taking.

Outside, her partner took his sweet time finishing with Giordano. Finally, he shook hands with the old man, then headed over and tugged on the passenger side door handle. He gave her a "WTF?" look, then stood there looking bemused until she hit the lock release. He was still frowning when he climbed in.

"What was that all about?"

"Nothing," she said. "None of your business. What did he say?"

"Nothing about you, so relax."

"*What?*" Ilsa's mouth went slack, then she spun angrily in his direction. "I-I meant the *number*, you overgrown jerk!"

Andy's lip quivered as he pretended his feelings were hurt. Then the corners of his mouth curled up, revealing those nauseatingly perfect teeth of his. "You know, it blows my mind that you're single. Seriously."

She inhaled sharply as she felt the sting of his rebuke. "I'm ... sorry. Sometimes I can be a real bitch."

"Wow," he said with a sage-like nod. "Did that hurt coming out?"

"Not as much as my *foot* will coming out of your *ass*! Now, did he *give* you anything or not?"

If Andy had any feathers, they remained unruffled. "He knows the McKinley's, but nothing about any religious ... issues." Then he held up his phone and showed her the picture of the number eight from their crime scene. "I showed him the burn mark. He's familiar with the city gangs and doesn't think it's a sign."

"Yeah, I did some Googling while you were talking. I got zip."

"Any word on the dad's condition?"

"Bad internal injuries, but he pulled through. He's stable but unconscious, and under heavy guard, obviously." She drummed her fingers on the steering wheel. "Soon as he comes to, we'll know. Until then, we got bupkis."

"Not necessarily," Andy said. His blue eyes sought and found hers as he held up a folded paper. "Merry Christmas."

"What's this?"

"When I pressed the good father about any religious connection, he declined to comment. *But . . .*" he opened the paper, displaying a hastily scrawled name and address. "He gave us a lead. Guy by the name of . . . Oleksander Apostol. He's some kind of high-end antique dealer."

Ilsa's mood turned as bright as her smile as she put it in gear. "Well, then, let's go bring Mister Apostol a little holiday cheer."

* * *

Andy's jaw felt like it had taken up permanent residence on his chest, as he and Dunbar were buzzed into *Apostol's Antiquities*. When they'd first arrived and he'd noted the diamond district store's dual-layers of outer security – heavy-gauge folding guards, backed by a row of inch-thick stainless-steel bars, shielding windows of three-inch-thick bulletproof glass – he thought the owner had gone a tad overboard.

That was, until he laid eyes on the treasures within.

The place was like an art museum. The walls were an endless parade of high-end oil paintings, most from Europe's Renaissance, Baroque, and Neo-Classical periods. At least, based on what he remembered from two torturous semesters of art history. Each masterpiece was nestled in its own, climate-controlled plexiglass cocoon, as was a series of Romanesque and Gothic art statues, a pair of spike-covered suits of plate armor, and a veritable arsenal of Scottish basket-hilt broadswords, Claymores, and daggers.

Curiosity got the better of him, and Andy finally paused in front of a gorgeous eighteen-inch cross, spot-lit atop a rectangular reinforced stand that came equipped with its own alarm system. The placard referred to it as a tenth century *crux gemmata*. It was solid 24-karat gold and very robust, with impressive sculpting and exquisite filigree work, not to mention topped off with a king's ransom in inlaid precious gems.

He did a doubletake as he checked the price, then wished he hadn't. It was worth more than his partner's house.

"Good evening," a decidedly feminine voice called out.

Andy straightened up as an elderly woman in a simple floral dress stepped forward to greet them. She was slim, an inch or two shorter than Dunbar, and had a slight Russian accent. Her posture and ease of movement suggested someone who'd been gifted with impressive spryness in their youth, and she had hair that appeared determined to not give in to the gray. Most impressive were her eyes, however; they were bright and inquisitive, and she zeroed him with them as she gave him a warm smile.

"We're closed. Except for the police, of course."

Andy stared at her. "You know we're cops?"

"Of course," she said, looking them both up and down. "Well dressed, but not overly so. Bold, inquisitive, athletic . . ." She studied Dunbar and smiled. "Tsk, tsk. And *so* stern."

Andy chuckled. "She's got your number, partner-o-mine."

"And yours," the woman interjected.

He smiled dashingly down at her and offered her his hand. "Andrew Alvilda, at your service, ma'am."

Her eyes glistened as she accepted. "Andrew, meaning virile or manly, and Alvilda . . . from the Danish . . ." She glanced up as if reading from a non-existent screen. "Meaning, 'a battle of Elves'. Yet, so little time left . . . *Very* interesting."

Andy wagged his brows at Dunbar. "See? She knows I'm manly."

She rolled her eyes. "Great, you're a manly elf. Good luck with that." She turned to the woman. "Mrs. . . . Apostol?"

"Elena," she replied, nodding.

"We'd like to speak to your husband, Olek, please. Is he here?"

Elena drew a breath and then shouted, "Olie, the police have come for you!" She grinned conspiratorially. "We originally immigrated from the Soviet Union, so I love doing that. A good scare always winds him up."

As if singing backup for Andy and Dunbar's half-stifled chortles, a voice rang out from a back room.

"The police? Are you behind again on your parking tickets, woman?"

Elena snorted. "More likely, they're here about the child support you owe one of your shavala mistresses!"

There was some unintelligible muttering in what sounded like Yiddish, followed by a well-dressed man in his mid-eighties emerging from the back. He was a wiry fellow around the same height as his wife, cleanshaven, with piercing eyes. He appeared fit for his age, but had a stooped look to him and moved with a shuffling gait, as if he carried a weighty burden.

Andy liked him immediately.

Elena nodded to her guests, then moved to intercept Olek. She touched him on the arm while he was still a few yards away and began whispering in his ear. He studied their visitors intently as she spoke, then nodded and whispered something back.

"Yes, yes, yes . . . I have this," he said, waving her off. "Why don't you go watch some more of your cat videos?"

She gave Andy and Dunbar a smile, one that morphed into an "oh-you'll-pay-for-that-later" smirk as she regarded her husband. Then, without further ado, she disappeared into a nearby office.

Olek momentarily considered the two detectives, then straightened like a soldier. "Yes, officers? How can I help you?"

Dunbar wasted no time in flashing her badge. "Mister Apostol? I'm Detective Dunbar and this is Detective--"

"Alvilda. Yes . . ." he studied Andy intently. "And, here you are. So?"

"Father Giordano sent us to you," Dunbar continued.

"Ah, Sean . . . a bright light in dark times. We go way back," Olek said, stroking his chin thoughtfully. "He sent you to me about what, exactly?"

"We're investigating the Christmas cannibal killings, and he thought you might--"

"Ugh!" The old man gave a shudder and hugged himself as if cold. "Horrible, unspeakable things. But I don't see how I can--"

Andy chimed in. "We're here about a number that keeps turning up at the crime scenes."

He pulled up the image on his phone.

Dunbar added, "We were hoping you'd loan us your expertise."

Olek declined holding the proffered phone, and instead leaned forward at the waist, with his hands resting on his thighs. He squinted at the image, then his head drooped, like he'd grown weary all of a sudden. A moment passed, then he sighed and pushed himself upright, gesturing for them to follow.

A few yards away stood a heavy door with a prominent "Do Not Enter" sign on it. He punched in a code on the electronic keypad and ushered them inside.

They passed through a narrow hallway lined with old-fashioned filing cabinets, a water cooler, and a mini-fridge, before ending up in what was obviously Olek's private office. Compared to the brightly-illuminated exhibitions outside, the space was dark and spartan, with black painted walls, a desk, computer, and a trio of chairs. Besides a framed photo of Elena, the only artwork in sight was an aged oil painting, displayed uncovered on the wall to their right. It was a portrait of an older man with craggy features and a long, flowing beard. He must've been a warrior of some sort, Andy deduced, as he wore an embossed steel helmet with cheek and nose guards. From the style of the painting, he could've sworn it was a Rembrandt.

If it was, it was one he was unfamiliar with.

As he turned back toward their host, a bright light emanating from an adjoining room caught Andy's eye. There was something in there, something interesting. He didn't know what it was, but it was sizable and undoubtedly old. A wave of curiosity washed over him and, for reasons he couldn't explain, he strode in with Dunbar trailing.

The attached space was twice the size of the office it adjoined; a good twenty-five-feet square. Its walls and ceiling were the same basic black, but there was no artwork hanging. The only furniture was a King-Arthur-style antique table made of dense black oak that was cordoned off by a series of burgundy velvet ropes supported by chrome posts. The table was circular and at least twelve feet across, with embossed evergreen trees decorating its foot-thick skirt and massive, yard-long legs that curled gracefully down, terminating in carved, beast-like feet.

Andy couldn't begin to guess how much the mammoth relic weighed, but it looked like it could support an elephant. Literally.

His already intense eyes lifted, then rounded. The table was impressive; but it was what was *on* it that intrigued him.

Illuminated by a series of overhead spotlights and protected by thick glass, lay what appeared to be the remains of some archaic horse-drawn carriage or sled. It had been badly burned at some point, which made it impossible to tell what its original design had been. Any body panels remaining were but shards. They lay in a crumbly pile, while the floorboards in the center had been reduced to little more than cinders. Even the runners were badly charred. The few sections that hadn't been blackened by whatever conflagration destroyed the once-elegant conveyance, showed it had originally been fashioned from some ancient gray wood, and engraved with strange runes.

Andy didn't know exactly what he was looking at, but it had a surprising effect on him. The thirty-year-old felt like he had when, as a child, he saw his first *Tyrannosaurus rex* skeleton. He'd been awestruck by the fact that creatures like that had once roamed the earth, but grew glum when he discovered there were no more of them.

The seconds ticked by, and Andy became aware of the pin drop silence in the surrounding room. He rubbed his nose and leaned forward, one hand resting atop a chrome stanchion. His eyes lit up. There was a brass nameplate affixed to the protective glass. He held his breath as he perused it, hoping for some revelation.

Sadly, there was nothing except a date.

"December 24th, 1968 . . ." he read aloud. "Wow, this looks old. Much older than that."

"It is," Olek said from the back of the room. His eyes got squinty and he wagged a finger at his visitor. "Please, don't touch, detective."

"Sorry," Andy said, not realizing he'd placed his palms against the tempered glass. "So, what is this, exactly? It looks, I don't know, Viking?"

"You wouldn't believe me if I told you."

"Sure, I would. I'm very trusting. Gullible, in fact." He made a face and gestured at his partner. "Just ask her."

Between Dunbar's headshake and the 'I'm not buying it' look in the old Russian's eyes, Andy could tell he was getting nowhere. He realized he was going to have to incorporate his top-tier negotiating skills for this.

"C'mon, *please*?" he pleaded with big eyes. "I really wanna know."

Olek's eyes bore a hint of gaiety. He ruminated for a moment, then relented.

"Very well," he said. Then, after a brief deliberation, "It's his sleigh. Or, rather, what's left of it."

"'His' sleigh?", Andy echoed. "Whose sleigh?"

"*His*," Olek said, pointing at the ceiling. "You know, 'Ho, ho, ho'?"

Andy's right eyebrow did the 'Mr. Spock' thing. "Wait, wait . . . you're telling me this is Santa Claus's sleigh? *The* Santa?"

A feeling of exhilaration tinged with nostalgia swept through him as the old man nodded. He didn't know if it was the time of year, the overgrown kid in him, or being surrounded by priceless treasures from all over the world. In all honesty, it didn't matter. All that mattered was Olek's affirmation. Deep down inside, he didn't really believe what he was telling him, but there was a part of him that truly wanted to.

"That is *way* cool, man," he said finally. "Where'd you get it?"

Dunbar's scoff sounded like escaping steam. "Oh, for crying out loud," she remarked. "Can we focus on reality, please?"

"Oh, it's real," Olek assured. "At least, according to the soldiers that sold it to me. They gathered up the pieces after it fell from the sky."

Andy felt his stomach tense. "Hold on. You're saying Santa is--"

"Shit, Alvilda!" Dunbar snapped. "Just *stop* it, will you?"

She blew out a breath, then turned to their host. "Mister Apostol, with all due respect, can we just focus on what we came here for, please?"

"Ah, I see it now," Olek observed. "You have no faith."

"Faith? Faith in what? Jolly old Saint Nick? Matter of fact, no, I do not," she acknowledged. "Nor do I believe in Jack Frost, the Tooth Fairy, or Tupac, okay? Geez!"

"Santa isn't his real name. Or even Nicholas, for that matter."

Andy did his best to avoid the looks Dunbar kept giving him as Olek moved around the room. On the far side of the tabled display stood an antique marble lectern that had previously gone unnoticed. It was an impressive antique all on its own; its base was in the shape of a lion, with a Greek column sprouting upwards to support its lavishly-carved, slanted top. On it, lay a large, leather-bound volume of some kind, its surface crosshatched with runic symbols.

Olek rested an aged hand on the big book's cover. "This has been in my family for generations," he said softly. "I will show you, if you wish."

Dunbar looked like she was about to explode. "Oh, for the love of God, I--"

"It *may* have a bearing on your case, detective," Olek said from beneath raised brows. "I simply ask that you keep an open mind."

"Why not?" Andy said, grinning disarmingly. "I'm game. Bring it on."

Olek leaned forward and blew gently on the book, dispersing a fine layer of dust that had accumulated on its cover. Then he carefully opened it.

Andy peered intently over the antique dealer's shoulder. The aged tome's pages were made of vellum and covered with flowery, hand-wrought medieval-style writing and images. Most of the former was in Latin, or some other language he was unfamiliar with.

Olek licked his lips, then breathed in through his nostrils before he began.

"The entity you call 'Saint Nick' or 'Kris Kringle' has been many things to many people over the centuries," he said, his age-spotted fingers gently turning the pages. "In the Netherlands, he was Sinterklaas. In Russia, Ded Moroz. During the Middle Ages, he was Father Christmas." He paused and indicated a colorful image. "Before that, during the fourth century, he was Saint Nicholas, and his day was December sixth. On the eve of--"

"Wait, did you say December sixth?" Dunbar interrupted.

"Yes, why?"

"Andy, that's the date the killings start each year . . ."

Olek cleared his throat. "May I continue?"

Dunbar pursed her lips and nodded.

"During the Reformation, this day was moved to December twenty-fifth, with 'Santa Claus' coming at the stroke of midnight on the twenty-fourth."

Andy snapped his fingers. "And the murders end each year on the night of the twenty-fourth!" He turned to his partner and nodded. "I studied the case file."

Dunbar inched closer. "Okay, Mister Apostol. You've piqued my interest. What else do you have?"

Olek resumed flipping pages. "Santa, or rather Father Christmas, actually predates Christianity by thousands of years." He stopped and touched a fingertip to an elaborate depiction of a bearded man wearing a horned helmet and brandishing a spear, while riding through the sky atop a winged horse with a pair of birds trailing him. There were what were presumably shooting stars swirling through the sky and a river and forest below. "All the way back to the midwinter pagan celebration known as the Yule. Back then, Wotan, also known as Long-beard, was the central figure."

The old man looked up. He had a faraway look in his eye, like he was peering through a portal into another space and time.

"Riding his eight-legged horse, *Sleipnir*, and carrying his spear, *Gungnir*, Wotan flew across the sky, bringing food and gifts to people in need."

Olek hesitated, his gaze descending to an image on the opposing page. It was a primitive village at night. There were trees and snow, and a large campfire in the center, with people gathered around it for comfort and warmth. Off to one side, hidden in the shadows of the nearby forest, lurked a pair of menacing eyes.

"Little did he know," he continued, "their need would be far greater than he imagined."

CHAPTER 5

Andy's head was spinning. It was his turn to take notes, but their host's words were flying at him in a never-ending barrage. Combined with his admittedly sorry printing skills, it was nigh impossible to keep pace. Finally, he raised his hand and requested a timeout. Then he stood there, running his tongue across his teeth, and jotting things down as fast as he could.

He tasted regret. It wasn't the first time he'd found himself wishing he'd taken his mother's advice, back when she'd realized he was going into the academy. She'd been right, of course, as she was about so many things. Learning shorthand would've been a sage move. Or at least cursive.

A few yards away and riding his marble pedestal like a pastor at his pulpit, a surprisingly long-winded Olek Apostol stood waiting with his hands clasped stop his stomach. Dunbar hovered close by, her wiry forearms folded across her chest, her black leather jacket draped over them.

As he finished reviewing what he'd written, Andy glanced toward their host. He wasn't sure if the old man actually bought into the fairytales he was regaling them with. He doubted it; he didn't. Still, they were interesting. After all, if there *had* been an historical figure that was the basis for the fabled Kris Kringle, who wouldn't want to learn about him?

Of course, regardless of his interest, and unlike his rather brash partner, Andy would never be impolite or rude to someone as helpful and forthcoming as the eccentric antique dealer had proven himself to be. Even if the old codger did believe he had what was left of Santa's sleigh sitting under glass, just a few yards from where they stood.

"Okay, just to recap," Andy said, clearing his throat. "So, Old Man Winter, AKA Wotan, became Father Christmas, who became Santa. So where does the number eight come in?"

"I'm getting to that," Olek said, returning to his oversized tome and flipping another page. "According to legend, Grandfather Frost, as some referred to him, was not alone. He had helpers."

"You mean elves."

Olek shrugged. "Elves, sprites, spirits of the forest . . . One of the strongest of these was a creature Wotan sometimes sent to punish the wicked."

Andy loudly snapped his fingers. "Oh, I remember this! His name was Krampus, right? He sneaked into naughty kid's houses to scare them."

"A watered-down version, used by parents to rein in disobedient children."

The old man indicated a full-page color illustration of a monstrous creature with horns and a tail, wreathed in flames.

"This deadly being also wore many guises," he continued. "In Russia, before the influence of Christianity, it was referred to as *Morozko*. It means 'snow demon'."

He turned the page, exposing an image of Morozko chasing terrified villagers.

"But the pagans knew it as something else. To them it was a cunning monster, born of ice giants. They named it Loptr, although you may know it by its other name . . . Loki."

"*Loki*?" Andy cocked an eyebrow. "Like, from the superhero movies?"

"Hardly so lovable," Olek said, shaking his head. "Eventually, Wotan discovered that Loptr's bloodlust could not be contained. It hunted anyone it pleased, even children. A confrontation between servant and master was inevitable."

He leaned back from the codex, gesturing at an image of what looked like clouds on fire. "In the skies over what is present-day Europe, they battled. Wotan cast down Loptr, binding him in chains of enchanted iron and hurling him into an active volcano, thereby banishing him forever."

The old man turned to his guests. "Thus, ended the Dark Ages."

Dunbar clicked her tongue. "Okay . . . so as long as we don't look in a mirror during a full moon and say this guy's name, we're safe, right?" She noted the recriminating look Andy gave her and pursed her lips. "I'm sorry; it's a neat fairy tale, but how does it relate to our number?"

Olek exhaled heavily, then turned one final page. "The rune you found . . . may I see it?"

"Rune? What rune?" She held out her phone. "It's just a number."

"Depends on how you look at it."

Olek reached out and gently turned her wrist ninety degrees. Then he pointed at an illustration in the book of a sideways figure eight. The "eight" was, in fact, a snake biting its own tail.

"It is the symbol of Loptr . . . Loki."

Just like that, a metaphorical light bulb went off over Andy's head and all the pieces fell into place. "So, we're dealing with a cult of serial killers – cannibalistic religious fanatics who worship this mythical demon."

Dunbar nodded affirmatively. "Makes sense. Each home they've chosen has had a big fireplace."

"Yeah, it's symbolic, represents his banishment. Maybe the consumption of flesh is some sort of ritual, like a sacrifice?"

"Could be," she concurred. "Trying to 'summon' Loki, to free him from his prison."

Andy's eyes lit up. "Hey, that's why the murders start on the sixth, and end before the clock strikes midnight on the twenty-fourth!"

"I don't get it."

"The Feast of St. Nick starts on the sixth, so it's a way of exacting some sort of half-assed 'revenge'."

"Okay, but why stop on the twenty-fourth?"

"Because, my dear Watson, on the twenty-fourth, Santa Claus is coming to town and he--"

"Could imprison Loki again, so the killers believe they have to stop. Bingo!"

Dunbar's eyes sparkled as she gave him an appraising look.

"An interesting hypothesis," Olek said as he observed their exchange. "But you're forgetting one thing."

Dunbar's smile faltered. "What's that, Mister Apostol?"

He indicated the charred sled.

"That's right..." Andy drawled. After a moment's deliberation, he decided it was best to humor their host. It was possible he'd been conned by the people he'd purchased the artifact from, and deluded himself into believing that what he had was valuable. Nothing wrong with that.

He approached the velvet ropes and took in the remains of the mysterious sleigh. "So, soldiers saw this fall out of the sky, like a meteor?"

The old man nodded.

Dunbar sucked in a breath. "So, you actually believe that Santa Claus – the *real* Santa Claus – died that day?"

Olek's expression was grim. "It heralded dark days for mankind. In fact, Egypt's 'War of Attrition' against Israel started only a few months later."

"Mister Apostol, I think it's great that you--"

"Are *helping* us," Andy cut in. "On a positive note, these cultists don't know Santa is gone, right?"

"I'm not sure I follow you."

"What I mean is, otherwise, they might just keep on killing, right?"

Olek nodded hesitantly. "If your theory is correct, yes."

Andy reached over and placed a hand atop the old man's shoulder. "So, we'll just keep that part to ourselves, okay?"

"Of course, Detective Alvilda." He checked his watch. "Forgive me, but if there's nothing else, it's very late and . . ."

"Say no more," Dunbar said. "You've been a great help and we can't thank you enough."

* * *

Olek Apostol's expression was somber as he watched Detectives Alvilda and Dunbar let themselves out. He was more than a little concerned for their safety. But then, these days, he worried about everyone.

He had good reason to.

His wife did her best to avoid wringing her hands as she wished the two officers well and bid them goodnight. The moment they were gone, she locked and bolted the store's heavy inside door behind them. This accomplished, she pulled the lever that lowered their storefront's portcullis-like wall of steel bars, followed by the one that activated its horizontal folding guards. The former came down smoothly, sinking into their respective housings with a series of thumps. The latter, on the other hand, made a terrible racket as they crawled along their integrated track. Even so, he felt better when they completed their journey with a shudder and settled noisily into place.

They were safe now, he decided; two old mice, shielded within their burrow-like vault. And a vault it pretty much was. With its reinforced walls and burglar-proof security measures, the place was built like a bomb shelter. It would take a T-34 tank to force its way inside.

That, or something equally formidable.

Olek found himself growing wistful as he watched Elena hit the button that lowered their store's streetside windows' light-proof inner blinds, then twist the dial that dimmed the display room's main lights, leaving only the accents on. He realized he was tired. Very tired. He glanced at their antique wall clock and made a face. It was unbearably late.

Fortunately, they did business by appointment only these days, and their schedule for tomorrow was light: five buyers only. All were regular customers – high-rollers who tended to party hard – and all had asked to be scheduled in the afternoon. He and Elena could sleep in late.

Olek looked about the place and his features tightened. They'd be staying here again tonight, in the spare room they'd set up as a bedroom, the last time they'd upgraded the store. It wasn't so bad; their makeshift suite had most of the comforts of home. True, their residence in Teaneck, New Jersey would have been preferable, but it was wide open and isolated; for the last decade they'd made it a point to stay in the store from the fifth through Christmas Day.

When friends or family asked why, they said it was because they didn't want to miss out on all the big spenders, out shopping for the holidays.

There was some truth to that. But not much.

Olek smiled as Elena walked quietly over to him.

"You didn't tell them," she said.

He threw up his hands. "And be branded a lunatic?" He shook his grizzled head and scoffed. "You heard them. They believe only what they can see. And then, half."

"Hmm . . . That female detective, she had some nice boobs on her, didn't she?"

"I hadn't noticed," he monotoned, playing along.

"And the other one, Andy . . ." Elena closed her eyes and started fanning herself, like she was suffering hot flashes. "God, he was *so* handsome. And tall! Makes me wish I was--"

"Yes, yes," Olek said, rolling his eyes. "Now, why don't you go make yourself useful and make me a sandwich?"

Her eyes danced with merriment as she kissed him on the cheek. "Anything for you, dear."

* * *

It was near-midnight, as Ilsa and Andy passed through the stationhouse doors. Nat King Cole's *The Christmas Song* was playing in the background, and the place was really bustling. Ilsa immediately took point, ignoring the looks her hunky partner was getting from the majority of the precinct's female cops, not to mention one or two of the males.

Seemingly oblivious, Andy followed blithely along, grinning and gabbing and munching away on the turkey-and-provolone breakfast sandwich she'd provided. After last night, she'd had no choice. She was used to being self-reliant and, when it came to meals, didn't like feeling indebted to someone, be they man or woman.

Ilsa realized she felt surprisingly upbeat. That was no minor feat, considering the nightmares that plagued her through much of her last sleep cycle. She couldn't remember the details, which was just as well. She preferred to focus on the fact that her and Andy's previous night's investigation – courtesy of that eccentric antiquities dealer – had produced potentially viable info. With any luck, and a butt-load of door knocking, they just might crack the case.

If they did, the two of them could be looking at career-changing opportunities. Saving lives was the ultimate goal, of course. But she also realized that, should they be successful, they'd find themselves the beneficiaries of major media coverage – the kind that made you a household name. Just the thought put an added spring in her step.

Her mood fell flat, however, as she entered Janus's office.

The big man wasn't there yet; he rarely showed up on time for his pre-shift briefings. Or beat-downs, as some of the dicks called them. He told everyone he liked to make an entrance, but she figured it was because popping in unexpectedly afforded him the opportunity to overhear things people might otherwise keep to themselves.

Wily old bastard.

Ilsa grabbed a seat and settled in, while always-curious-Andy took to exploring the place. His attention was immediately drawn to the 400-gallon freshwater aquarium that occupied a good portion of one wall. Hands on his hips, the tall Texan-turned-Californian leaned forward and peered intently into the tank. It had a heavy screen cover that was securely locked and a fluorescent light that ran much of its length, but was currently turned off. The water was clear and the décor minimal – a backdrop, smooth pebble substrate, and an elaborate, four-foot hunk of driftwood.

Andy's blue eyes contracted as he looked around, then widened as he met the curious gaze of a big, grayish-brown fish, lurking behind the driftwood with its belly on the bottom.

Ilsa shuddered. She was familiar with the beast. It was carnivorous and sizable: forty inches long and close to fifty pounds.

I guess all those live rats Janus keeps feeding it are paying dividends.

"Wow, that is one big, ugly-ass fish," Andy muttered, then whistled through his teeth. "It almost looks like a coelacanth." He turned to Ilsa. "What is it?"

A chair shifted noisily. "That's 'Wolfie'," the captain's pet," a nasally voice interjected. "Dumb name for a wolf fish, if you ask me. He brought it back alive from a fishing trip to Suriname. Must've cost a bundle."

Andy's eyes ping-ponged from his partner to Ramirez, then back again. She could tell he was gauging her discomfiture, after which he gave the intruding detective a nod. "Interesting. What does it eat?"

"Oh, I dunno. Why don't you stick your hand in there and find out!"

"Or, I could shove your face in there instead." Andy retorted. He winked at him, then plopped down into the seat next to Ilsa, his eyes still on Ramirez and a chilling smile on his face.

Ilsa was about to say something, then thought the better of it. She loathed her Puerto Rican peer with a passion. It wasn't a professional thing; the thirty-two-year-old was a halfway decent investigator – if you discounted his brutal methods, that is – but he was a consummate chauvinist. Not a day went by when the sexist remarks he directed at her and half the women in the city didn't make her want to grab him by his greasy hair and bury her fist in that weasel's face of his.

And, of course, she couldn't help feeling bad for his partner, who sat quietly a few yards away. Detective Tokaido was the polar opposite of Ramirez, and not just because of the size difference.

At six-foot-four and a solid three bills, Tokaido had seven inches and one-hundred-and-thirty pounds on the obnoxious Queens resident. But it was their opposing personalities that truly set them apart. Unlike the belligerent Ramirez, the big Japanese had nothing to prove. He was polite and professional, with a cool disposition. She envisioned him like a snow-covered mountaintop: stoic and enduring.

Which was probably why Janus put the two of them together, she surmised. Tokaido was there to mitigate things; to make sure someone with a cool head was present to resolve any problems his partner might cause. And, when needed, to do damage control.

"Hey, Dunbar," Ramirez called out.

What the hell ... Did that son of a bitch just read my thoughts?

"I forgot to ask how your vacation was. I heard you traveled the globe."

"Parts of it. What's your point?"

A leering look came over the goateed detective, and he patted his lap with both hands. "Hell, if you want to see the world, hembra, all you got to do is sit them nalgas right here! You know?"

Ilsa made a show of batting her eyelashes at him. "Yeah, but then everyone knows I'd end up singing, *'It's a Small World'* ..."

It was the mother of all burns, with Andy and even Tokaido nearly falling from their chairs; they were guffawing so loud. Ramirez turned an angry shade of scarlet, then purple as he clocked the malicious grin on her face. Even the reclusive wolf fish seemed to be enjoying the raucousness; it rose from its hiding spot to look around.

Ramirez's feral eyes swept the room. He must have realized he had no comeback and, desperate to save face, decided to focus his attention on Andy instead.

"So, Alvilda," he said. "You see that gym she's got? Mierda!" He ran his tongue across his upper lip in what could only be described as an obscene manner. "Tell me, did she let you press those big 'dumbbells' of her?" He leaned back hard in his chair and acted like he was struggling to hold a gigantic pair of breasts. "Spot me, Tokaido! I'm doing negatives!"

Ilsa felt her temper build, but before she could rise to the bait, Andy responded.

"Actually, I bet you're more into hoisting Tokaido's ginormous *nuts*," he remarked. Not missing a beat, he turned to Ramirez's shocked partner. "Oh, c'mon. I saw you in the locker room, big guy. Those things are like hairy honeydews. The girls must love you."

Tokaido blushed and stared at the floor, then grinned and nodded shyly.

"So, what do you do, Ramirez?" Andy continued. "Juggle them while you slob his knob, or does that come later?"

The veins in Ramirez's neck jutted out as he sprang from his seat. "What the *fuck* did you just say, cabron?"

Andy got up slowly, a predatory smile on his face. He moved uncomfortably close, until he towered over the smaller man. "Oh, I'm sorry. You couldn't *hear* me down there?"

"Oh, that's how it is?"

"Yeah, that's how it is."

"Yo, you better watch your ass, newbie. This ain't LA. You don't know who the fuck you messing with."

All of a sudden, Andy's on-again-off-again Brooklyn accent reemerged.

"Oh, please. What are you gonna do, change your *tampon* in front of me?"

Ramirez opened his mouth to say something, but his flustered expression became one of trepidation as the office door burst open.

Like a brewing storm cloud, Captain Janus stomped into the room.

At six-foot-two and a solid two-fifty, Janus was no-nonsense walking. He had glowering eyes that lurked beneath beetling brows and a brawler's reputation. He was proud of it, too. At one point, he'd boasted to Ilsa that he represented the "ultimate three Bs of badassery: big, bald, and black". She didn't know about all that, but experience had taught her he was a Brama bull, brimming with testosterone and easily provoked into charging.

"Hello, ladies," Janus said, his dark eyes jogging from face to face. "Something going on I need to know about?"

"No, sir," Tokaido said. "Ramirez was just welcoming Detective Alvilda to the squad."

"That's very touching. Now sit your asses down; we got work to do."

After picking up a stack of papers from his desk, Janus moved behind it. On the wall behind him was a large map of Manhattan, with dozens of tiny colored flags pinned into it.

"Okay, first off, nice job by Dunbar and Alvilda last night," he said, eyeing the topmost report. "They got us our first live one."

"Uh, sir?" Andy asked, raising his hand.

Janus's eyes zeroed him like iron rifle sights. "You're new, kid, so just this once, I'm gonna cut you some slack. Let me explain how things work around here. This job comes with a lotta stress." He pointed at his brow. "See this head? It needs hair." Then he reached into one of his desk drawers and came out with a large jar crammed with cash. "See this? This is my hair transplant fund. Every time you interrupt me you put fifty bucks in it. You got me?"

Andy nodded hesitantly.

"Good," Janus said with a smile. "Those are the rules. I talk, you listen. When I'm done, if you still have questions, *then* you ask."

"Sorry, sir."

Janus picked up a second report and started perusing it. "Okay . . . toxicology on Dr. McKinley is negative. Wealthy, no priors, devout Christian and family man. Alvilda, you asked about his lacerations . . ." He reached down, held up a blackened fireplace poker sealed in plastic. "This was found near the fireplace. It was supposed to be just for show, but sulfur on it matches that found in McKinley's wounds."

His gaze fell on Ilsa and he caught the look in her eyes. "Yes, Dunbar, he's awake. Still in local holding, pending psych eval." He looked around the room. "Questions so far?"

Ilsa cleared her throat. "Yes, sir. Has Dr. McKinley been crossed off as a suspect?"

"Based on your report, yes. He is, however, our best, make that our *only* witness."

"Yes, sir. We'll head straight there."

Janus came back around his desk and leaned back against it, with his thick arms folded atop his chest. He drew a deep breath, then let it out slow. "Okay, listen up. At this point, we believe we're dealing with some sort of serial-killing Xmas cult that has no prior association with their victims."

Ignoring their confused expressions, he held up a stack of gory crime scene photos. "Past investigations were dead ends, because every 'suspect' was found with a quart of their loved one's innards wedged in their gullet."

He handed Ilsa the photos. She suppressed her gut reaction as she saw what was on them and took a set, before passing them on.

"Husband with an eviscerated wife," Janus continued. "Mother with a half-eaten kid. That's how it's been, year after year, with the killers all choking to death on pieces of their victims."

He looked around the room. "Dr. McKinley's survival changes things. I put a call in to the medical examiner, who confirmed the amount of flesh missing from each victim far exceeds what was found inside their supposed killer." He glanced back over his shoulder at the wall map. "Which means, some sick SOBs are butchering people, then framing their loved ones for the crimes."

Janus's baleful expression turned rueful as he held up the report. He shook the pages for emphasis, then slapped them down on his desk. "For ten years they've gotten away with it. Well, they've hit *my* precinct now. And it ends here." He pushed himself upright and passed out everyone's assignments. "It's the twenty-third. That means we've got two more chances to catch these fucktards. If we don't, they'll disappear for another twelve months." He pointed at his people, made it a point to catch each of their eyes in turn. "That's not happening. Not on my watch, and not on yours. You got me?"

He nodded approvingly as he waited for the chorus of, "Yes, sirs!" to finish.

"Good. You have your assignments. Ramirez and Tokaido, I want you reviewing case files." He rubbed the back of his neck as he spoke. "See if this new angle shows any pattern that might indicate where the next attack could take place."

"Yes, sir," came the stereo reply.

Ilsa stood ramrod straight as Janus turned to her and Andy. "Dunbar and Alvilda, go see McKinley. He's pretty banged up, but see if you can get anything out of him." He lowered his voice and added, "Dunbar, tell him his daughter is safe. Use it to break the ice. You know, be 'maternal' . . ."

"Aye, sir," she said, ignoring Ramirez's snickering.

"Oh, and follow up with this crazy antique dealer," Janus said, flipping through their report once more. "The one who thinks he's got Santa's sled. See if he--"

"--will let you touch his Yule log?!?" Ramirez tittered.

Janus's expression darkened and he reached for his money jar. "Ramirez . . ."

"B-but that was just a joke! I--"

"*Jar*, Ramirez. *Now.*"

The other three detectives bit their tongues as their colleague got up, muttering Spanish curses as he reached into his wallet. He counted out a bunch of fives and tens and reluctantly stuffed them through the "hair jar's" narrow opening.

"Thanks for your contribution," Janus said good-naturedly. "Now, all of you, get the *hell* outta my office and go find those scumbags."

* * *

A few miles from the precinct, perched atop an old brick building, the figure watched and waited. It was crouched behind an aged concrete parapet, its bent body hidden beneath a ragged cloak that clung to its oversized frame. Its eyes glittered within the blackness of its cowl, and it pulled the hood tightly about its face, trying to shield itself from the omnipresent light sources that threatened to dissipate the nothingness it preferred.

It leaned forward and peered down from on high, its crimson eyes gleaming. Far below, three uniformed constables had gathered together on the snow-coated stone. They spoke and joked and stamped their feet in an effort to maintain their bodies' warmth. One raised a cigarette to his lips, savoring the toxic smoke he drew into his lungs.

The figure studied the men's faces, observing the movements of their fleshy lips and the pulsing of the hot blood that flowed through the veins beneath their skin. Its gaze fell to the weapons they wore suspended from their waists and a humorless smile creased its craggy lips. Its muscles tensed as it prepared to rise, but then it vacillated.

The door behind the three constables opened and two more men emerged from the squat building across the way, out into the windswept night. The first was a convincing "Santa" impersonator, adorned in ridiculous scarlet garments, trimmed with faux fur. Everything about him was false, from his skull cap to his boots, even his whiskers.

It was the second individual, however, that caused the hackles on the back of the figure's neck to rise. He was tall and old, with a real beard that stood out against the blackness of his robes. As he turned, smiling jovially and patting the imitator that accompanied him on the shoulder, the ancient crucifix that hung suspended from a chain around his neck swung into view.

A cleric.

The figure uttered a low rumble of annoyance and shrank back down, until only the ruddy glow of its narrowed orbs was visible. The moments ticked by and it remained still, the falling snow collecting atop its broad shoulders. Finally, after an eternity of jocularity, the clergyman and his outlandishly dressed companion climbed into their waiting conveyance and disappeared into the night.

CHAPTER 6

Outside the precinct, Andy followed a few paces behind Dunbar, zipping up his bomber's shearling collar as he went. A gentleman by nature, he would have preferred taking point. It was an instinctive thing; he didn't feel comfortable bringing up the rear. Especially now. As he bowed his head to the wind, however, the sight of the denim-covered work-of-art in front of him convinced him that, for the time being at least, he could make an exception.

A moment later, he reconsidered and averted his eyes. The last thing he wanted was to get caught ogling – make that *admiring* his partner. He'd never hear the end of it.

The young Californian gave a half-smile, as he realized it really didn't matter. This late in the game he wasn't looking for a relationship, or for *anything* for that matter. There was no point. Still, whether he liked it or not, Dunbar was starting to grow on him. Some men may have found an aggressive and athletic woman like her intimidating, but not him. He found the combination of assertiveness and uber-fitness a powerful aphrodisiac.

Not that he'd ever tell *her* that, he thought with a smirk.

Of course, there was more to life than just the physical – something Dunbar obviously had locked up. There was no doubt in his mind that her looks, style, and overall deportment would have garnered his mother's approval.

Andy chuckled, imagining them meeting, then his hand went to his chest and he sighed. She probably would have referred to the headstrong hellion as *fetching*. His lips quirked up at the thought. Did anyone from this century even *use* that term anymore?

He doubted it.

Still, he liked Dunbar's fire, as well as her innate sense of independence. She'd grown up an only child like he had, and it showed. She was used to taking care of herself and not relying on anyone. Of course, taken to extremes, such an attitude could be off-putting, and it probably explained why she was single. Still, if she found a man capable of weathering her storm, he was betting she'd blossom into something amazing.

A shame he couldn't stick around to see it.

Andy's heart skipped a beat as the object of his reflection unexpectedly slowed and looked his way.

"So, what's with the Brooklyn accent? I mean, you're originally from . . ." She pointed at his Star of Texas belt buckle. "I don't know, Dallas, correct?"

"Yes, ma'am. But before I moved to LA, I lived in Bay Ridge for seven years."

"Wow, you get around," she said, rubbing her gloved hands together, then slipping them inside her leather jacket's pockets. "But the accent only pops up once in a while. Is that just to bust balls?"

Andy shrugged, then switched to Bensonhurst mode. "Oh, I can turn it on and off whenever I want. But it does tend to come out if I got a beef with someone. You know, force of habit, I guess."

"Ah . . . oh, one more thing." She paused by her SUV's door and gave him an inscrutable look. "I appreciate you taking my back in there with 'Squiggy', but I can handle myself. Don't get any ideas."

"Hey, like I said, we're partners. Don't read into it."

She nodded her appreciation, then allowed him to hold her door as she climbed in. "Okay. Just making sure you weren't motivated by any *primal urges*."

"'Primal urges'?" Andy feigned a flabbergasted look, then went full-Goombah on her. "Fuhgeddaboudit!"

***

Andy's heart was lodged in his throat as Dunbar tore up the west side like an out-of-control drag racer. The way she sped, cut corners, and weaved around other cars, not to mention taking the occasional light, he figured she must've been a New York City taxi driver in a previous life. The only time she came to a full stop was when an ambulance unexpectedly crossed their path, its lights and sirens screaming.

Thank God they'd cleaned and salted the streets the day before.

"Do you know why I prefer the graveyard shift, this time of year?" Dunbar asked breathlessly.

Andy grimaced as she skidded around another car, his hand gripping the Forester's overhead grab handle so hard, he was sure he'd deformed the metal. "Because we're *dead!* I mean, because *it's* dead?"

She snickered, took another turn, then glanced his way. There was an aroused, almost exhilarated look about her, and he could've sworn he saw a hint of drool at the corners of her mouth.

"I *hate* traffic, not to mention anyone or anything slowing me down," she growled, jamming the gas down again. The SUV's engine roared like a caged lion as they accelerated down a deserted strip. "But now, it's so peaceful. The rat race of Christmas fades, and I can actually hear myself think."

"What *is* it with you and the holidays?"

"We're here," Dunbar announced, slowing and pulling smoothly into an available space. She cut the ignition, pocketed her keys, then threw him a wry look. All of a sudden, her gaze dropped unabashedly to his crotch region. "Let's go, big man. Oh, and I hope you didn't pee on my leather seats."

* * *

Andy peered pensively up at the psychiatric holding station. He'd read up on the place, shortly after his transfer had been approved. It was an early twentieth century construction: an armory, originally, if memory served. He gave a mental shrug. That would certainly explain its forbidding, fortress-like design.

Now, of course, the place was a squat, brick-and-reinforced-concrete prison. A medical jail where violent offenders – the insane and the potentially so – were held for clinical analysis, pending official dispensation.

Andy's lips tightened as he contemplated the ominous structure. He'd heard disturbing stories about the things that went on in there – exaggerated, no doubt – and he wondered what kinds of unpleasantness really awaited. The wind, of course, was eager for him to find out, and lashed his exposed face and neck repeatedly with its icy whips, spurring him on.

The veteran Dunbar had no such reservations. Already three paces ahead, she tramped forward, her military boots tamping down the snow while flurries fell around her. When she got to the entrance's stone steps, however, she hesitated.

"That's weird; the lights are out."

Andy followed her gaze up a nearby telephone pole. Its wires had been severed and hung limply in the wind, and the distribution transformer near its top was a wreck. Sparks spat from its exposed innards, and he smelled ozone.

Dunbar made a dismissive sound and started up the steps with Andy close behind. Halfway up, his lead foot slipped back and he barely caught himself. There was some sort of viscous liquid trickling down the stairs.

Oil?

He touched it with a gloved hand, rubbing it between his fingers, then reached for his flashlight. His eyes flew open wide as he espied the sticky redness. Atop the landing, Dunbar was already reaching for the building's heavy metal door.

"Ilsa, wait!" he shouted as he fumbled for his gun.

It was too late. The moment the door opened a dark form tumbled out. It landed on his stunned partner, causing her to exclaim loudly as she staggered back. Her rear end hit the cold stone hard, while she punched and shoved at the husky figure on top of her.

Andy was there in a millisecond, his weapon drawn as he bodily hauled her assailant off her. He mouthed a curse as he hurled him onto his back, then realized what he was looking at.

It was a uniformed police officer.

Or rather, what was left of one.

"Shit!" Dunbar spat, pushing herself away from the blood-soaked corpse with a shudder and clambering to her feet.

The dead cop was Caucasian, his age indeterminate. He had no radio, no gun or gun belt, and no chest, for that matter. The front of his patrolman's jacket, uniform shirt, and most of the muscle underneath were gone, ripped away, exposing ruptured ribs and even a portion of one of his lungs.

Dunbar recovered her poise and felt for a pulse.

"He's gone," she confirmed with a spasmodic headshake. "Call it in. We--"

Both detectives' heads snapped up at the sound of distant gunfire, followed by a series of muted screams. Dunbar's teeth bared as she whipped out her Glock, and the partners rushed inside, flashlights in hand and weapons ready.

The scene that awaited them was worthy of one of those post-apocalyptic zombie movies. Except that nothing was moving.

The lobby looked like the remains of a ten-car pileup. The reception desk was smashed, its surrounding wooden chairs and dividers flattened like matchsticks, and the drop ceiling overhead had literally dropped. Its shattered gray tiles lay mixed with the rubble below, and what framing remained hung like eerie metal cobwebs, twisted and deformed.

Draped atop the debris, lay the bodies of office and medical personnel, as well as two more police officers. Their wounds were horrific; two had been disemboweled, with two more missing arms and legs. Those that still had faces stared blankly upward, their agonized expressions highlighted by an eerie strobe effect; the result of sparks intermittently spewing from a damaged overhead conduit.

Andy gnawed his lower lip as he performed a visual sweep of the area. The wrist of his gun hand rested atop his opposing forearm as he swung his pistol and high-powered torch back and forth, scanning for threats.

To his left, Dunbar checked an intact cop's body, searching for signs of life. She looked down and shook her head gravely.

"His gun's empty," she noted, then held up what was left of the dead man's other hand. "Radio's shattered, and his hand with it."

Andy grabbed his cell phone, then mouthed a curse as he saw he had no bars. His brow knitted up like an old tire tread as he considered the building's thick stone walls. They'd get no signal without a router, and the communications desk had been annihilated.

But by whom?

He took a step, then realized that, in addition to all the blood spatter, the floor beneath his feet was littered with spent shell casings and two more police radios. Both were badly broken, to the point they looked as if they'd been hit with a sledge hammer.

Dunbar's jaw ratcheted open as she took in the devastation. "What the *hell* happened here?"

"I'd say it's *still* happening!" Andy shouted as a distant scream echoed up and down a nearby hallway.

Side by side, the pair started forward. Almost immediately, they heard a garbled voice coming from a room to the right and made for its open doorway, sidearms at the ready. In the center of the room, a uniformed patrolman staggered around, his back to them. He had his gun in his right hand and was waving it to and fro, while muttering to himself.

As he spun in their direction, Andy recoiled. His face looked like raw ground beef. His cheekbones were exposed and his eyes were gone, their empty sockets staring out from a bloody backdrop.

"Jesus," Dunbar said, holstering her weapon and rushing toward him. "Here, let me help you--"

"Keep away!" the blind officer shouted hysterically.

A moment later, Andy and Dunbar found themselves diving for cover as he started capping off rounds. Without his sight, he was firing at random, and they could hear him muttering the 'Our Father' in-between potshots.

"Asshole!" Dunbar shouted from behind a support column. "We're fucking cops!"

"No, you're not! You're with *it!*"

From the shelter of an upended desk, Andy caught his partner's eye and mouthed the word '*it?*'. Then, from somewhere down the hall, they heard a loud rumble followed by a muffled scream.

"Fuck this shit," Dunbar snapped. She stepped out from behind the column. "Look, buddy, we're NYPD and we're here to help you!"

"I don't believe you! Keep away!"

Andy felt a spearpoint of panic as the wounded man squeezed off another round. This one zinged through the air less than a yard from his partner's head, and he heard her gasp loudly at the realization.

"*There* you are . . ." the blind cop said as he zeroed her.

"Whoa!" Andy shouted. Before Dunbar could react, he sprang between them, the distraught cop's 9mm pointed at his heart. "C'mon, pal," he cajoled. "You don't want to do that. We're the *good guys.*"

The blind officer hesitated. A second later, a deafening bellow resounded throughout the building.

"You're right. It's better this way."

Andy's scream of denial came a moment too late, as the mutilated officer took a step back and, in one smooth motion, raised the pistol to his temple.

Blam!

Andy rushed forward, only to stand powerlessly over the spasming body. He remained there, gaping in disbelief, lips quivering and hands shaking.

Before he could give voice to the emotions welling up inside him, Dunbar grabbed him and spun him roughly around.

Seizing him by the collars of his dress shirt, she yanked it open, popping buttons and exposing both his bare chest and the religious medal resting on it.

"You, asshole!" she snapped, then shoved him angrily away from her. "You're not even wearing a vest!"

Andy stared numbly at her. He was still trying to process the senseless death he'd just witnessed, coupled with the incensed look on his partner's face, when more cries of terror echoed up and down the halls.

This time, however, they came from different directions.

He drew a huge breath and bore down. A heartbeat later, he felt the barfly's equivalent of a triple-shot of adrenaline, spiked with a cold dose of reality, shoot through him. It freed him from his momentary funk, as well as the net of indecisiveness that had settled over him. "We'd better split up," he advised. "I'll check the back, you hit the holding cells."

Dunbar nodded. "Okay, I'll call it in."

His sidearm in one hand and flashlight in the other, Andy loped around a nearby corner and disappeared from view.

* * *

After stepping outside just long enough to make a frantic call to Emergency Services, Ilsa reentered the warzone that was the city's psychiatric holding center. She picked the furthest corridor from the one Andy chose and raced down it without hesitation. Weapon ready, she moved nimbly forward, her senses on high alert.

As she pondered their situation, the muscles of her jaw systematically contracted. They were obviously dealing with some sort of terrorist attack. There was no other explanation. She had no idea how many scumbags were involved or what was driving them, but to assault a government building that almost always had armed cops on hand, they had to be fanatics.

And, from the look of things, heavily armed ones.

Their motive, on the other hand, was a bit more obvious. They were after Dr. McKinley; nothing else made sense. The wounded surgeon had undoubtedly seen one or more of their faces. His testimony could put the kibosh on what she suspected was a large and well-funded organization – one responsible for a decade of headline-grabbing murders.

No worries.

Ilsa doublechecked her Glock's safety, then felt for her spare magazines. She smiled a predatory smile. The bastards were in for a rude awakening. Or, as Captain Janus would put it, *'the fuck stops here.'*

She ignored the crunch of spent brass underfoot as she worked her way down the lightless corridor. Fifteen yards further, she came upon the remains of yet another freshly murdered cop. She smelled him before she saw him, his bowels vented and skull crushed, lying in a pool of blood. His spent Sig Sauer was still gripped in rigid hands.

No perp bodies yet and no blood trails. Hmph. Looks like LA was right. Whoever these assholes are, they're wearing military-grade body armor. I guess headshots are the order of the day. Glad I practiced.

She stopped as she reached the first holding cell and stood there staring. It had been opened, but not via its heavy steel door. A large swathe of its reinforced bars had been pushed outward, leaving a makeshift hole over five feet wide.

No, make that *pulled* outward, she thought, studying the pattern.

What the hell is going on here? Is there some sort of supersized 'Jaws of Life' type tech out there that can do this?

Ilsa shined her light through the plume-like opening, then inhaled sharply. The detainees were still there – six or seven of them, from the look of things. They were piled up in the far corner, a fleshy hillock of bleeding and broken bodies.

They were dead. Every single one of them.

She could feel her heart starting to pound and focused on drawing slow, calming breaths. This situation was getting more fucked up by the minute. She focused her Surefire on the collective creek of blood that meandered out of the cell, and gritted her teeth as she stepped carefully over it.

Then she saw the tracks. Someone had tread in the gore, leaving behind an easy-to-follow trail.

A very big someone.

She did a doubletake then swallowed nervously. The tracks were exactly the same as the ones she'd abused Andy about the previous night, the ones they'd found pressed into the ice outside the McKinley's apartment building. Huge, hoof-like ovals, over one-foot wide, except these were outlined in coagulating crimson.

What in the actual fuck?

Ilsa felt the hairs on the back of her neck prick up, then chided herself for being a superstitious idiot. Obviously, there was a logical explanation for the draft-horse-sized tracks. She was acting like a frightened child.

C'mon, girl. Woman up!

She commenced following the hoofprints, picking up the pace as she realized they would soon run out of "ink". They were nearly gone, when she noticed they'd curved toward a nearby examination room. The door to the room rested on the floor outside. From the look of things, it had been yanked right off its hinges.

Steeling herself, she counted to three, then sprang into the room, weapon ready. Her chest heaved in relief as she realized there was no one there. No one, that is, except the person she'd come to find.

It was McKinley. He was propped up in his hospital bed. He had a series of straps restraining him, and one arm extended in greeting.

"Doctor McKinley, thank God!" she cried, rushing into the room. "We--"

Ilsa came to a screeching halt as the beam of her flashlight illuminated the surgeon's face. His eyes, skin, and hair were all a ghostly white, and lips were drawn back in a frozen grimace – a death mask of unadulterated horror. His arm – the one she thought had gestured to her – was extended stiffly outward. Tightly gripped in his lifeless fingers was the old rosary he'd been clutching the last time she'd seen him.

"Jesus, what happened to--"

The gunshots interrupted Ilsa's soliloquy. There were two of them, back-to-back: a double-tap. She frowned. They sounded deeper and louder than the pop-pop sounds made by the usual 9mm rounds. More like a . . .

"Andy!"

Any thoughts for her own safety were forgotten, and Ilsa pounded purposefully down a lightless hallway, searching for the source of the gunfire. Moments later, she found her partner. His body was silhouetted by a faint glow that permeated the end of the hallway via an open door.

He was slumped against the wall in a seated position, a dazed expression on his face. Her heart skipped a beat when she saw his eyes flutter and she rushed to him. Dropping to her knees, she ran her fingers deftly over his chest and abdomen, checking for wounds.

"Andy . . . are you hit? Are you *shot*?"

The sound of her voice caused his eyes to come into focus and he stared blinkingly at her. He shook his head slowly from side to side, like he was attempting to rid himself of something, then pushed up off the floor, trying to regain his feet. She put her arm around him and helped hoist him upright.

Lord, he was heavy.

Still out of it, Andy rested one palm against the wall and concentrated on breathing. After a few controlled inhalations, he gave her a nod of thanks.

"Did you ... did you see it ... him?"

A line appeared between Ilsa's brows. "See who?"

"Kid was right ... Big bastard in a long trench coat. Nailed him center mass but he just kept coming. Ran me over on his way--"

His voice trailed off as he glanced left, and Ilsa followed his wide-eyed stare. Five yards away, the facility's thick metal EXIT door was gone, allowing the frigid night breeze and snowflakes to invade the otherwise warm hallway. She could see a streetlight outside and, past a nearby wall, the illuminated windows of an office building.

Guns at the ready, she and Andy advanced on the doorway. Her brows hiked up as she noted the damage to its frame. The broad hinges were gone, shorn away with the door itself. Before them lay an unfenced platform, coated with snow. There was an adjoining flight of steps that led down to the alley and, to the right, a concrete wheelchair access ramp.

Ilsa signaled to her partner, then pointed across the alley. Their missing door stood waiting, propped up at an odd angle against the base of a fifteen-foot brick wall. At first glance, it appeared intact, but their flashlights soon pinpointed a tremendous dent in its center. It looked like the equivalent of a medieval battering ram had slammed into it, deforming the surrounding metal as it blasted it free from its frame.

Eyes wide and jaws set, the pair stepped out onto the slippery landing. The omnipresent wind continued to harangue them and flurries obscured their view. Then, suddenly, there was a tremendous whooshing sound and Ilsa's peripherals got the distinct impression of something large and dark passing overhead. They swung their weapons up but saw nothing.

If there was something, it was gone.

Ilsa pointed to the door and surrounding alley, signaling Andy to go first while she kept her Glock trained on the roof. If someone was up there, she had no intention of getting caught flatfooted.

Once Andy reached the alley, she followed him down, her eyes still sweeping the rooftop and surrounding windows. He crouched down to study something, then gestured for her to join him.

She shook her head in befuddlement. He'd found more of those oversized hoofprints, a series of them, in fact, each spaced a good six feet apart. They started at the base of the steps and made a beeline for the brick wall on the other side. The tracks were fresh and had a faint pinkish tinge – likely left by the same psychopath responsible for McKinley's death.

Ilsa's eyes zoomed in on the wall, itself, and she felt her heart start pounding again. There was a series of sizable gouges in the bricks and mortar, starting at around the seven-foot mark and traveling upward, all the way to the top. They looked fresh. She exchanged looks with Andy, who was undoubtedly thinking the same thing she was.

They were handholds.

She resumed pointing her Glock at the roof, but when her partner stumbled to one side and had to catch himself, she realized he hadn't recovered from his collision with the intruder. She moved to his side, giving him time to regain his equilibrium, while simultaneously using her peripherals to keep watch.

Andy drew a breath. "Dunbar, no . . . no *man* could've done this."

Her head snapped up. "What do you mean, 'no man'?"

When no answer was forthcoming, she grabbed him by the shoulders. "Hey, I'm talking to you," she said, shaking him. "What did you *mean* by that? You're not making any sense!"

Andy's face was a study in incredulity as he took in the pockmarked wall, the shattered door, and the bizarre tracks that went from the wall to the frosted landing and back again.

"None of this makes sense."

CHAPTER 7

Dawn was barely a ghostly gleam on the horizon, when Andy and Dunbar made their way to the *Ne'er-Do-Well* diner. It was a homey little place he'd started frequenting, just a few blocks from the precinct. Ever the gentleman, he tried holding the restaurant door for his headstrong partner but she blew right past him and opened it herself.

"Look, we need to get our facts straight so they match the report," Dunbar muttered. They were standing near the hostess's station, waiting to be seated. She looked around, then lowered her voice to a whisper. "We've got over a dozen dead, including five cops from three different precincts. This thing's gonna go nuclear, and we don't want to get burned, okay?"

Andy shook his head. "Or fall off the wagon. Because, frankly, I need a drink."

From across the room, the hostess spotted the pair and immediately headed their way. Andy remembered her from his last visit. Her name was Pam – an attractive brunette with a passion for the theater. She puffed out her chest and flashed him her most dazzling smile as she approached.

It dimmed as she laid eyes on Dunbar.

"Andy, I'm glad you stopped by," she said, then indicated his partner. "Girlfriend?"

"Hey, Pam. No, this is Detective Dunbar, my new--"

Pam lit up like Independence Day. She entwined her arm around his and led him toward a windowed booth, chatting happily all the while and acting like Dunbar didn't exist.

"You taking class later?" she asked, standing in front of the booth.

He smiled down at her. "I think so. Why?"

She drew awkwardly close and murmured in his ear. "Listen, I know it's short notice, but it's almost Christmas and I was hoping you'd come by and help me clean out my chimney."

Dunbar rolled her eyes and pushed brusquely past. "Get a chimney sweep, sister. Or better yet, a gyno. Now, if you don't mind, we're on the clock."

Pam's face darkened. She opened her mouth as if to say something, then spun on her heel and returned to her podium, leaving them to seat themselves.

The corners of Dunbar's mouth crinkled with amusement as she hung up her coat and looked around. Then she pulled up an Adobe file on her tablet and showed it to Andy. "Okay, so our report covers all the basic facts. I took out your little 'Secret Service' routine--"

"Why?"

"Because the captain will send you in for psych eval, that's why." She studied his face before continuing. "I also deleted your references to 'monstrous hoofprints' . . ."

Andy frowned. "Well, what would *you* call them?"

"Some asshat wearing cosplay boots, to conceal his shoe size and brand, and to make himself look taller."

"And him taking two to the chest like they were spitballs?"

Dunbar shrugged. "Big guy, high on PCP and wearing Kevlar. It happens."

"And the door? And the holes in that wall?"

An exasperated look came over her. "Rusty hinges, an explosive charge, and/or they were there before we got there. How the *fuck* do *I* know?" She lowered her voice. "Look, that's for forensics to decide, okay? Be smart. You *get* me?"

Andy leaned back in his seat, a scowl on his face. His partner's attempt to palliate his report didn't sit well with him. Admittedly, he hadn't gotten a good look at the person that bum-rushed him. It was dark and he hadn't had a chance to bring his flashlight to bear. But whoever it was, they were incredibly fast and strong, not to mention impressively agile for someone that size. The SOB was seven-foot easy. Men that big often suffered from a pituitary condition resulting in uncontrolled growth. They usually ended up clumsy, with some requiring a cane to walk, and many ending up half-crippled.

This guy wasn't. He was a runaway rhino.

Andy exhaled through his nostrils, trying to dispel his mounting misgivings. Hopefully, in addition to checking the blood, the lab would do a DNA workup on the track marks themselves. That might shed a little light on things.

He glanced up from his musings to see Pam passing by with another pair of patrons. She seated them, gave him a smile and his partner a '*You bitch,*' look, then returned to her station.

"Quite the ladies' man, aren't you?" Dunbar observed, peering at him over the top of her menu.

Before he could reply, a tall, super-fit waitress sauntered over. She was an aspiring actress, if memory served; although, for the life of him, he couldn't recall her name. She beamed at him as she sidled up to the booth, then tossed his partner a perfunctory nod.

"Hi, Andy. Taking class later?"

He grinned affably. "With you there? Wouldn't miss it for the world."

"Good. Afterward, could you come by my place, before your shift?" Her lips parted and she started twirling a strawberry-blonde lock around her fingers. "It's the holidays, and I was hoping you'd help me put up my stockings."

"Um, that's really tempting."

"So, is that a yes?"

"Tell you what. How's about if I help you take them down instead."

"*Down?*"

"Yeah, right after Christmas. Then I'll be all yours."

"*All* mine?" she asked, her eyebrows rising.

He winked at her. "Absolutely. For as long as I live."

Dunbar made a rude noise. "What in the actual *hell?* Is this a diner or an escort service? Can we place our order, please?'

The server's bright expression dulled as she looked the other woman up and down.

"Sorry, Andy," she said. "I didn't realize you had your *aunt* with you. Your usual?"

"Yes, ma'am," he replied, denying the grin that was literally begging to surface.

Suddenly, the girl's eyes lit back up. "Oh, I almost forgot. I got a bag of those marshmallows you like for your cocoa. You know, the jumbo ones?"

Andy smirked despite himself.

"And you, *ma'am?*" the waitress asked, focusing on Dunbar.

"I'll have a coffee, black, and an OJ," she replied coolly. "And egg whites and spinach on an everything bagel."

The girl was barely out of earshot, when his partner wheeled on him. "What the shit, Alvilda? You've been here less than a month, and every chick in here wants to play, 'Mister and Missus Claus' with you?"

Before he could formulate a response, she added, "And what is this 'class' nonsense?"

He thought it over, then decided it was best to come clean. "Uh, most of the girls here attend the dance studio I joined."

Dunbar went poker-faced. "'Dance studio'? As in ballet?"

Andy cleared his throat. "Actually, it's ballroom dancing."

"Ballroom dancing . . ."

"Yep. Taken classes since I was eight. Don't knock it."

He watched as one of her eyebrows crept up.

"Let me guess. Your mom was a prima ballerina and made you suffer through lessons every day."

Andy paused as the waitress came prancing over and proudly handed him an oversized mug of steaming hot cocoa. There was a plum-sized marshmallow floating in its center, and he made it a point to ooh and aah at it before she wiggled off.

"Actually, no. I was clumsy because of my height and she thought it might help my coordination. It did. And *now* . . ." he shifted nimbly in his seat. "It helps with my martial arts. You know, speed, balance . . ."

"Your mom's a smart woman."

"She was."

Dunbar's face crumpled. "Oh, geez. I'm so sorry. How long?"

"Three years," Andy said on a sigh. He hesitated, then added, "She was a gifted psychic. Saw her own end coming, too. A brain tumor, of all things."

"A psychic? Look, I-I'm sorry, but I don't believe in such things."

"You don't seem to believe in much of anything," he remarked. His face became devoid of expression, and he stared out the window at the darkness. "What's up with that?"

"I'll tell you what I believe," Dunbar said. She glanced over his shoulder at the nearby kitchen. "I believe your would-be-girlfriend better not screw with my food, or she's gonna get my foot up that perky little ass of hers."

"Chill out. It's almost Christmas," Andy said with a chuckle.

His pugnacious partner's evasiveness was hardly lost on him, but he decided to let it slide. A part of him wanted to know what she was hiding, but he respected her privacy.

Still, hating Christmas? Who does that?

He decided to distract himself by playing with his mega marshmallow. Placing his spoon atop it, he pushed it under and held it there. In his mind it was an ORION-class submarine, trapped at the bottom of the ocean. A submerged volcano had split the seafloor nearby and magma was pushing its way up, superheating the surrounding seawater.

The sub had to do an emergency blow. It was life or death. Surfacing in three, two, one . . .

Andy released his confection-based vessel so it could bob to the surface. He waited eagerly for it, but when it did what popped up wasn't a marshmallow.

It was an eyeball.

A huge, horrifying eye with a vertical pupil. It was covered with distended veins and, instead of rich cocoa, floated in a bubbling mug of blood.

Dark blood. The venous kind.

Andy uttered a startled cry and rocked back in his seat. Denial kicked in like a tripping circuit breaker and he averted his eyes. Ramrod straight, he sat there blinking furiously. When he finally looked back down, his cocoa was normal.

What the . . . hell?

"Hey, you okay?" his partner asked. The concern on her face was evident. "You just turned sheet white."

He cleared his throat. "Uh, yeah, yeah. I'm fine. Um, what were you saying?"

Dunbar gave him a clinical look, then shrugged. "So, she was a psychic, huh. Could she talk to the dead, things like that?"

Andy contemplated his cocoa, then did the prudent thing and set it aside. "No, her gift was precognition."

"Yeah? Did she know you'd become a cop, and a reckless one at that?"

He vacillated as the waitress returned with their order. He gave the girl a friendly nod as she set their plates down, waited for her to leave before replying.

"Yes."

Dunbar tasted her sandwich. Apparently satisfied it wasn't poisoned, she nodded. "She wasn't afraid you'd die? I saw your file. Those gunfights in LA . . . in a two-year span you shot and killed what, two heroin dealers and a child trafficker?"

"They all drew on me," he said simply.

"And your mom was okay with it?"

"She said it wasn't my time."

Dunbar studied him through hooded eyes. "Ah, so you're saying she *knew* when you'd die."

"Yes."

"And she told you."

"On her deathbed."

Dunbar finished another bite, then took a sip of her coffee. "So, is that why you walk around all badass, like you're Wyatt Earp, sans vest?"

Andy regarded her with those chill blue eyes of his. "If we're going with a Tombstone analogy, I'd go with Doc Holliday."

"Come again?"

"Holliday's tuberculosis made him among the deadliest of gunfighters. He was already dying. What more could they take from him?"

"So, since you know when your time is up, until then you're invincible."

"What's your point?"

Dunbar ran her tongue over her teeth. "So, uh, when, exactly, is your demise scheduled? I mean, as your partner, I think I should know." She gave him a sardonic smile. "Unless you're going to post it on social media, that is . . ."

"I'll send a tweet," Andy said with a smirk. "Hashtag: peace out."

"Well, for your sake, I hope it's soon," she remarked, angling her head toward their waitress and hostess. The two were in full gossip mode and, every so often, glanced hungrily in Andy's direction. "Because, *'Glamazon'*, over there, thinks you just proposed."

A minute later, an impish grin spread across Dunbar's face. "You know what? Maybe I'll help you out," she said, rising.

She walked over to the two women, got the check, and initiated a tête-à-tête. From the curious stares he kept getting, Andy could tell he was the topic of conversation. All of a sudden, his partner leaned in and whispered in the tall waitress's ear. A shocked look came over the girl, and when she glanced back at him her eyes were huge.

Dunbar stepped back to take a quick call, then headed back to the booth with their visibly distressed server in tow. She had an ill-concealed smirk on her face as she grabbed her leather jacket.

The waitress wore a chagrined look.

"Andy, I-I just wanna say I'm *so* sorry for how I acted before," she said. She took the check back from Dunbar and tucked it inside her apron. "If it's okay, your meal is on me."

Andy's jaw went into freefall and his eyes started doing the pendulum thing, from her face to his partner's and back again. "W-what? What did--"

The server placed a reassuring hand on his shoulder.

"It's alright. And I want you to know, I think the world of you."

She gave him a sad-yet-sympathetic smile and walked away.

Andy stared after her, then sucked in a breath and turned to Dunbar. "Okay, what the hell was *that* about?"

"I told her your secret," she said smugly. "You're safe now. C'mon, we got a call."

Andy wore a befuddled look as he grabbed his coat. "Secret? What 'secret'?" He glanced toward the kitchen and saw Pam and their waitress standing there, chin-wagging for all they were worth. Their expressions spoke volumes. "Wait, what did you tell her . . . *them*?"

"Don't worry about it," Dunbar said, chuckling as she headed out.

Andy caught up to her, his eyes narrowing. "Oh, I get it. You told her I'm gay. Ha, ha . . . very funny."

She shook her head.

"No? Okay, so you said I smell. That I have a tiny dick . . ."

Dunbar mimicked his exaggerated sniffing from the other day, then gave his crotch a quick squint. "No, but do you?"

"What?!? Which one? No, of course not!" he exclaimed. Man, the smugness of her grin had him fuming. "Seriously. I have to *eat* her – I mean *here*! What did you say?"

"I'll tell you on Christmas Day," Dunbar said, practically shaking with laughter as she opened her SUV door. "It'll be *my* gift in *your* stocking. Now, move that overgrown ass."

Andy held his tongue as he got in. But as his partner pulled out, he stared wordlessly out the window, his features contracting around his frown.

It was going to be a long two days until Christmas.

CHAPTER 8

An uneventful fifteen minutes later, Ilsa braked into a spot across the street from an upscale apartment complex. She checked her cell phone for additional data before setting it in its stand, then reached inside the glovebox for her placard. Outside, it was graveyard still. The flurries had finally stopped and even the wind was sleeping.

Hallelujah.

She decided a breath of fresh-albeit-frigid pre-dawn air would be a nice pick-me-up. After setting her SUV's heating system to compensate, she cracked her tinted window a hands-breadth and peered intently up at the darkened structure.

She'd never been inside this particular building. It was a mid-twentieth century construction; a fifteen-story, brick-and-concrete-faced high-rise, whose eminently desirable Central Park location was eclipsed only by its far-from-desirable prices.

As always, in New York it was money, money, money.

Thank God her parents had gifted her a home and the means to pay for it.

Ilsa's tired eyes were still combing the building's exposed walls when she felt Andy shift beside her. He was impatient, that one: always energetic and easily bored. She imagined his future wife – that is, if the egotistical stud-muffin ever decided to settle down – would have her hands full keeping him happy.

And by happy, she meant in *and* out of the boudoir.

Her imagination started getting the better of her and she smirked as she put it to bed. Man, she needed a date. She needed to let the cat out of its cage, to give it something to sink its teeth and claws into. It had been ages – something that sitting next to Mister Flat-Abs was a constant reminder of.

Speaking of which . . .

"So, why exactly are we here? Andy prodded. He leaned forward in an attempt to see what she was looking at. "You got a text?"

Ilsa cleared her throat as she nodded. "After the holding station, it dawned on me that our perps might be hitting buildings from the outside." She lowered her window a few more inches and scoured the apartment building's assorted floors and fire escapes.

Everything seemed quiet.

"I talked to a friend at dispatch, asked for info on any and all calls that came in about cat burglars or rappelers, no matter how crazy they might sound. Ten minutes ago, someone reported seeing a man--" She used two fingers from each hand to form quotation marks. "'Running up the south side' of this place."

Andy wore a dubious look, but joined her in looking as best he could. "Makes sense . . . McKinley's door was still in one piece. But how many guys do you know that can punch holes in bricks?"

"Besides you?" she said with a fleeting grin. "Could be anything. Maybe some military-grade rock-climbing shit. Who knows?"

"I'd like to believe that. But after what we saw, what *I* saw . . ."

"Look, I know you took a hit, but I need you frosty. Like coal eyes and a carrot frosty, okay?" Ilsa's brows lowered like blinds atop her eyes. "Janus is right. We're dealing with some sort of Satanic cult. I don't know who they are, but they're organized and dangerous, and we need to find them and shut them down. *Hard*. You get me?"

To her surprise, Andy was uncharacteristically silent.

The brooding respite lasted mere moments, however, as his wandering gaze flitted to the distant skyline.

"It's almost dawn. Looks pretty dead to me. Maybe we--" He hesitated as a blood-curdling shriek echoed down to them. "--should get our asses in gear!"

Forgetting her partly-open window, Ilsa yanked her keys out and sprang from the Forester, Glock in hand. She was already halfway across the street, her eyes scanning the complex's assorted floors and her thumb pressing her key fob, when Andy caught up to her. His jaw was set and he had his custom Colt 1911 in hand.

"Anything?" he said on an exhale.

Her keen eyes caught a hint of movement above them – something dark. "Fourth floor! She yelled, pointing. "Move it!"

They hit the nearest entrance, a side door that, from the look of things, led to the building's laundry. Andy gave the door a yank, only to find it securely locked. He gritted his teeth, then seized the metal handle with both hands and started heaving back with everything he had.

The lock held for two impressive tugs. On the third its mechanism snapped like balsa wood, and the big Californian nearly tore the metal and glass barrier right off its hinges.

"Way to go, Gargantua!" Ilsa exclaimed, clapping him on the shoulder. "You're proving more useful by the minute!"

Adrenalized now, the two stormed into the building like gangbusters, scaring the bejesus out of a headphones-wearing college kid in the process.

Eschewing the elevator, they bounded up the nearest stairwell, with Andy calling for backup. As they burst onto the fourth floor, they found themselves in a long corridor with no one in sight.

There was another ear-piercing scream. This one was cut short.

Fear that they were too late welled up, but Ilsa clamped down on it; desperation would only impair her judgment. She jogged down the hallway, her eyes ricocheting from one apartment to the next. In her head, she was visualizing the building's layout, hoping to match the window she'd seen outside with the corresponding residence.

Eventually, she narrowed it down to a door some ten yards away. She loped toward it with Andy watching her six. Signaling for silence, she leaned in and pressed her ear against the cool wood.

She was in luck. She heard something. It was . . .

Her eyes flew open wide and she uttered a high-pitched squeak, like she'd swallowed a gasp.

"Break it down!" she whispered.

Andy nodded, then hauled back and hit the apartment door with a front heel kick that would've staggered a moose. It flew open wide and the two sprang in, weapons ready.

"NYPD!" Ilsa shouted to whoever was within earshot. "NYPD! Come out with your hands up!"

There was no answer.

Grim-faced, the partners started forward.

Ilsa reached for the nearest light switch, then proceeded to navigate the mound of books that had spewed from a fallen bookcase, while Andy fanned out to her right. The place reminded her of the McKinley's. It was spacious, with high ceilings and lots of holiday decorations.

And it had been similarly trashed.

She tried going straight, but found herself taking a roundabout in order to bypass a flattened coffee table. She shook her head. Broken furniture was everywhere, making navigation difficult and stealth impossible. As her grandfather would've put it, it looked like one hell of a donnybrook had taken place.

Her ears pricked up. Directly ahead, a familiar song was playing on an old-fashioned record player. It was an LP of Frank Sinatra's classic *"Santa Claus is Coming to Town"*. She knew the song well; it was one of her parents' favorites. In fact, it had been playing on the radio, that day the family headed to Saint Patrick's . . .

Ilsa's jaw tightened at the unwelcome recollection. She attempted to distract herself by focusing on her feet but her brain decided to start an argument, centered around whether or not she should turn the phonograph off.

Probably best to leave it on, she reasoned, as the noise masked their advance. Also, should the song end unexpectedly, any intruders on the premises would instantly be alerted. Still, her subconscious argued, it brought back a lot of unpleasant memories. Why not silence it?

Her emotional waffling ended abruptly as she stumbled over a black-clad pair of legs, protruding from beneath an inverted couch. She pitched forward, managed to catch herself, but then slipped on the pool of blood her feet ended up in.

"Fuck!"

She'd have ended up sitting in it, if Andy hadn't made a quick grab. She mouthed an embarrassed 'thank you' as he hoisted her up, then blanched as she bent down and gave the victim a cursory look. It was a woman, but there was no point in checking for life signs; her eyes were wide and staring and her throat had been torn out.

All of it. To the point, you could see her bloodstained cervical vertebrae.

Ilsa clocked the look of abject agony on the victim's face and felt the anger within her build. Whoever did this was going to pay.

She started to step, acutely aware of her gore-coated soles sticking to the carpeting. Any urge to look down or back was instantly suppressed; she had no desire to see the trail she was leaving.

Just then, "Ol' Blue Eyes" finished crooning. The LP had run its course, as evidenced by the rhythmic static that followed. Ilsa was glad. She figured the reduced background noise would make it easier to hear, and she was right. A moment later, there was an audible thump, and both her and her partner's heads shot up.

The noise had emanated from an adjoining room, six yards away.

Ilsa signaled to Andy, who was in the middle of double-checking his weapon's safeties and spare magazines. He nodded grimly and together they stalked forward, two hunters on quick cat's feet.

As they approached the room – stepping around a defiled Christmas tree in the process – Andy paused and waved a hand in front of his face. "What is that *stench*?" he whispered.

Ilsa smelled it too, but shushed him.

When they reached the door, the first thing she noticed was the damage to its frame. There was a series of deep, dirt-filled gouges on the left, right, and top portions of the doorway's thick molding, like something big and filthy had been forced through it.

The second thing she noticed was the door itself was ajar. The crack was small, but by angling her head she could see part of a furiously burning fireplace. She squinted and leaned closer. She could hear strange squelching sounds, and was just able to make out a hint of a dark outline at the periphery of her field of view. The outline shifted noticeably, until the shape of what looked like a shoulder became visible.

Ilsa's eyes narrowed. There was someone in there.

A second later, she spotted a bare foot lying on the floor and corrected herself.

Make that two someones.

She signaled Andy that they had potential suspects, then indicated she was about to do a push-in. To her surprise, a concerned look came over him. His lips tensed and she expected him to say something, but then he just nodded.

Ilsa readied herself, then did a countdown with her fingers. *Three . . . two . . .* just before *one*, she sucked in a huge breath and, a moment later, bodychecked the door with everything she had.

It blew open and the two detectives barreled in, weapons hot.

Ilsa's lips curled back from her teeth as she laid eyes on their suspect. "Got you, you son of a-a . . ."

What she saw next sent her whole world into a tailspin.

There was a man sprawled on the floor, directly in front of the room's antique fireplace. He was gaunt and dressed in a t-shirt and sleep pants, and his chest was heaving. She could see he was practically covered in blood – Lord knew what injuries he'd suffered – but it was what stood *over* him that gave her pause.

There was a second man, an impossibly huge one, hunched over the battered homeowner. He had him gripped around the ribs with one hand and was holding him at an odd angle, so that his head and torso remained in a semi-upright position. She couldn't see the larger man's face; his back was turned and he wore a long, black cloak, the hooded kind that concealed the wearer's face and form, like you'd see at a Renaissance fair or in one of those old space saga movies.

The cloak itself looked mausoleum old. It was badly frayed along its edges, and the tatty strings that draped from it lay upon the floor like a fringe of rotting rat tails. Despite its fabric being the color of pitch, it had a dull shininess to it. She realized it was the result of caked layers of filth; dirt, ash, and cobwebs, all held in place by an outer crust that served as a binding agent.

It was dried blood spatter. Tons of it.

A sense of overwhelming dread filled Ilsa and she stood there gaping. She knew the moment they'd burst in that they'd found their killer. She also knew that, whoever the giant before her was, even with his back turned he radiated evil on a scale that made serial killers seem like newborns. He was old too; she didn't know how she knew, but she could sense it. There was a timelessness about him and, accompanying that immutability, a rapacious desire to kill.

And feed.

Feed?

It was then that the true horror she and Andy faced revealed itself. The cloaked figure shifted its weight to one side, exposing more of the homeowner's face. She realized there was something over his nose and mouth, encompassing them in the manner of an oxygen mask. Whatever it was, it was tubular in shape, but appeared slimy and flexible.

It struck her as organic. In fact, it reminded her of a big sea lamprey. She was familiar with the disgusting parasites; she'd cut one off a Lake Erie salmon, just last summer.

But this was no lamprey.

The tube was amber in color and semi-translucent. In fact, backlit by the fire, she could see things moving along inside it. They were irregularly-shaped, globular objects that, responding to the pull of gravity, flowed down its length in regular pulses. She didn't know what the objects were, but they were being forcibly pumped down the homeowner's esophagus, like a stomach pump in reverse.

The thing shifted again, and its profile came into view. As it did, she followed the tube from the victim's face up to its point of origin. What she saw next made her stomach clench.

It was the figure's tongue. It was long and hollow, and being used to push hunks of regurgitated matter down the victim's throat.

The chest heaves . . . oh, my god.

Suddenly, Captain Janus's reveal about a member of each family choking to death replayed inside her head. Ilsa's eyes opened so wide, her eyelids felt like they'd split. She tried to speak, but her lips were numb. She tried to move, but her limbs refused to obey. A sickening feeling came over her.

This person, this . . . *thing* had her under its spell.

She was helpless.

As it finally became aware of her and her partner's presence, or perhaps it had simply decided to finish its awful repast first, the thing dropped what it was doing. Literally.

Its leech-like tongue separated from the homeowner's pallid face with a vile sucking sound and disappeared back inside its mouth. Then it released its grip, the still-twitching body falling to the floor with a moist thud, reminiscent of a soaked sack of topsoil.

Still hunched over, it turned in their direction. Ilsa could see its eyes, deep within the confines of its cowl. They burned like embers, and in them she read two things:

Disdain and death.

Theirs.

"Shit!" Andy spouted as he broke free from the spell that held him. Out of the corner of her eye she saw him whirl in her direction. His lips moved and she heard him say her name. His voice sounded tiny, like he was a mile away.

"Dunbar! *Dunbar!*"

As the thing roused itself, Ilsa felt her lips begin to work again. She stared up at it. "W-what . . . What *are* you--"

She froze in mid-sentence as it rose to its full height and peered contemptuously down at them. It was enormous, over eight feet tall from heel to cowl. In between the edges of its cloak, she could see portions of its body. It had an impossibly massive build, and looked to weigh at least nine hundred pounds. Its chest was incredibly broad and layered with thick cords of gristle, on top of which lay patches of indigo-colored scales. Bristle-like hairs protruded both in-between and around the scales, giving it the appearance of both reptile and mammal.

Ilsa met the thing's gaze and froze, like a bird entranced by a viper.

Beside her, she heard Andy curse and gag as the foulest stench yet inundated them. He turned to her and spotted the shock and disbelief on her face.

"It's not a man!" he shouted, taking aim as the unholy apparition took a step. Its thick-furred legs ended in huge hooves, and it was so heavy the entire room shook.

"Shoot it, Dunbar!"

Ilsa tried to move, tried to raise her gun, but she didn't have the strength. Her Glock was so heavy; she couldn't lift it. All she could do was stare into--

Those eyes.

"Shoot it, damn it!" Andy cried out. "Shoot the fucking thing!"

A split-second later, LA uttered the foulest curse she'd ever heard and cut loose.

The resultant tumult was music to Ilsa's ears. The booms from her partner's weapon, coupled with the creature's unearthly bellow, shook her free from her daze. She blinked hard as she felt herself regain control. Then her face contorted with uncontained fury and she opened fire.

The combined report from the two guns was deafening. Slug after slug slammed into the walking nightmare, an unrelenting barrage. It snarled menacingly, then raised its apelike arms in front of its face as it gave ground. Ilsa expected it to drop, but as a round struck it then smashed into a nearby wall, creating a golf-ball-sized hole and casting up a puff of plaster, she realized their bullets were having no effect.

Its skin was too tough. All they were doing was pissing it off.

They needed a more vulnerable target.

Ignoring Andy's shouted warning, Ilsa aimed for the thing's face.

It must have deduced her plan, because before she could pull the trigger, it came for her. She froze as she saw it grow exponentially in her sights. The next thing she knew, one of its huge hands was encompassing her head.

There was no time to react, no way to escape.

It had her.

Out of nowhere, Andy uttered a bellow worthy of a character from an Edgar Rice Burroughs novel and threw himself between them. His M1911 spat fire, striking the creature solidly in the throat, with the impact sending Ilsa stumbling backwards. Her feet went out from under her and she landed hard on her right side. Shaken but undeterred, she tried firing from a seated position but couldn't, for fear of hitting her partner.

Meanwhile, the creature, furious at having missed its mark, launched a devastating strike at Andy's chest. Its claws were like thick-ridged meat hooks and ripped through both his heavy bomber and the tissue underneath. Then something strange happened. LA's yelp of pain was tailgated by a loud hiss and the thing yanked its hand back.

Confused as to why it had broken off its assault, but grateful for the respite, Ilsa sprang to Andy's side.

Less than three yards away, the creature stood stock still. A confused look spread across its misshapen face and its ruby eyes blinked as it peered at its raised paw. Its banana-sized fingers peeled open, revealing Andy's religious medal, pressed into the flesh of its palm. Smoke began to rise from it, and the thing let out a howl of anguish. It clawed furiously at the medal as it lurched back.

A heartbeat later, and with astonishing speed, it seized the dead homeowner by the legs and flung him at Ilsa and Andy like a boomerang.

Both detectives were caught flat-footed. The still-warm corpse plowed into them with the force of a one-hundred-and-fifty-pound bowling ball, knocking them off their feet and depositing them in a tangled pile of limbs. Then, before either could even think about regaining their feet, their assailant leapt headlong into the open fireplace and vanished.

Ilsa grunted as she pushed Andy off her – no mean feat – and clambered to her feet. She stood there, mouth open and chest heaving, her smoking Beretta hanging impotently at her side.

She couldn't believe her eyes.

It was gone. Just . . . gone.

She turned to her partner to gauge his reaction, then let out a gasp. He was pale and teetering like an axed tree, ready to fall. She reached him just as he collapsed into a nearby chair.

Andy blew out a breath and looked down. The front of his shirt was gone and a trio of ten-inch gashes ran down his chest. Oddly, there was almost no blood seeping from the wounds.

"Jesus, you're hurt," she said, indicating the angry-looking slash marks. She looked him in the eye and shook her head. "You know, you *really* need to stop throwing yourself in harm's way for me."

"Ah, it's just a couple of scratches," he said, shifting in his seat. He winced, then his usual grin resurfaced. "Like I told you, it's not my time."

Ilsa drew in a lungful to castigate him, but her ire was snuffed by the sudden influx. No matter the swagger, it was hard to stay mad at a guy who'd just thrown himself between you and a demon with murderous intent.

Having caught his breath, Andy attempted to stand. The notion turned out to be a tad premature on his part, and she ended up helping him to his feet.

"Thanks," he muttered sheepishly.

"You're insane," she pointed out, then indicated the still-burning fireplace. "Speaking of which, what the hell *was* that?"

Andy frowned as he studied the front of his ruined bomber. Although the tough leather and thick shearling had thwarted what might otherwise have been a lethal blow, it didn't stop the poor guy from mourning the loss of his favorite jacket. "That, partner-o-mine, was your *'Hannibal Heifer',*" he said on an exhale.

"I'm fucking serious!" Ilsa snapped. "You saw it, right? The face, the fangs, that . . ." she glanced at the mutilated homeowner and shuddered. ". . . that *tongue*?"

"Yeah, I saw it," he said, folding his arms across his chest. "I assume we'll be editing this report, too?"

Ilsa paced the room, trying to harness the chaos running rampant inside her head.

"This is insane," she said, rubbing her temples with her fingertips. "It was *here* and now it's *gone*." She stopped in front of the antique fireplace and gestured erratically at the crackling flames. "And unless I hit my head and imagined it, it jumped right into the fire a-and disappeared!"

Andy's mouth was a hard line as he moseyed over to her. He bent at the waist, eyed the soot-stained wall at the back of the hearth, then gave her an enquiring look. "Think it burned up?"

"No, it was enormous. There would be, I mean . . . no." She drew her lower lip between her teeth. "Do you think it somehow uses fireplaces to . . ."

"To what?"

"I-I don't know. Maybe to-to move around?"

"Like a secret passageway or something?"

As the ramifications of her words struck her, Ilsa felt like an idiot. Frankly, if Andy hadn't been by her side and seen what she'd seen, she'd have believed she was ready for a Section 8. Not that a rubber room might not still be in both their futures.

"I-I don't know what I mean. It's just a thought, a feeling." She looked up and caught the faraway look in his eyes. She could tell he needed grounding as much as she did. "Andy, *look* at me. Is that the same thing you shot earlier?"

He nodded. "Yep. Ten-ringed it twice. Then it ran me over like the F-train."

Ilsa's hands came up and she started mussing her hair. "This is impossible, isn't it? Am I losing my mind?"

"Hope you like company," Andy chuckled. He gave her that lopsided grin of his. "So, now what?"

"Well, we're not telling anyone what just happened. That's for sure," she said with a scoff. "If we do, *we'll* be the ones in psychiatric holding."

"So, what then? You saw it. I-I really don't think it's human." He held his empty pistol up for emphasis. "How do we stop something that Plus-P hollow points can't?"

Ilsa pulled out her phone, then stashed it as she heard the sound of approaching sirens. "We'll stay until the EMTs and forensics get settled. Then we need to find help." She glanced down to find the dead man's eyes on her and looked away. "Help from someone who can tell us what the *hell* we're dealing with."

She watched as Andy bent down to retrieve his fallen medal. Behind him, a blackened figure eight had been gouged into the wooden floor, right in front of the fireplace.

"And I know *just* the person . . ."

CHAPTER 9

Andy's dark and dismal mood stood in stark contrast to the sun's early morning brilliance as he and Dunbar returned to *Apostol's Antiquities*. Technically, their shift was already over, but after what they'd been through, this couldn't wait.

His blue eyes perused the antique establishment's now-familiar storefront. As it had been during their previous visit, the place remained brightly-lit. He managed a smile as he pictured the pair of wisecracking coffin dodgers that owned it. They were quite the team, those two – impish and energetic.

Still, he couldn't help but wonder; did they *ever* sleep?

He checked his look in the passenger seat's sun visor mirror, while Dunbar did her usual "no makeup needed" prepping. The haggardness that greeted him left something to be desired. Granted, his five o'clock shadow wasn't helping any, but it was small potatoes compared to the undead eyeshadow he'd been wearing of late. Insomnia was the thing; for the last week, he'd found it impossible to sleep. He'd been plagued by disturbing dreams, and spent night after night tossing and turning.

Now he knew why. It was that thing, that ... devil.

It had to be.

At a spiritual level, he'd somehow anticipated their clash. At least, that's what his mother would have said. He didn't have her gift, of course, so he didn't know if that made sense, or how it might have happened. What he did know was that their confrontation had been incredibly draining, and not just physically. Ever since then, he'd felt like a candle that was running out of wax and headed for a burnout.

Sadly apropos, he realized. Then he scratched idly at the bandage covering his wounds.

Damn, they itch.

After she'd seen him come close to taking a tumble down the stairs, Dunbar had been on him like white on rice. She was like a seeing eye dog – refused to leave his side. The ER doctor she'd dragged him to had been mystified by his gashes, which were already showing signs of infection. The curious resident kept pressing about how he'd come by them. Finally, his partner made up a whale of a tale about a bear escaping its enclosure at the Central Park Zoo.

Poor Andy was quite the hero, she'd explained in dramatic fashion. He'd been mauled while shielding an innocent young maiden from harm.

An innocent young maiden . . .

He smiled with his eyes. He didn't like telling lies, but there was a hint of truth to her whopper. A hint.

A hundred stitches and a handful of antibiotics later, and they'd been on their way. Of course, once they were back in her SUV, Dunbar had announced she'd be driving him home after they clocked out. He was in no shape to take the B train back to Brooklyn, she said.

She could be quite the mother hen when she wanted to be, he thought, giving her a surreptitious glance. And, she looked damn good in that turtleneck sweater, he amended. The 2XL 'I Love New York' sweatshirt he'd snagged at the hospital gift shop, on the other hand, left something to be desired. He shook his head and sighed as he adjusted what was left of his bulky bomber. It was ruined, of course, but at least the shearling liner still kept him warm.

Andy's expression turned thoughtful as he considered the warranty Cabelas offered on their merchandise. He figured the odds of his coat being covered under "factory defects" were slim-to-none. They had impeccable customer service, but he could already picture one of their phone reps telling him, 'Sorry, sir, but that sounds like something along the lines of an act of God'.

He stifled a snigger. It *was* something like that. Except, of course, said "act" had come from the opposing side . . .

"What are you grinning about?" Dunbar asked. She studied his face as she pulled her keys from the ignition.

"Oh, nothing. Just something that struck me as funny."

Her perfectly groomed eyebrows lifted as she climbed out. "Really? Because I saw what 'struck' you earlier, and, let me tell you, it definitely was *not* funny."

"Ah, so you've got 'dad jokes' now, eh?"

Her eyes twinkled as she afforded him a quick once-over. It was obvious she had lingering concerns over his condition. The light in her eyes faded, however, as she looked ahead, then pointed at the door to *Apostol's*.

It was unlocked and ajar.

Dunbar's Beretta appeared in her hand as if by magic.

Eyes slitted, Andy opened the door to the halfway point and held it while she slipped inside. After checking their six, he followed suit. He advanced slowly, grinding his molars as he did. He was used to danger, thrived on it, in fact. But he realized that, after last night, he didn't know how much more madness he could handle. Another incident like that, and he might have to put in for early retirement.

Ha, ha. Imagine?

A few yards away, Dunbar fluttered the fingers of her free hand to draw his eye and signaled her intention to go right. Andy took left, freeing his .45 as he did. He looked around. Nothing looked out of place, nor did anything appear damaged. In fact, everything seemed perfectly normal.

That was, if your definition of normal was being the curator for the fine arts section of the Louvre.

"Holster your guns, detectives," a voice called out. "We're perfectly fine."

A moment later, Olek appeared from behind one of his medieval suits of armor displays, a rag and bottle of glass cleaner in his hands. He wore a tight-lipped smile, but greeted them affably before guiding them to the rear of the store. To Andy's bemusement, there was a small table and chairs waiting for them, along with china plates, teacups and saucers, and a small tray of high-end pastries.

Olek's wife emerged from the back offices carrying a ceramic teapot. She smiled warmly at the two of them.

"Do, sit down," Olek said.

Andy exchanged looks with Dunbar. "You were expecting us?"

Their host stood beside the table as Andy seated himself, then gestured proudly at his wife. "My Elena is a gifted clairvoyant. Except, of course, when it comes to my whereabouts..."

His piercing eyes focused on Andy's, causing the big cop's grin to falter.

"You have some experience with psychics, Detective Alvilda?"

"Call me Andy," he replied. He beamed at Elena as she filled his teacup. "Thank you, ma'am."

Dunbar was the last to sit. She wore a thoughtful look, but smiled pleasantly as she accepted tea from their hostess.

Realizing he was starving, Andy decided to forego standing on ceremony and reached for one of the sinful looking pastries. It turned out to be the most mouthwatering cannoli he'd ever tasted, and it was all he could do to keep from grabbing a handful and stuffing them in his mouth, while cramming more inside his jacket pockets for later.

He cleared his throat and alternated chewing and sipping his tea, while Dunbar drank and fidgeted. *Watching her figure, no doubt.*

The seconds ticked by, with neither of them feeling comfortable enough to initiate a conversation while Elena was still present.

Olek studied the partners' faces, then seated himself. "So, what can I do for you?"

Dunbar raised a supercilious brow. "What, don't you know already?"

The old man's smile faded as he stirred his tea. "I should think by now your eyes would be a bit more open."

Andy scoffed. "Oh, after what we just saw, our eyes are *wide* open. Believe me."

"Wait, you saw it?"

"*Saw* it?" He indicated his blood-spattered bomber. "We *shot* the damn thing."

Andy watched as the color drained from the old man's face. A look of alarm followed, and he sprang up with surprising speed.

"Elena, turn on the extra cameras," he said. "Quickly! I've got the doors!"

Andy and Dunbar rose, their faces matching masks of confusion.

Elena moved hurriedly to the back, while Olek rushed to the entrance. He hit the levers that activated the store's protective outer measures, then opened its front door. He checked the gates and bars, then took a moment to touch the mezuzah on his door jamb. His eyes swung heavenward, then he closed the heavy door and securely bolted it.

Andy gave him an analytical look. "You're Jewish, Mister Apostol?"

"Why?" Olek deadpanned. "You looking to convert?"

"No, just surprised. Seeing how you have a bible on Santa Claus."

The antique dealer's voice took on an educator's tone as he keyed a security code into an alarm pad by the front. "Ded Moroz is not about religion, my young friend. What he represents transcends mere sect; it's about spirit, tradition." He licked his lips, then, apparently satisfied with his preparations, walked over to them. "It's about faith in the goodness of man, the joy of family, being with loved ones we normally can't due to time, space, or circumstance."

He rested his hand on Dunbar's shoulder. "It's about *belief*."

She looked at Andy and shrugged as Olek turned and headed toward his office.

"You better come with me," he called back to them.

* * *

Ilsa felt like she was back in high school in the principal's office as she balanced on the edge of a chair facing Olek Apostol's desk. On the surface, she was calm, but inwardly she was chafing. She and her partner had come looking for desperately-needed answers to even more desperate questions and she was in no mood for delays.

Andy, on the other hand, looked like a well-behaved Catholic schoolboy, sitting beatifically in a pew in church.

Other than an initial glance toward the adjoining room, where the remains of that "Santa sleigh" were housed, he hadn't moved. His hands lay neatly folded in his lap, and his expression was so serene it made her want to vomit.

How the hell does someone who was nearly killed twice in twenty-four hours manage to stay so calm? God, he can be so annoying!

Finally, their host returned. He was toting a steaming mug of Java, which he stirred as he walked. After seating himself, his gaze fell on one of the monitors on his desk.

Ilsa had clocked the display when she sat down. There were a dozen live feeds from external security cameras on it – infrared, motion-sensing – the works. It was a lot of protection, even for someone who dealt in high-end art.

Olek cautiously sipped his coffee, then set it on a coaster next to a framed photo of his wife. "Okay," he said, blowing out a breath. "Tell me everything."

Ilsa took off like a racehorse out of the gate.

"We've had a busy night," she began. "Multiple incidents with fatalities, which is a first. We--" She hesitated as she noted Olek rechecking his camera feeds. "Is something wrong, Mister Apostol? You look like you're expecting someone."

"What? No, no . . . you drove here, right?"

She nodded.

He made a dismissive gesture at the monitor and swiveled toward her. "It's past dawn. We'll be fine. Go on."

Ilsa exchanged glances with Andy. "We've been playing catch-up, it seems. This is the official case file," she stated, leaning forward and placing it on his desk. "We'd like you to take a look."

"Sure, if it's alright," he replied. His lips formed a tight line as he opened it and started perusing the contents. "You said there were multiple incidents?"

Andy cleared his throat. "Yeah, last night before we came to you, we got a report that a group of Christmas cannibals hit a fancy apartment." He indicated the crime scene photos. "Usual MO. Family was killed, wife partially eaten."

Ilsa watched as Olek licked suddenly dry lips.

"Was there a . . . fireplace in the apartment?" he asked.

Andy got up and started flipping through file photos. "Yeah, a big one. You can see it here. How did you know that?"

"Any survivors?"

"A little girl and her dad. First time a spouse wasn't found dead from being force-fed."

Olek's eyes ping-ponged back and forth between them. "Force-- Wait, you-you've *seen* what it does?"

Ilsa blanched. "Unfortunately. It has some sort of nasty, I don't know . . . siphon for a tongue? It uses it to puke portions of its victims down family members' throats." She shook her head in disgust. "It asphyxiates them, presumably to frame them for its crimes."

"God help us," Olek said with a shudder. "Anything else different about the first scene?"

Andy shrugged, then handed him a separate group of photographs. "Other than the clawed-up doc and this giant hole in the wall? No."

"Da . . ." The old man eyed the images.

"We think it escaped through the opening," Andy stated. He glanced at Ilsa for affirmation, then sat down and rested his chin on the knuckles of one hand. "Climbed down or jumped."

"Seems likely. And the next scene?"

Ilsa leaned forward. "Psychiatric holding station. Whoever or whatever 'it' is, it broke in the back and killed everybody."

"Everyone?"

"*Everyone.* Five cops, six medical personnel, and seven prisoners."

"Did it . . . feed?"

"No, just ripped them apart. Armed people. People with *guns.*"

Andy snapped his fingers. "And McKinley. Don't forget about him."

"Right," Ilsa said, nodding. "One person wasn't mutilated. The dad who survived the first attack."

Olek's brow creased up. "And what happened to--"

"*This,*" she said, holding her cell phone at arm's length.

"O moy . . . Bog."

"Sheet-white, rosary in a death grip. Look at his face. It's like he died of fright."

Olek's hand trembled as he reached for Ilsa's phone. Then, just as his fingers closed on it, there was a loud bang.

Something had struck the store's outside door.

The sound of Ilsa's phone clattering to the floor was overshadowed by creaking noises, as she and Andy sprang from their seats.

"It's okay, it's okay," Olek said, his hand on his heart. He pointed at a figure on the monitors. "Just a homeless man I help from time to time." He exhaled slowly, then gripped his armrests with both hands and pushed himself upright. "I'll be right back."

"I'll go with you," Andy said.

* * *

Andy left Ilsa reviewing case notes and accompanied Olek from his office to his store's display room. Not wanting to look like a loomer, he hung back a few paces, pretending to watch disinterestedly as the old man stopped by the table in the back and picked up the tray of pastries.

Andy's mouth watered as he caught sight of the remaining cannolis, but he kept quiet. If anything, he'd ask their host where he'd procured the sinful delicacies before they left.

Whistling, Olek marched to the front door, pastries in hand. When he got there, he killed the alarm, then pulled the lever that disabled the store's outermost defenses, its horizontal folding guards. As they rattled along their tracks, he opened the front door and stepped into the available two-foot-wide space. Only a row of inch-thick bars separated him from whatever was out there.

It was a homeless man, just like he'd said.

From six feet back, Andy studied the unfortunate fellow. He couldn't make out enough details to be able to pick him out of a lineup – his face was backed by the morning sun – but his trained eyes did their usual pan-and-scan routine, regardless.

Olek's gruff-looking visitor was in his mid-sixties, Caucasian, and of average height. He had silvery hair and wore a USMC cap paired with, of all things, an old Russian military winter coat and mittens. He was sweaty and out-of-breath, no doubt courtesy of the beat-up snow shovel he leaned on.

"Good morning, Vincent!" Olek said good-naturedly. How are you this brisk winter's day?"

The near-toothless smile he got back made Andy reaffirm his commitment to both brush and floss, morning and night.

"Cold, but not as cold as I'll be when I'm in the ground," Vincent said with a hoarse chuckle. He indicated the surrounding sidewalk. "I cleared your walkway for you. I hope it keeps you from getting sued."

Olek gripped one of the security bars and looked left and right.

"Thank you, that's excellent. I'm sorry, I can't have you in for our usual breakfast, but here . . ." He eased the pastry tray between the bars and handed it to him. "Take this, with my blessing."

"Geez, thanks, but I-I can't accept this. This is silver!"

"So, it is . . . Tell you what, why don't you swing by later and I'll buy it back from you?"

Vincent's look of discomfiture turned contemplative. "Really? I don't know . . . how much?"

"How does forty dollars sound?"

"Forty bucks? I don't know . . . can you go sixty?"

Olek grinned approvingly. "How's about we split the difference and call it fifty?"

"You got it. Spasiba!" Vincent said. He grabbed a pastry, stuffed it into his mouth. "You rock, Oleksandr!" He took a step back, then glanced at Andy and nodded. "And a merry Christmas to you, officer. Catch you later!"

CHAPTER 10

Ilsa had her nose buried in crime scene reports when Olek finally returned with her partner in tow. She glanced up, gave Andy a questioning look, got a hoisted eyebrow in response.

Olek shrugged and reseated himself. "A harmless old man who served his country," he said. "He deserves better."

"You're a good man, Mister Apostol," Andy observed.

Ilsa cracked a smile, but it was fleeting. "So, back to the case . . ." She held up an eight-by-ten from the holding station. "Whoever or whatever this thing is, it's strong enough to tear apart cell door bars."

"My goodness," Olek said, swallowing nervously. "Was there a, uh . . . a fireplace there too?"

"No. But there was at the house we just came from. It didn't enter through there, however. It scaled the building's walls."

"You know about the flames?"

"We've, uh, considered that it might have had some sort of 'secret passage' leading to the fireplaces. But that doesn't make any sense. It's huge; there's no way it could fit."

Andy shook his head. "Nothing about this makes any sense."

Ilsa shifted forward and rested her palms on Olek's desk. "Mr. Apostol, several times you've referred to this thing as an 'it'." She pegged him with a hard stare. "I need a straight-up answer, and no elaborate fairy tales, please."

"Very well."

"Is this thing like the monster from your stories?"

Olek's already lined face creased even more deeply. "Your adversary is not human." He paused to gauge their reactions. "You said you fired at it?"

Ilsa scoffed. "More like emptied our guns into it. Barely slowed it down. In fact, Andy saved my life. It was a miracle it didn't rip him apart." She turned to her partner. "Show him."

"Uh . . . really?"

"*Show* him."

Andy sighed, then hoisted up his sweatshirt and loosened the medical tape on his bandages.

Olek blanched. The wounds were puckered and inflamed and, coupled with their array of stitches, had a Frankensteinian look to them. "Good lord. It had you in its grasp and you *survived*? How?"

Andy lowered his sweatshirt. "Because it inadvertently latched onto *this*." He extracted his religious medal from his pocket and offered it up. "I don't know why, but it dropped it like it was a red-hot ingot."

"Saint Nicholas . . . interesting."

Ilsa rolled her eyes. "You're not gonna give us another Kris Kringle lecture, are you?"

Olek's eyes twinkled. "Well, Saint Nicholas *is* the patron saint of children." He looked around his office and smiled. "And pawnbrokers . . ." He examined the medal closely. "This is silver, da?"

Andy nodded slowly. "A gift from my mom."

"I'll give you a better chain for it. Keep it with you at all times."

Eyes tight now, Olek resumed flipping through the case file. A minute later, his forehead furrowed. "Detective Dunbar, can I see the dead doctor's picture again, please?"

Ilsa handed him her phone and watched as he enlarged the photo. He started muttering something about "aged eyes", then fished a jeweler's loupe from his desk drawer.

"Fascinating."

"What?"

"It's an antique rosary," Olek replied. "Hematite and silver, from the look of it. Fairly valuable, too."

"So, religious stuff can stop it?"

He handed her back the phone. "It didn't help *him*."

"No, but he wasn't dismembered like the others."

"His *body* wasn't," Olek emphasized. "His soul, on the other hand..."

Andy made a grunting sound and started cracking his knuckles. "Look, we've seen this monster of yours. We know it's real. We just need to know how to stop it."

The old man shook his head. "I-I don't know if you can. It's so strong now, and brazen... Scaling buildings? Multiple attacks?"

"Yeah, why is that?" Ilsa asked. "In ten years, that's never happened."

Olek's incisors dented his lower lip. "Something interrupted its initial feeding. Most likely the rosary. That, and McKinley's fierce love for his child."

"Is that why it fled through the window instead of going back into the fireplace?"

"It prefers the fire. You remember my story about how Wotan threw Loptr into an active volcano?"

Ilsa nodded. At this point, she wasn't ruling anything out.

"Howsoever it freed itself, I suspect it can now use flames to move from place to place."

Andy's eyes lit up. "Ah, so the fireplaces are like portals, right? Like in *'Stargate'*?"

Ilsa coughed a loud "Uber nerd!" into her hand. "You got issues, Alvilda..."

Andy grinned. "Okay, so why didn't it leave the same way?"

Olek paused thoughtfully, then dug into the case file. He came up with a photo from the McKinley's living room. "That's why... see?"

"The fireplace?"

"The screens. They're closed. Must've happened during the struggle." He stared at Andy, waiting for the light to come on, then added, "They're made of iron."

Ilsa felt a twinge of excitement. "And iron keeps it away?"

"Certain potent religious items and metals are anathema to creatures from the other side." He indicated Andy's medal. "Silver, like that keepsake, or that big cowboy belt buckle of yours..." he said, pointing at his waist, "... can cause pain, but cold iron can actually kill them."

"What do you mean by 'cold iron'?"

"Iron found in a natural state, like especially pure iron ore. It is forged with low or no heat and hammered into shape. It's why cemeteries are surrounded by iron fences – to keep the dead inside."

A line appeared between Andy's brows. "Okay, so it can't use the fireplace at McKinley's and goes through the windows. But why did it follow him?"

"He saw it," Ilsa said.

Olek blew out a breath. "I think there's more to it than that. Its behavior has changed. It's becoming bolder, more aggressive..."

A disturbing possibility suddenly dawned on Ilsa and she steepled her hands. "Mister Apostol, have you *seen* this thing?"

"Hmm?"

"*Seen* it. As in, in person."

Olek's weathered eyes found hers. "Only its aftermath. It was at a base I was stationed at, fifty years ago."

"In Russia."

His eyes took on a haunted look and he nodded. "It was the reason Elena and I fled to the West. It started slaughtering families in our home town. Happy families. People we knew."

Ilsa's brows cranked down a notch. "How did you manage to come here? The Soviet Union wasn't exactly handing out travel visas."

"I was a bright young engineer who had what your government called 'valuable military knowledge'. They were glad to have us."

"I'm sure. So, this, this . . . 'demon', for want of a better word, has been in Russia until ten years ago?"

"No."

Olek opened his desk drawer and extracted a large scrapbook. He opened it and started flipping through yellowed newspaper articles.

"For decades, I tracked clusters of unsolved murders and incidents of cannibalism across the globe." He paused to moisten his finger with saliva, then continued. "England, France, even America; your 'Jersey Devil' with its hooves and habit of flying up chimneys . . ." He closed the scrapbook. "Ten years ago, it showed up here, in New York."

Andy's eyes rounded. "Wait. You don't think it was tracking--"

"Us? I hope not. But no. I don't think so."

Ilsa frowned. "So, what brought it here?"

"Something must have attracted it. According to my research, this can only be done via a blood sacrifice." He shifted in his seat. "A willing one. That's what gives it its power. That and . . ."

"And what?"

Olek drew a deep breath, let it out slow. "There is great evil in the world, detective: the evil of men. Cold, cruel men who worship dark things and prey upon the weak, the downtrodden, the children. They seek dominion over others and they care not whose blood they spill." His arms and shoulders tensed and he began to grow visibly upset. "Their evil is spreading. It is here now, infecting this great country. And this creature, be it demon, dark elf, or Loptr himself, is also here. It feeds on fear and hate and it will not leave."

He paused, his eyes scrutinizing their faces, like he was searching for something. Then he shook his head vehemently and pointed toward the room where the charred sled lay. "Don't you understand? Its nemesis is no more, and less than two days from now marks the fiftieth anniversary of its escape!"

"Okay, okay, calm down," Ilsa said. "What does it matter that it's been fifty years?"

Olek pressed two fingers to his wrist, checking his pulse, then began massaging his temples in an effort to relax. "The half-centennial is significant. Eckartshausen called fifty 'the number of the Illumination'. And it is. It is also the sum of the square numbers on the sacred triangle of Pythagoras, as well as the number of the Feast. And in the Old Testament, God promised Abraham if he could find just fifty righteous people in Sodom and Gomorrah, he would spare both cities."

He stopped and sighed. "Abraham failed."

"Yes, but New York City isn't Sin City."

Olek held up a finger. "I beg to differ. But for all its vices, and as big as it is, the five boroughs are but a tiny bite of a much larger, and rather rancid, apple."

Ilsa cocked her head. "I'm not sure I follow you."

"Think politics, my dear. Can you imagine Abraham if he was alive today, in Washington, wandering the halls of Congress, trying to find fifty honest men? Just fifty?"

He gazed meaningfully at her.

"So, you're saying, what, that we *deserve* this? That we've brought it on ourselves?"

"Evil begets evil, detective. And let us not forget that God also directed Israel to hold a jubilee every fifty years, on the Day of Atonement. On that day all debts were to be settled in favor of the debtor, and all those in bondage set free."

Ilsa nodded. "I see. Okay, so after being imprisoned for so long this thing feels that it's owed a little payback. I get it. So, let's say the fiftieth year passes like every other year. What then?"

Olek folded his arms across his chest. "For the last forty-nine years its rampages have ended on Christmas Eve. I-I don't know why. Maybe it fears Sinterklaas will come for it. Maybe it doesn't know that he's . . ."

"And when he doesn't come?"

"According to legend, once it has claimed its final victim, it will return to the pit to gather its strength. And when it comes again, its reign of terror will not stop." He leaned forward in his seat and hung his head in his hands. "It will strike wherever and whenever it wishes, both day and night. No chains will be able to bind it, and no one will be safe. Not men, not women, and especially not children. Its presence will usher in a new Dark Age: one that will never end."

He stopped talking then, his face lapsing into shadow.

Andy exploded up out of his seat. "Well, *fuck* that!"

Ilsa did a doubletake; she'd never seen him lose his cool before.

"Screw this shit," he snarled. "Let's go find the son of a bitch and kick his ass!"

Olek held up his hands. "Find it how?"

Andy's eyes slitted and the skin on his chin took on an orange peel consistency. "Do you have a map of the city?"

Olek rummaged through his desk drawer. "Only a subway map. Will that help?"

"Perfect."

Ilsa moved beside Andy as he spread the map across Olek's desk, then reached for a Sharpie and started marking it.

"Now, I've only been on the case a few days," he said. "But I couldn't help noticing that the previous three attacks have been here, here, and here . . . See the arc?"

Ilsa's face lit up. "It's following a curved line. That's fantastic! But . . . if that's true, the region where it strikes next measures three square blocks. We can't stake out an area anywhere near that size."

"So, let's tighten the noose. What do we know about its chosen victims?"

"Big apartments with fireplaces . . ." She nodded approvingly. "Ah, I see where you're going. That narrows it down. But still--"

"What else do we know?" he pressed.

Ilsa nibbled her bottom lip. She'd never seen Andy's assertive side before. She had to admit, she liked it.

"It targets families so it can pawn off its attacks. And most importantly, people who--" She snapped her fingers. "Celebrate Christmas!"

"Which means, you're safe," he said, waggling his eyebrows.

"Bite me," she smirked. Just then, an idea came to her, and she reached for her phone.

"Who is she calling?" Olek whispered.

Ilsa gave the two men a coy look, then turned sideways as her contact finally picked up. "Hey Steve, it's Dunbar,"... "Thanks, I need a favor. I need real estate records for all residential properties in grid 3A." She saw the inquisitive look on her partner's face and signaled for patience. "No, I want only residences that have fireplaces. Yes, big ones. Thanks."... "Yeah, send it to me ASAP."

Olek sniffled, then reached into his breast pocket for a handkerchief. "So, this means you will have a list of possible locations?"

"Hopefully, a short one. But that still leaves us with a serious problem."

"Which is?"

Ilsa gave Andy a meaningful glance. "What do we do when we find it? Bullets don't penetrate, and I sincerely doubt Alvilda's dance moves will phase it."

"Hey, you haven't seen my chicken dance."

Olek cleared his throat. "Perhaps I can be of service."

He got up and moved to a metal cabinet situated in the nearby hallway. Reaching for his keys, he unlocked its top drawer and extracted a cloth-wrapped bundle – one with a bit of weight to it, based on the way he handled it.

Olek carried the object to his desk and carefully unwrapped it. It looked like a foot-long pewter-colored rock of some kind. It was pockmarked and scarred, yet there was a sheen to it, despite its condition and color.

"What is it?" she asked.

"A very rare meteorite," he said, tapping it with his finger. "Old as creation, and pure iron."

"*Cold iron* . . ."

'The coldest. From the frozen void of space."

Andy reached down and read the meteorite's attached price tag. "Holy shit, this thing goes for twenty thousand bucks?"

"Forget the price," Olek said. "It may help."

Ilsa reached down and hefted the hunk of space rock. "So, what are we supposed to do, hit it over the head?"

The old man chuckled. "See me after closing."

* * *

The setting sun hung menacingly atop the Manhattan skyline as Ilsa pulled up, yet again, in front of *Apostol's Antiquities*. Her lips were a taut line as she contemplated the store's illuminated sign. She'd been there so many times over the last few days; she felt like she should register for their damn mailing list.

Not that she planned on shopping there, obviously. The annuity she received from her parents' investment accounts took care of her mortgage, property taxes, and general expenses, but despite what that cock waffle Ramirez went around telling people, she was far from rich.

Ramirez . . . what a douchebag.

Now, *there* was someone destined to end up old and alone. That is, if he and the rest of New York survived the growing supernatural threat that would soon imperil everyone.

Old and alone . . .

Ilsa tried to distract herself from the gravity of their situation by envisioning the quaint couple that owned the place. It took a while, but she felt a smile trying to break through. How had Andy jokingly referred to them? Oh, yes . . . 'artful coffin dodgers.'

The husband's Kris Kringle fantasies notwithstanding, she personally found the pair utterly adorable. The wife, with her sarcastic wit, was obviously the spice in their relationship – as any woman worth her salt should be. A veritable cougar, that one. As for the seemingly henpecked husband, Ilsa considered herself a fair judge of male virility. She'd bet good money Olek still had plenty of what her grandmother once referred to as "fire in the flak locker".

Geez, at their age, I wonder how often they do it?
Cancel that. I don't want to know . . .

Andy's chest scratching drew her back from her reverie. Without looking, she reached over and gave his hand a light smack – someone had to stop him from aggravating his wounds – then clocked the time on her dash. Normally, at this hour, she'd still be in bed. But Janus had approved them switching to a four-to-twelve today so they could meet up with *Apostol's* owners. She hoped the changeup ended up being worth it.

Turning off the ignition, Ilsa eyed her partner in the SUV's illuminated rearview mirror. "By the way – and I assume you have a car – why *is* it that you never drive?"

Andy gave her an affronted look. "What, and lose my spot in Bay Ridge?"

She groaned and he grinned.

Then they both grinned.

Great, we're turning into the Apostols . . .

CHAPTER 11

Andy was still smirking as he and Dunbar were once again welcomed inside *Apostol's Antiquities* by a tense-but-smiling Elena.

"He's in his office," she advised, hurriedly bolting the door and resetting the alarm.

In an attempt to ease the tension, Andy bowed like a courtier, then handed her the bag of bagels and Starbucks he'd picked up along the way. She accepted the gift with a smile, graciously thanking him and Dunbar, then escorted them back. The museum-like display room they passed through was its usual self – brightly lit but barren. Elena explained that, for security reasons, they were seeing clients by appointment only. Especially during this time of year.

That made total sense. And now more than ever.

"Ah, detectives, just in time," Olek said breathlessly. He had an impish air about him as he rose from his seat and ushered them to theirs. As they settled in, he left the room.

He returned a few ticks later, carrying a cloth-covered tray about the size of a clipboard. He set it carefully on his desk, then, with a magician-like flourish, pulled the cloth away.

Both Andy's and Dunbar's lips parted and they leaned forward in their seats. On the tray were two opened boxes of rough-looking pistol rounds.

"Happy Hannukah," Olek said, smiling proudly.

Andy's eyes gleamed at the realization. "Oh, you *shouldn't* have."

Ilsa twisted at the hip, her brown-green eyes falling on the metal wall cabinet in the nearby hall. "Wait, were these made from your--." Her jaw slackened at the mischievous grin she got back. "H-how did you manage this?"

"It was nothing," Olek said with a flippant gesture. "A wealthy client who hunts and makes his own rounds. He considers himself a gunsmith."

"Hmm." Andy picked up one of the bullets and scrutinized it from projectile to primer. "Will they feed properly?"

"He assured me they will. They're half-jacketed solids . . . cold iron and copper cups. He said penetration will be phenomenal . . ." He slid the boxes forward. "Forty-five ACP for you, and nine-millimeter for the lady."

Dunbar wasted no time. Slipping her Beretta M9 from its shoulder holster, she ejected its fifteen-round magazine and began popping out hollow points. Twenty seconds later, there was a series of snicking sounds as she replaced them with the experimental ammunition.

"We might actually have a chance now," she said.

Andy enthusiastically followed suit. "Oh, I wanna see him eat a few of *these*!"

"Only thirty rounds each," Olek advised. "I'm sorry, it was a small meteorite . . ."

"Are you kidding?" Dunbar offered him a dimpled smile. "I could *kiss* you!"

Their host's eyes bulged, and he gave the nearby hallway a darting glance. "Shush! Are you trying to get me killed?"

Dunbar's cheeks pinked and she resumed reloading with lowered eyes. Once she was finished, she ejected the round currently in the chamber, then slapped the mag back in and pulled the slide smoothly back.

Olek nodded his approval. "So, how did your real estate check go?"

Andy held up the tablet he carried. "Just got the report," he said, then turned and handed it to his partner. "We have six possibles."

"*Six*?" Olek's lips turned down. "How will you know which one is the target?"

"Process of elimination," Dunbar replied.

Andy watched her tanned fingers work their magic. He had to admit, with one hand or two, she was quite the typist.

Another skill he'd failed to acquire . . .

"Two families are out of town," she announced. "Of the remaining units, one is empty, and the tenants in another are Hindus."

Olek gave one of his earlobes a couple of tugs. "That still leaves two, da? I would advise against splitting up."

Andy scoffed. "Oh, don't worry. Seen *way* too many horror movies for *that* to happen!"

Dunbar wore a touch of a smile as she paused what she was doing. "At Detective Alvilda's suggestion, I'm checking social media . . . By the way, nice profile pic," she commented, turning the tablet around and showing him his Facebook account. "But lose the Speedo."

She ignoring the cool look he gave her and resumed checking.

"Okay, Mrs. Harmon on seventy-eight posted something about catching her husband 'plowing the au pair'." She stifled a titter. "Looks like *they* won't be celebrating anything." Then her eyes took on a gleam as she explored the last account. "The Stansons, on eighty-first, however . . ."

Dunbar turned and held the tablet so everyone could see. On it, a live video played of a family of five belting out, *"A Tyrannosaurus for Christmas"*, in front of their tree. The kids were wearing dinosaur pajamas and everyone was smiling and laughing as they separated gifts into piles.

"I think we have a winner."

As the video feed continued, Olek glanced apprehensively at a nearby wall clock. "Shouldn't you be there?"

Andy copped a quizzical smile. "Already? The attacks usually take place closer to midnight."

He followed the old man's gaze back to Dunbar's tablet. On the screen, Mister Stanson had opened their fireplace's screens. He added a Firestarter log to the existing wood and bent to light it, while his children cheered happily.

Olek shook his head. "It's dark and cold out. Once that fire is lit, it can come at any time. It could be there now . . ."

Dunbar's eyes sprang to the store's security monitors.

It was pitch-black outside.

"Shit, let's go!"

Andy grabbed his gear, stuffed any remaining bullets in his pockets, then gave their host a quick salute and a sincere thank you.

Then he followed Dunbar out.

* * *

The snowman-shaped clock on the wall read half-past-ten when it began.

Despite the place's obvious festiveness, the surrounding apartment lay dark and quiet. The holiday lights had been dimmed, and the only sounds to be heard were an occasional crackle or pop from the fireplace, as a burning log split and settled before giving up the last of its essence.

All at once, the dying fire flared brightly. Its flickering flames grew and grew until they practically touched the top of the hearth, then a hand appeared in the center of the blaze.

It was a hideous hand, long and gnarled, with bluish-black fingers the size of plantains that ended in cruel claws, reminiscent of sickles. The "skin" that covered the hand was more a collection of tumorous bumps, with mangy patches of fur decorating its back, as well as the visible portions of its wrist and forearm. The hairs themselves were long and bristly yet, despite the intense heat, not a single strand was singed as a result of the licking flames.

Further and further the hand reached until it, and the ape-like arm accompanying it, protruded from the fire almost as far as a man is tall. It lowered then and, with the taloned tip of a finger, began to score what looked like an octad into the surrounding parquet.

No sooner had the sounds of its despoiling ceased, when the arm withdrew and the figure emerged.

Its monstrous form was twisted and bent and, due to the inglenook's restrictive size, it had no choice but to crawl through the hearth on all fours. Hot ash and embers spewed from its limbs and torso as it moved, littering the floor and clouding the air with smoke and a sulfurous stench. Impassive, the figure rose to its full height and surveyed the room in which it stood.

Directly overhead, a tiny red light, affixed to a small, whitish disc that was attached to the ceiling, began to blink. An instant later, the disc emitted a high-pitched squeal, so shrill and loud that it was painful. The squealing ended almost immediately in a low cracking sound, followed by what remained of the disc and its contents spilling from the figure's calloused palm onto the floor below.

It looked around, then licked its gore-coated lips.

Its time had come.

Moving with impressive soundlessness for its size, the creature skulked through the apartment. Eventually, it focused on a trio of bedroom doors. From within the blackness of its cowl, its eyes glittered like Mexican fire opals.

The doors to the first two rooms were gayly decorated with images of extinct dragons. It ignored them. For now.

It knew from experience they would be occupied by its quarry's offspring. Although the children's youthful flesh would make for a sumptuous feast, it preferred to target the adults first. It had nothing to do with concerns for its safety – its strength was peaking and there was naught to fear – it was innately cautious and, when possible, preferred to avoid discovery. Whereas, the parents would put up a struggle or attempt to summon assistance, the younglings would inevitably cower under their beds, remaining there like the veal calves they were, until it came for them.

And it would.

Oh, yes . . . it would.

Foamy saliva spilled from the corners of the creature's mouth in anticipation, and it lapped at the drool with the bulbous tip of its tongue-like proboscis.

Yes. . . the adults first. Then their succulent progeny.

Outside the parents' door, it cocked its misshapen head like some hellish hound and listened. The breathing it detected was slow and regular. Its offering was inside and fast asleep – plump sheep for the shearing. There was no need for terror tactics on its part.

Foregoing its usual approach, it opted for stealth. It reached down, its ham-sized hand enveloping the gilded brass doorknob, and twisted.

Its lips spread into a rictus grin, revealing rows of hooked fangs.

The door wasn't even locked.

Pushing it gently inward, the creature bowed its head and bent its knees to enter, then rose and scanned the room with its luminescent eyes. There was a lone figure, softly snoring beneath quilted bedding, and, scattered on the floor en route to the bed, a woman's shoes, dress, and assorted undergarments.

It inhaled slowly, relishing the scent of artificial pheromones the females of this world used to anoint themselves. It had no idea why they did so. It suspected it was done in the hope of confusing predators by disguising their scent. It was an inane notion. For it, the pungent smell only made its prey easier to track; once its senses homed in on a target, there was no escape.

The creature felt the omnipresent hunger within it build and its patience came to an end. As silent as the shadows it favored, it crossed the room in two strides and seized the concealing comforter. Ripping it away in a single swipe, it reared back with its free hand. Its glittering eyes brimmed with expectation and it held its breath, waiting for its horrified victim's inevitable scream. Once she did, it would open her from chin to crotch and gorge on her innards.

To its surprise, however, what stared up at it was not a woman.

It was a man. A tall, fully dressed man who was wide awake.

As their gazes met, the creature blinked in what, for it, passed for confusion. It realized it had seen this particular human before. Twice, in fact. He was--

"Hi, there," the man said with a humorless smile. "You must be the 'Grinch'."

Then fire and thunder exploded from his hand.

* * *

The sinister gloat Andy wore as the monster yanked back the blankets was so diabolical, the twenty-nine-year-old's own mother wouldn't have recognized him.

Like most peace officers, he was a firm believer in the law and in due process. But right now, the rule of law no longer applied. The thing peering down at him was no man. It was a remorseless killer and a consumer of human flesh. There could be no redemption for it, no trial by a jury of its peers.

It was a mad dog. And like all mad dogs, it needed to be put down.

He'd been aware of its approach from the moment it hauled its considerable bulk up and out of the apartment's old-fashioned fireplace. It had taken every ounce of willpower he possessed to control his breathing, and to not shiver with anticipation as it took the bait and fell for their ruse. But despite his eagerness, in the back of his mind, a lingering fear remained.

That fear that Olek's meteoric bullets would fail to penetrate.

Or worse, misfire.

That anxiety disappeared faster than a bag of cash on Capitol Hill, as his first round slammed into the thing's broad chest. On impact, the .45 ACP slug gouged out a ragged, two-inch-wide wound channel, sending blood spatter the color of fresh guacamole spraying in every direction.

Andy sent three more rounds to keep the first one company, then sprang out of bed. The behemoth's roar of pain and rage as the cold iron slugs tore into it was even louder than the gunshots and it staggered backwards from the ferocity of the assault. Its balance gone, it missed the doorway altogether and fell through the surrounding drywall, leaving a jagged hole big enough for Dunbar's SUV to pass through.

Andy's expression intensified as he peered through the opening. Their enemy had taken a knee.

His eyes turned to twin murder holes.

It was hurt. He had a chance to finish the job. And he would. This ended now.

With his M1911 extended sword-like before him, he stormed through a billowing wall of gunsmoke and plaster dust. The adrenaline gushing through his veins had left him so emotionally detached that he felt like a cyborg from one of those *'Terminator'* movies. All things considered, he thought darkly, he could probably pass for one. He only hoped he'd prove a fraction as effective.

The sound of fast-moving footfalls to Andy's right told him Dunbar had emerged from the kids' bedroom to join the fight. Rather than afford the creature the opportunity to recover, he put the last three rounds in his mag into its knees, then paused to reload while it bellowed in agony.

Oh, the pain's just beginning, child killer.

With its cloak perforated and blood streaming from a half-dozen wounds, the thing forced itself upright. The majority of its weight rested on its oversized knuckles and it uttered a shuddering snarl as it gathered itself and prepared to charge.

Before it got the chance, it was subjected to a dual-pronged assault.

Andy's mirthless smile got bigger and bigger each time he pulled the trigger. With the creature's attention primarily on him, his partner could focus on pinpoint accuracy, while he blasted away at it like Clint Eastwood in a scene from *The Outlaw Josey Wales*. It was a lethal combination. His heavier rounds tore up the thing's stomach region and groin, while his partner's lighter, faster 9mm slugs peppered its thighs, ribs, and the side of its neck.

The blitzkrieg continued unabated, with droplets of olive-green ichor spritzing in every direction, and the creature roaring and raging. Despite being blinded by pain and blood spatter, it continued to claw at the air, feeling about for something to rend. Then, out of nowhere, two of Dunbar's rounds nailed it in the side of the head, slicing through its heavy cowl and burying themselves in what passed for its brain.

There was a moment's silence as it stood there, seesawing back and forth. Then, with a groan reminiscent of a chainsawed redwood, it came down hard on its back, flattening a loveseat in the process.

Andy stayed where he was, his chest heaving and his angular face coated with an oily blend of sweat, dirt, and gunpowder residue.

He couldn't believe they'd done it. And not a moment too soon, he realized as he checked his weapon. He'd put two full magazines into the resilient son of a bitch, leaving him just six rounds in mag number three.

He blew a breath through bowed lips and watched Dunbar do the same. She looked cleaner and less bedraggled than he did, but her expression was no less intense. It was a life-changing moment for both of them, something they'd remember until the day they died.

Andy tried to say something, but came up dry. He imagined the taste of fresh orange slices to get his saliva going again, then swallowed to clear the grit from his throat. He opened his mouth to speak, but hesitated. The wet, squishing noise that came out didn't sound like him at all.

Because it wasn't.

There was something happening to the remains of their Sasquatch-sized nemesis. Teeth gritted, the tall Californian tramped toward it, switching out his last mag as he did. He stopped six feet from the corpse and waved a hand in front of his face, trying to clear the last of the gunsmoke. As he did, he heard a series of plopping noises.

His Nordic blues quickly pinpointed the source of the unfamiliar sounds.

What he saw made him want to vomit.

Their bullets were bubbling up and out of the creature's assorted wounds and dropping, one by one, onto the debris-strewn carpet. Then, before his disbelieving eyes, its bleeding stopped altogether and the holes left behind began to close. Before he knew it, its malice-filled eyes reopened. Then a growl so deep he felt it in his bowels rent the air and it began to rise.

"Fuck!" Dunbar shouted. "He's doing a *'Deadpool'*!"

"Hit him again!" Andy cried.

His partner needed no invitation, and started capping off rounds, one after another. Realizing he was apt to run out of ammo, he strove for accuracy, and was rewarded with a choking sound as his second shot hit the thing right in the mouth. Its face contorted in obvious pain, and it started making disgusting retching noises.

Clutching its throat, the creature threw itself in the opposite direction. With a thunderous crash, it plowed through the nearest wall, ending up in the hallway outside. Hunks of drywall and pieces of stud settled all around it, but it didn't stop there. It uttered a leonine roar and took off like a runaway locomotive. Screams and crashes echoed throughout the building as it fled into the night, and the two partners stared down the hall after it in astonishment.

"Well," Andy said, shaking his grime-streaked head, "That was some--"

CHAPTER 12

"—fucked up *shit!*" Janus bellowed.

Ilsa and Andy were sitting front and center in the captain's office, their faces drawn and eyes lowered. The shouting had started five minutes earlier, and since then no one had dared say a word. Even the hungry wolf fish which, upon hearing its master's voice, emerged from its hiding place, had tucked tail and hid.

The only ones who seemed at all comfortable were Detectives Ramirez and Tokaido. The two were seated in the back, and neither moved nor spoke. The latter had a troubled-yet-tranquil expression on his face, like someone nursing a drink while watching a hurricane unfold on television. Ramirez, on the other hand, wore a sadistic smirk.

Given his track record, Ilsa figured he was relishing her and Andy's turn on the hotseat. Probably turned him on. In fact, she thought, while suppressing a shudder, if she spun in her seat, she'd probably clock the loathsome toad sporting an erection.

Gross. I bet I'd have to squint really hard to see that roll of quarters. Nah, too generous. Make that a pack of 'Certs'. A partly-used one . . .

On the surface, Ilsa remained impassive. But inwardly she was cackling.

Sadly, her attempt to distract herself was waylaid by a loud bang, as a furious Captain Janus slammed their report down on his desk. He snorted angrily, then snatched up a remote and unmuted his office's television set.

"It's Christmas Eve," he snarled. "And *now* I have to deal with *this*?"

It was a news broadcast from one of the regional networks. They were showing footage of the damage done to the building where she and Andy confronted the creature. The piles of debris the news anchors kept focusing on made it look as if the place had suffered a full-fledged artillery barrage, and sound bites collected from its traumatized witnesses made it seem like they'd barely survived one.

Ilsa inhaled deeply then let it out slow.

If they only knew . . .

Janus froze the image and sent the remote clattering back onto his desk. Then he turned back and thrust a thick finger in her face.

"What the *fuck*, Dunbar?" he demanded. "You used to be solid. Then 'Pretty Boy LA', here, shows up, and you turn into, what . . . *Dirty Harriet*?"

Out of the corner of her eye, Ilsa saw Andy shift. His lips parted, but then his gaze flicked to the money jar on the captain's desk and he clammed up.

A wise move. Now was not the time to roll the dice.

Still foaming at the mouth, Janus took a step back and started gesticulating wildly. "You put a family in protective custody, trashed half the building, and shot up the place to boot! People were hurt, vehicles damaged; we're looking at--"

He hesitated as Ilsa held up a crisp Ulysses S. Grant. ". . . what is it, Dunbar?"

Janus's eyes lit up as she rose, added her "donation", and then returned to her seat. "We saved their lives, sir," she said. "The stakeout worked. Our perp--"

"Yes, it worked. But where is this--" He snatched back up the report. "'Roid-raging bouncer wearing body armor'? The building's lawyers are gonna milk the city until its *udders* hurt, and *you* let the man get away!"

Ilsa felt a spike of alarm as Andy raised his hand.

"But, sir. It's not a man. It's--"

Janus eyed him from beneath beetling brows. "You interrupted me, Alvilda."

Ilsa cleared her throat. "Sir, what my partner meant was--"

"And you did, too, Dunbar . . ." He jerked his thumb twice toward the hair jar, then smirked at the irate look on her face.

Ilsa shook her head, then uttered a sigh of resignation and dug back into her pocket. She was glad she'd hit the ATM on the way in. She'd had a feeling she was going to be needing cash.

Janus started toward Andy, then paused en route to snatch the hundred-dollar-bill she held up with impressive speed. "Y'all feel free to keep it up," he said with a smile. "I'm like Captain-fucking-America right now. I can *literally* do this all night."

As much as losing a buck-fifty irked her, Ilsa was far more worried about the words that were about to come out of Andy's mouth.

She had reason to be concerned. The room grew deathly quiet as Janus pulled up next to her partner. He loomed over him for a moment, glowering, then his face fell and he smiled a humorless smile.

"Okay, sunshine, you're on her dime," he said, inclining his head in Ilsa's direction. "What did you mean by, 'It's not a man'?"

She tried desperately to signal Andy, but his focus was entirely on his captain.

"It's *not*," he began. "It's like, I don't know, an elf . . . a dark spirit of the forest or something like that."

Ilsa wanted to facepalm herself as Janus's dark eyes contemplated Andy. He looked around the room, his expression unreadable. Then he burst out laughing, with Ramirez and Tokaido following suit.

"An elf . . . like one of Santa's little helpers?"

"No, sir." Andy shook his head vigorously. "This thing *hates* Santa. And it's *huge*, like eight feet tall, with fangs and red eyes and--"

Any pretense of humor vanished as Janus gave voice to the groan Ilsa had been holding back. "Okay, that's enough," he said, holding up his hands. He drew his lower lip between his teeth, then exhaled through dilated nostrils. "You know, Alvilda, when the LA guys told me you were crazy, I thought it was a *good* kinda crazy." He leaned forward and pointed at his bald head. "Not *this* kind."

Andy stiffened. "Sir, did you review the video footage from the holding station?"

"Of course. Buncha scared rookies losing their minds, screaming and firing wildly in the air."

"W-wait . . . it doesn't show up on film?"

"That's *it*," Janus said icily. "Your gun and your badge, detective."

"Sir?"

"You're off the case and suspended, pending departmental review and full psych eval."

"But--"

The cords in the big man's neck tightened. "Your gun and your badge, newbie. *Now*."

The room went coffin quiet as Andy stood up. He unclipped his detective's shield and laid it in Janus's hand. No one said a word; even Ramirez looked shocked.

Andy licked his lips. "The, uh, the gun is mine, sir."

"Fine," Janus said. He studied the gold shield, then snapped his fingers. "Tokaido and Ramirez will escort you to your home, where you will *remain*. You got me?"

"Yes, sir."

Janus fixed Ramirez with a hard eye. "Make sure he stays put."

"Oh, with pleasure, sir," the goateed detective reveled. He glared up at Andy. "Let's go, pretty boy."

Ilsa sat there, pressing her tongue against the inside of her cheek, as her partner was escorted out. She took a moment to mull over her next course of action, then sprang up and approached her captain. "Sir, permission to speak?"

"You're off the case, too, Dunbar," Janus said, not even looking at her.

"Me, sir? But what did I--"

"Don't try and play me," he warned. "You knew Alvilda was 'cuckoo for cocoa puffs', and you told nobody."

She started to object, but a wagging finger stifled her.

The tension grew. Eventually, Janus's fierce gaze directed downward and his voice softened. "Look, I know how the holidays are for you. Take a few days off. It'll do you a world of good."

"But, sir, the killer is still out there. Maybe we can--"

"Can *what*?" Her superior's heavy jaw clenched and unclenched. "You've read the case files. In ten years, the killings always stop when?"

She bit her lip as she waited for him to continue.

"Before midnight on Christmas Eve. He already took his shot tonight. Face it, Dunbar, it's over."

"But, sir, there's still a little time. Maybe we can follow up on--"

"Look, you and 'Calamity John' stopped him from getting his last victims," he pointed out. "It's not a big win, but it's a win of sorts. So be happy."

Ilsa frowned. "So, what happens now?"

Janus shrugged. *"Now,* the psycho disappears into the woodwork, like he has every other year. He got away. As for me . . ." He indicated the disheveled pile of papers on his desk. "I've got to deal with the repercussions of your little shootout. Now get out."

"Yes, sir."

* * *

Ilsa's mood was as depressed as her vehicle's brake pedal as she came to a stop. She glanced right before starting forward once more, and imagined Central Park's benighted trees all waving at her as she drove past.

Hmph. At least they aren't flipping me off . . .

As if the nearby woods could read her mind, a dash of icy powder splatted across her windshield. She gave a small start, then keyed her wipers, clearing it. According to her instrument panel, the weather outside remained clear and crisp, although the wind had kicked back up.

A glance up ahead brought a scowl to Ilsa's face. The traffic lights lining Fifth Avenue appeared to be of like mind; a seemingly endless row of glittering red dominoes, all conspiring together to slow her roll.

She scoffed and shook her head. You'd think, with everything she'd endured of late, not to mention it being Christmas-fucking-Eve, that the Universe might cut her some slack.

No such luck.

Thanks for nothing, Santa. You suck, fat man.

Ilsa checked the time, then resorted to sucking on her teeth in an effort to relieve tension. It was barely one AM and she had no idea where to go or what to do with herself. She wasn't about to take Janus's advice and go home. That would be crazy. Even if there wasn't an indestructible demon on the loose who viewed human beings as bipedal cheeseburgers, what would she do there? Sit on the couch, her knees pulled to her chest, and watch Netflix until the walls closed in?

Her eyes moistened at the thought.

God . . . she'd never felt so alone in her life.

Her thoughts drifted to Andy, and she decided to call and see how the big idiot was holding up. She sat her phone in its dash cradle, put it on speaker, and tabbed his number.

As luck would have it, she got his voicemail.

Hi, this is Andy and you know what to do. If you don't, I can't help you.

Ilsa smiled at the sound of his voice. She hadn't realized how much she missed LA's annoying chirpiness. That is, until she'd been deprived of it. Good Lord; she'd only known him a few days. How the hell had *that* happened?

Ignoring the tightness in her chest, she cleared her throat.

"Hey Andy, it's . . . Dunbar. Sorry about what went down. Hope you're holding up okay, and that those two crotch-grabbers kept their hands to themselves." She forced herself to chuckle, then hesitated.

Up ahead, the twin spires of St. Patrick's Cathedral jutted skyward like serrated horns. Her pseudo-smile faded.

"Give me a call if you feel like talking. Bye."

Ilsa had no idea how she'd ended up there. But with nothing better to do, or perhaps hoping for some sort of "divine inspiration", she pulled up in front of the church. She threw it in park, checked her mirrors and messages, and looked forlornly around.

There was no one. Just the cold and the dark.

She decided to leave her phone in its cradle and climbed out. A sudden gust of briskness cut into her, causing her to shiver. She folded her arms across her chest – a fruitless attempt at offsetting both the numbing temps and her growing anxiety – and approached the pockmarked granite steps.

She was barely halfway there, when the past rose up like a gray-colored tsunami and knocked her right on her ass.

When she reopened her eyes she was a precocious six-year-old again, wearing a pretty blue Christmas dress with white fur trim.

She couldn't wait to see St. Patrick's in all its glory, to the point her mom and dad had to practically restrain her as she tried bursting from the backseat of their chauffeured town car. New York City wasn't all puppies and kittens, her father lectured. Then he gave one of her pigtails a playful tug and leaned down to kiss her on the forehead.

She could still feel the warmth of that kiss as she skipped along between her mom and dad, holding their hands and gazing wide-eyed up at Manhattan's never-ending neons. Holiday cheer was everywhere, and everyone they passed wore jubilant smiles. Even her oft-strict parents engaged in a bit of jocularity as the family moved along, working their way through the crowd, toward the mile-high church where they attended mass.

The gaiety ended when they reached the cathedral's steps.

Ilsa was the first to spot the three men passing on the left. The bald-headed, swarthy one in the lead was the meanest-looking of the bunch, and he shot her dad an intimidating look in passing. As she stared up at the man, she found herself studying his face. He radiated menace and had a series of strange tattoos on his face. They made it seem like he was crying.

That struck her as odd, since the tears were black.

Her dad refused to be drawn in and ignored the man, focusing instead on guiding his family up the stairs. They were late compared to some parishioners, he explained, and he wanted to get decent seats so everyone could have a good view.

All of a sudden, from behind them came the sound of screeching brakes. A big, burgundy-colored car pulled up so quickly, it jumped the curb before careening to a stop. Several people on the sidewalk had to dive out of its way to avoid being struck. They were still lying prostrate on the frigid sidewalk, when the vehicle's rear doors simultaneously flew open.

Two dark-skinned men jumped out of the car and made for the bald man and his companions. Ilsa felt a twinge of fear. The newcomers had intense eyes, as dark as the black scarves covering the bottom half of their faces, or the scary-looking weapons they carried. She knew nothing about firearms; only that these were big and black.

One day, she would know them as UZIS.

By the time the first group spotted the new arrivals, they were barely ten feet away. One of them shouted something colorful and their hands all went inside their coats. They produced guns of their own, like the kind she'd seen policemen carrying on the TV shows her father liked to watch. But unlike the police they were too late.

They were all too late.

Ilsa's dad, realizing the impending peril, yelled a warning and tried rushing the girls inside to safety. His cry of alarm was drowned out by a litany of Spanish curses, followed by the deafening shriek of automatic weapons fire.

The drug dealers sandwiched between the frightened family and their assailants bore the brunt of the assault. In seconds, they were annihilated to a man, without any of them getting off a shot. Of the sixty 9mm rounds fired, nearly half missed their targets.

A few pitted the cathedral's aged stone steps, before careening skyward.

The rest found far softer targets.

Unable to get clear of the crossfire, Ilsa's mother was the first to fall. She was half-dragging, half-carrying her child up the steps when she emitted a high-pitched yelp that stopped as soon as it started.

Ilsa felt her mother's grip on her slip. She looked up, just in time to see her pitch forward and collapse onto the unbosoming stone. Her face and right shoulder looked funny, like she was wearing two of those rotten tomatoes they'd tossed in the trash last week. Her legs kicked a few times, but she made no attempt to rise.

Ilsa's squeal of terror became a whimper as her dad scooped her up and made a break for it. With his back to the shooters, he managed three steps before his body shuddered like a giant was shaking him. He uttered a series of pain-filled grunts, followed by a loud, barking cough. The next thing she knew, her father, the strongest person she knew, dropped.

There was a deafening silence, interrupted by the sound of a car's doors slamming, its engine revving, and its tires screeching. Through a cloak of smelly smoke, Ilsa peeked up over her father's shoulder. All around her, people were shrieking and running like frightened rabbits. Halfway down the street, the burgundy car corkscrewed its way around other vehicles, as the assassins made good their escape.

Ilsa's eyes fell on the three men lying by the curb. Their bodies were twisted up like disarticulated rag dolls, and the surrounding sidewalk was airbrushed with what she began to realize was blood. She saw the first man's face and wished she hadn't. His formerly belligerent eyes were now wide and unblinking, and the black tears on his face were paralleled by real ones – some clear, some crimson.

Concern for her mother hit her like a jolt of electricity and she twisted against her father's protective arms, trying to find her. She spotted her, crumpled on her side, not five feet away. Her eyes were half-closed and there was a ragged, grape-sized hole in her right forehead.

And blood. There was so much blood.

She couldn't believe all the blood . . .

Ilsa turned to her dad, who'd somehow managed to turn sideways as they fell, crashing down on his ribs instead of her. His eyes were closed and he wasn't moving. She placed her hands against his chest and tried nudging him awake, the way she did every Christmas morning. She felt warmth and wetness and her palms came away coated with a gushy, dark-red liquid. It was sticky. So much so, in fact, that her fingers felt like they'd been glued together.

With a shriek of horror, she seized her father by the lapels and started tugging. He was so heavy; she could hardly move him. She called out to him, asked him, begged him, *pleaded* with him to open his eyes.

He finally did.

His face was as pale as a piece of paper, and a trickle of blood oozed from one nostril. He smiled weakly at her, then patted her on the head, trying to comfort her.

Ilsa felt hysteria take the helm. Then she heard herself screaming at him.

Why? Why had he done this? Why had he put himself in harm's way like that?

His pain-filled eyes met hers, then he gently gripped her chin between his thumb and forefinger.

"Because that's what dads do," he breathed.

As she watched, his smile ebbed and clouds coated his eyes. There was a long, drawn-out wheeze, which she realized was his final breath leaving his body.

She went into shock immediately. All of the sounds around her increased in volume and frequency, until they merged into an awful high-pitched hum, so loud it was painful. She felt her world begin to collapse and the borders of her eyes followed suit. Soon, she viewed the world through a blackened tunnel, with a narrow kaleidoscope of chaos churning at the far end.

Numbed, Ilsa watched dispassionately as a surprisingly young Father Giordano rushed out of the cathedral. His astonished eyes met hers, and he shouted at the altar boys accompanying him to go and summon help.

He started toward her. His lips were moving and she could hear him calling out. At least she thought she could. She couldn't understand a word he was saying; it was all so much mishmash.

Curious passersby and concerned bystanders gathered around her and her parents. She could see them stepping back to avoid getting blood on their shoes, but she didn't care. She didn't know if it was just her parents' blood or if she'd also been shot. Perhaps, she had been, she wondered. Maybe she, too, was dying.

It didn't matter. In fact, nothing mattered. The people she loved most had been torn from her, and there wasn't anything anyone could do about it.

Or was there?

Out of nowhere, a figure in scarlet appeared. He looked familiar, and through a veil of tears she focused on him. Her traumatized eyes blinked in disbelief and she felt the tiniest spark of hope ignite within her breast.

It was Santa Claus!

He was there, less than twenty feet away. She could see him, jostling his way through the crowd.

She couldn't believe it. He was trying to get to her, to help!

Her heart started doing handsprings in her chest. She'd been wrong; of all the people in the world, surely *he* could do something! After all, he was the maker of Christmas miracles, wasn't he? Maybe he could use his magic to undo this awful tragedy!

The hope she clung to faltered, however, as Saint Nick took in the carnage. Their eyes met and she saw the panic in his bloodshot baby-blues. It flowed from him, like March snow melting in the sun. She drew a breath to encourage him but her vocal cords seized up. All she could do was mouth the words '*Help me*'. Based on his ruthful expression, she thought he was going to. But then, to her dismay, he shook his head sadly and, mumbling to himself, turned his back on her and her dying family.

Ilsa's heart sank as she watched him waddle off in seeming slow motion, his big red coat bouncing up and down, the fluffy ball at the end of his hat swinging back and forth. Before she knew it, he'd vanished into the crowd, taking what remained of her hopes with him.

All that remained was the opened can of beer he'd dropped. It lay on its side, making soft chugging noises as it added its foamy contents to the already-stained sidewalk.

Ilsa was despondent. In her moment of need, the one person she thought she could count on had deserted her.

Goodbye, Santa!

Her tears flowed freely as she tried to wave, but for some reason her arm refused to obey her commands. Then things got really confusing. She sensed Father Giordano trying to take her from her father. She stubbornly refused and clung to his still-warm body with the strength of a frightened koala. She noted the consternation on the priest's oval-shaped face, then her expression hardened. She'd never realized how similar his beard was to Santa's.

Giordano tried to calm her, to reason with her, but whatever words he was speaking were dampened by the hysterical thumping of her heart.

Louder and louder, it became, its twin beats increasing in rapidity like the rest of the racket, until its pulses merged to the point that they began to sound like a blaring car horn. There was a series of sharp toots, then the horn's repeated trumpets converted into a single, sustained note that shook her until her teeth rattled.

A . . . horn?

"Hey, you gonna move that piece of crap or what?"

Like a squid's tentacles, whipping around its prey and drawing it toward itself, the chilling male voice hauled the child in her out of her dreams and thrust her back inside the woman she'd become. She shuddered as she regained her senses and gazed fearfully about the city street, her hazel eyes blinking.

The car horn flared yet again, and her foul temper with it. Jaw set, she wheeled angrily on the yellow cab's impertinent driver.

"What the *fuck* is your prob--"

Ilsa's words died in her throat, and her anger with them. In their place came undulating waves of dread, running up and down her spine like the clammy legs of some giant centipede.

The taxi's "driver" was her mother.

Or a zombified version, thereof.

Her dead eyes were sunken inside her skull but they were still there, glittering in the shadows as she peered at her daughter. Her teeth were cracked and black, her skin a leprous shade of gray. Worst of all was the puckered bullet wound adorning her brow; it bubbled and oozed an unholy ichor reminiscent of rancid crude oil.

The thing that was her mom smiled. "Well, sweetie? *Are* you or *aren't* you?"

Ilsa literally leapt free from her nightmarish dream-within-a-dream. She rocked back on her heels, then leaned forward with her hands on her thighs, shaking and gasping like she'd just completed a marathon. Her eyes spun wildly in their sockets as she looked furtively around, trying to make sure that what she was seeing was really real.

"Yo, lady. I ain't got all night," the stern-faced driver prodded.

Her lips curled back from her teeth, then she turned and gave the cabbie the stink-eye, while opening her jacket to display her badge and gun. His eyes popped, then he shook his head and muttered something unintelligible, before closing his window and pulling around her double-parked vehicle.

Still weirded out, Ilsa stood there, inhaling through flared nostrils and exhaling through her teeth. Then, just as she felt her heartrate begin to normalize, one of the cathedral doors opened. As if cued, Father Giordano emerged, along with some wealthy patron.

The two men shook hands, then the priest's head swiveled in her direction. She saw the inside corners of his eyebrows slant upward as he recognized her. She realized then that she had no animus left and gave him a polite nod, before turning and seeking shelter inside her Forester.

After clicking her seat belt, Ilsa sat there for what seemed like hours, her eyes closed and hands gripping the steering wheel as she strove to center herself. She was scared. She'd never had flashbacks like that. At least, not since she was little. And *never* with her mother showing up as *The Ghost of Christmas Past: The Undead Edition*. What in tarnation was going on with her? Was it stress? Was she losing her mind? Did it have something to do with the demon?

The demon.

She opened her eyes, sucked in a breath so huge her ribs ached, then let it out in a rush.

Yes.

It was the only thing that made sense. There was some sort of causality between it and the things she'd seen. There had to be. The nightmares she'd been experiencing started right before it hit her precinct; a few days prior to its abortive attack on the McKinleys, in fact. And these . . . *visions*, for want of a better word, began right after their confrontation. She had no idea how such a thing was possible – perhaps Elena, the antique dealer's wife might – but some way, somehow, it had managed to either spiritually or psychically latch onto her.

Had Andy suffered similar incidents?

She was willing to bet he had.

Their opponent was ageless and smart. It realized it was faced with enemies who knew it for what it was. It *had* to. Especially after they'd put it down for the count using custom-made bullets.

She ground her molars.

The ugly bastard is playing mind games. He's toying with us, probing for weaknesses, trying to demoralize and destabilize us.

Ilsa's expression hardened. Well, "Loptr" was about to discover he'd fucked with the wrong bitch. His divide-and-conquer techniques might work on the timid, but they were not about to derail her. And she was pretty sure they wouldn't work on her death-defying partner, either.

Speaking of which...

She reached for her phone to see if LA had gotten back to her. He hadn't. But she did have a missed alert.

An alarm notification? Wait, it was...

"Shit!"

* * *

CHAPTER 13

Ilsa Dunbar arrived home to find hell waiting for her.

A half-block out, she jammed on the brakes and skidded into an available space. After blowing out the breath she'd been holding, she sprang out of her SUV and rushed headlong toward the waiting nightmare.

She could see it up ahead. It was her house.

And it was an inferno.

Her chest felt like there was an elephant sitting on it. A big one. She didn't know how, but she'd experienced an awful premonition even before she'd read the notification on her phone. She'd raced there like she was trying to qualify for the Indy 500, all the while praying that it was a mistake, a glitch of some kind.

As always, her prayers went unanswered. Even from a mile out, there was no mistaking the infernal glow and plumes of smoke, climbing into the night sky.

Once she'd gotten close, she realized she'd have to go the last hundred yards on foot. Police and fire department personnel had created an impressive bulwark of vehicles and barricades that covered half the block, ostensibly to keep civilians at bay. Badge in hand, she weaved her way through the crowd, circumventing a huge fire engine in the process that was turned Evergreen-style, obstructing both sides of the street.

Ilsa began to cough, then found herself blinking uncontrollably. It was a side effect of the unseasonably warm wind that blew stinging smoke and motes of soot into her eyes.

She knew what was fueling that breeze. She'd never hated wind more.

After passing the hushed throng of onlookers, she made for her front door and the enormous turntable ladder truck parked directly outside. Everywhere she looked, uniformed officers, firefighters, and EMTs were shouting into radios and megaphones as they cleared and, in some cases, carried, residents out of other brownstones. She saw a long line of ambulances waiting, but was relieved to see that, so far at least, they had few takers.

Up ahead, she spotted a couple of cops. She started toward them with the intent of introducing herself, but stopped short as she caught a head-on view of the destruction.

Her beautiful home. The house her parents had worked so hard to afford. The place they'd lived in, loved in, and ultimately left to her . . .

It was no more.

The lower level and first floor had been gutted by the conflagration, their windows and frames shattered and, judging by the litany of creaking sounds, their floors on the verge of collapse. Thick firehoses from multiple ladders flowed like a bed of anacondas, up the steps and inside, while firemen inside used axes, hooks, and halligans to tear away at whatever regions of the house they could reach, dousing flames and dodging smoldering debris as they went.

They had the lower floors pretty much under control, but the second floor and attic were a veritable firestorm. Towering sheets of orange fire had climbed as high as the roof, and men from a pair of ladder trucks were poised on extending platforms thirty feet in the air, blasting away at the searing flames with high-pressure hoses that packed enough punch to drill through drywall. Soon, the brownstone's shell had taken on so much water, it started flowing down the front steps and into the street, like a creek overrunning its banks.

Miraculously, although the homes to the left and right of hers had suffered substantial damage, the fire appeared confined primarily to her residence.

Miraculously.

Frustrated by how powerless she felt, Ilsa gritted her teeth and stood there staring, all-but ignorant of the chaos around her. Between the roar of the fire, the pummeling of the hoses, and the crashes of falling pieces of debris, she could hardly think let alone hear. The pair of uniforms approaching her had to yell her name repeatedly before she finally turned and replied.

She recognized them. Officers Brown and Lopez. They'd been in her class in the Academy. Good guys: family men with decent reps. The neighborhood called them the "Beefy Boys", because of their big appetites and burly physiques. Lopez was the quiet one with the mustache and the Puerto Rican flag tattooed across his barrel-shaped chest. Brown was the taller of the two, African American, with big arms and a bigger smile.

He wasn't smiling now, of course. Neither of them was.

Lopez licked chapped lips. "Geez, Dunbar, is that your place?"

He muttered an apology as she nodded. She wanted to say more, but before she could formulate a more substantive response, she clocked a gurney toting a body being guided toward a nearby ambulance. An arm flopped out from beneath the concealing blanket. It was a dark-skinned arm. A girl's arm.

That same feeling of dread came over her again and she rushed to the stretcher, pushing past a pair of startled EMTs in the process. Before their cries of protestation had faded, she yanked the covering back. Horror overtook her face.

It was Kareema.

Ilsa uttered a choking gasp. "Oh, God. Kareema? *Kareema?*" She reached out and shook her gently, praying for a response. There was none. The ashy complexion, the unfocused eyes, and the dilated pupils all told her something she refused to accept. "Oh, no. Oh, God . . ."

The nearest EMT, a raven-haired woman, swallowed nervously. "I'm sorry, ma'am. She's gone."

"Are you sure?" Ilsa asked, her gaze still locked on her friend's youthful face. With her peripherals, she saw the EMT nod. Her head swiveled mechanically on her shoulders and she zeroed the woman with eyes as hard as agates. "*Are you sure?*"

The EMT's thickset partner cleared his throat. "Yeah, we're sure."

Ilsa took a couple of steps back and stood there, watching helplessly as the pretty teen's body was prepped for transport. What would happen to Kareema now? Would someone notify her mother? Should she do it? She didn't even have the woman's number. Was it listed as an emergency contact somewhere? She had no arrest record. How would she find it?

As a Cuisinart of questions roiled through her head, she noticed Brown and Lopez still standing there. She could tell from the way they stared at the ground and seesawed back and forth that they were sympathetic. But there was something else. The pair had something on their minds.

Finally, Brown gave his partner a shrug and the two came over to her. Lopez was holding something by his hip. It was a translucent evidence bag containing something the size and shape of a laptop.

Brown gnawed his lower lip. "We, um, hate to ask this, but..."

"But what?"

Lopez avoided eye contact as he handed her the bag. "FDNY pulled her out of your house. She, uh... she had this."

Ilsa unzipped it and did a doubletake. It contained the ornately-framed eight-by-ten from her mantle, the one of her and her dad, back from when she was five. He was wearing that silly Santa Claus suit of his and a goofy smile to match. Both the frame and print appeared in good shape. The glass was soot-stained and stank of smoke, of course, but that was easily remedied.

"The frame's solid silver... pricey," Brown explained. "We thought maybe, she, uh--"

Ilsa shook her head vehemently. "No. Kareema would *never* steal from me. She tried to save this. She--" Overcome with emotion, she bowed her head and hugged the photo to her chest.

Embarrassed by her show of vulnerability, she backed away until she felt the edge of the gurney. The EMTs exchanged looks, then went around to the ambulance's far side to give her space. She focused on taking slow, calming breaths, while trying to fight back the tears that shimmered in her eyes. It was to no avail.

Then Justin showed up.

She'd only seen the drug dealer in mugshots and on Kareema's phone, but there was no mistaking that face. How he'd gotten past all the cops, firefighters, and other emergency services personnel was anyone's guess. *What* he was doing there, and at that particular moment, was of far greater interest.

Ilsa placed the bagged photo atop the gurney as Justin strutted up to her. Her wet eyes bored into his as she sized him up. Late twenties, athletic, streetwise and street-smart, he reeked of smugness, rubbers, and the crack cocaine he sold.

Just looking at him made her want to vomit.

An obviously feigned and exaggerated look of surprise came over him as he caught sight of the body on the gurney. He made a show of staggering back, his hand over his heart.

"Oh, snap! Is that Kareema?" he yelled. His pearl-white teeth flashed against a background of mahogany skin as he smirked and stuck out his tongue. "Man, that's some fucked up shit." He gave Ilsa a leer that would've done Ramirez proud, then added. "I never got to break that bitch in!"

Ilsa's lips curled back from her own teeth, then she hauled back and blasted him in the face with everything she had. Justin had four inches and forty-pounds on her, but she dropped him like a smelly dishrag. He emitted a frightened squeal as he landed flat on his back, but before she could continue giving him the beatdown he deserved, Lopez and Brown were all over her.

There was a brief but intense struggle as the two cops fought to restrain their incensed comrade. Eventually, it got to the point that Brown had to seize her around the waist in a reverse bearhug. He hoisted her in the air and held her there, legs kicking and fists flailing, preventing her from gaining the leverage she needed to break free.

Justin cradled his face in his hands. He looked down at all the blood and screamed. "You crazy bitch! You broke my fucking nose!"

Ilsa uttered a snarl reminiscent of an enraged panther as she again tried and failed to get her hands on him. "I'm gonna break a lot more than that, you pedophile pimp!"

After a final bout of ineffectual struggling, she realized she was getting nowhere. Not without taking down two of her own, at least. She sucked in a lungful, then let the air rush from her lungs like a balloon deflating.

She tapped out on one of Brown's steely forearms, to let him know she was calm. Far from convinced, he did a one-eighty and put her down, but both he and Lopez remained between her and the object of her ire. It was a wise move, as one look at Justin regaining his feet caused her temper to flare again. Jaw set, she paced back and forth like a caged lion.

"You're gonna pay for that shit," he seethed. He pointed at the two uniforms with a blood-and-snot-streaked hand. "I'm gonna sue. Y'all *saw* it!"

"I didn't see shit," Brown said. He glanced confusedly at his partner. "Did you?"

Lopez shook his head. "Looked like self-defense to me. I distinctly saw him raise his hands to her. Didn't you?"

His partner stroked his chin thoughtfully. "You know, I think you're *right*." He turned to Justin. "You had your hands up, didn't you?"

"Oh, I get it..." the dealer scoffed. Ilsa watched as his usual smugness returned. He picked at his nose, then flicked what he'd removed onto the frozen asphalt. "We'll see what my Jew lawyer has to say about this."

"*Try it*," Brown said. He leaned forward, his expression frightening. "We'll tell the whole city how a little girl dropped you like the used condom you are." The corners of the big man's mouth curled up. "I say you fell trying to rob the place. You get me?"

Justin's expression closed up as he mulled things over. Finally, he shook his head ruefully and turned to leave. Five paces into the wind, he spun around and, with both hands, flipped them all the bird.

"Man, fuck all y'all!"

Brown shot him a huge smile. "Yeah, you be careful on that ice now! It's slippery!"

Cradling the photo frame in her arms, Ilsa walked over, her gaze directed downward. "Thanks, guys."

"Man, don't sweat it," Brown said. "That punk-ass gives men of any color a bad name."

She nodded, then watched sorrowfully as the ambulance pulled slowly out. Its tires made a series of loud crackling sounds as it carried its burden across sheets of fresh ice, formed from the fire's runoff.

Lopez pursed his lips. "Hey, Dunbar. Anything we can do?"

Ilsa shook her head slowly.

"Sorry. It's a fucked-up Christmas Eve, huh?"

She gazed up at what remained of her home, the flames reflecting in her eyes. "It's not my first."

She turned sideways, trying to decide what to do now, when something captured her interest. It was on the nearby sidewalk, to the left of the closest ladder truck.

Ignoring Lopez's follow-up query, she proceeded there and peered about. The area was a mess, with chunks of rubble scattered across the walkway, not to mention hundreds of footprints from civilians and first responders. Still, there was something there.

She was positive. She'd seen it illuminated by the fire's flickering light. A familiar shape, embedded in the soot-stained snow . . .

She finally found what she believed was a portion of it, but the lion's share was covered by a section of firehose. Straddling the heavy gray hose in a sumo stance, she gripped it with both hands and, with an effort, wrestled it a foot to the left. Her eyes contracted, then expanded to the size of hen's eggs.

It couldn't be, but it was. There, embedded in the ice at her feet, was the monster's calling card – a cloven hoofprint the size of a large dinner plate.

Inside her head, Ilsa could hear the thing's deep-throated roar. This time, however, it had a drawn-out, stop-and-start quality to it, like it was mocking her. Her vision began to swirl like the flurries falling all around her and she looked fearfully about.

Instinct took over and, without regard for Brown and Lopez, she took off like a sprinter at the starting gun. She made for her SUV, dodging firefighters and cops alike as she slipped and slid on the ice-encrusted asphalt. She hit the Subaru's auto-start from thirty yards out and jumped in, locking the doors before her ass had touched the seat.

Panting now, she clicked on her seatbelt and pulled out. She executed a quick K-turn, then tore off down the street. She had to get out of there. She needed space to breathe and to think, to figure out how she would--

How she would *what?* What was she going to do?

The enormity of the menace she faced hit her like a hook punch to the temple. She felt dazed and pulled into a nearby bus stop, nearly clipping a Mercedes in the process. She sat there, a death grip on the steering wheel and breathing like a fish out of water as she tried and failed to come to terms with her situation.

The creature knew where she lived.

She didn't know how – maybe it had tracked her by scent like a bloodhound does – but it did. Not finding her there, it torched the place in retaliation. And even though poor Kareema's body showed no signs of the trauma it usually dished out, it had ultimately caused her death.

Her face knotted. It had to be stopped – tracked down and destroyed – but how? Should she inform her superiors and risk ending up in a straightjacket?

Nope. That was *so* not an option.

Point of fact, Captain Janus was wrong. Their "Christmas Cannibal" was *not* going to slink off into the sunrise with the intention of returning again next year. It was still here, still killing. and, from the look of things, it wasn't about to stop. It had unfinished business and her name was at the top of its itinerary. It was just a matter of time before it came for her.

She had to prepare.

Her hands shaking, Ilsa felt inside her jacket pockets. She came out with a handful of bullets and fished through them. Most were her usual hollow points, but there were four . . . five . . .

Damn. Only six iron rounds left.

She'd expended a lot of ammo the previous night. For all the good it did. She wondered how many Andy had left.

Andy!

God, if she'd ever needed someone's help, it was now. She reached for her phone, but after checking her mirrors decided to pull out first.

It was best to keep moving.

Putting the Forester in gear, she sped off. She checked the time, then voice-dialed Andy's phone.

C'mon, LA. Pick up, pick up, pick up . . .

Voicemail. Damn.

She tried again and got the same thing.

Third time . . . busy signal.

"Fuck!"

CHAPTER 14

Olek Apostol was seated in his office, going over the day's sales receipts and invoices, when the doorbell rang. He frowned as he checked the time, then switched screens to bring up the external cameras. A sigh slipped from his lips as he spotted the familiar form of Vincent, the old Vietnam veteran. He was standing out front, making a show of brandishing the silver pastry tray his host had "loaned" him the other day.

Olek smiled sorrowfully. As a veteran, it pained him to see one of his own living under such circumstances. It meant nothing to him that, at the time the two men had served, his country – the then Soviet Union – and the United States were politically and ideologically opposed. In his mind, soldiers were soldiers and, beneath their uniforms, they were all brothers in arms. To see a fellow vet alone and adrift, with no family or friends to provide support or lodging, cut him to the quick.

So, he did what he could. He offered food and drink and, as opportunity permitted, money. It was the least he could do. He and Elena had been blessed in so many ways. After his time at the United States military's science division had come to an end, they'd put down roots and started what would eventually become a thriving business. And raised a large family to boot.

He felt privileged to have the resources to be able to help others less fortunate. And, admittedly, he enjoyed how Vincent always tried to make it seem like he wasn't receiving charity. The man liked to earn his keep.

Olek respected that. A fellow needed to keep his dignity about him. A warrior, most of all. Nowadays, you couldn't walk the streets donned in armor. But your self-respect was something you could and should have girding you at all times.

He touched a button on the wall for the outside intercom and advised his visitor he'd be right there. Then he reached for his wallet.

How much had they settled on to keep his prized pastry tray from ending up at the local pawn shop? Was it forty dollars?

No, the wily old soldat managed to haggle his way up to fifty. I remember now.

Chuckling, Olek opened his billfold and extracted a crisp Ulysses S. Grant.

He whistled a merry tune while heading toward the front of the store. When he got there, he disarmed the burglar alarm and pulled a lever, deactivating the horizontal folding guards that prevented would-be burglars from reaching the inside door. Even without the guards, no one could get past the secondary barrier of inch-thick stainless-steel bars; but there was no sense in providing some inebriated individual the temptation to break a window or deface the place. Of course, all that security came with a price, he realized, wincing at the terrible screeching sound the steel guards made as they rattled along their track.

What a racket! That thing needs oil even more than my knees!

An idea came to Olek then. The grin that tailgated it added yet another crease to his already cross-hatched face, but he didn't care. He was pleased he'd come up with another chore he could tag onto Vincent's ever-expanding to-do list.

THE SLEIGH

Still smiling, he unbolted the store's inside door and swung it slowly open, the fifty-dollar bill in hand.

"A little late, my friend, but--"

The sight that greeted him caused Olek's smile to vanish, along with a hefty chunk of what hope he still had for humanity's future. While he'd been waiting for the steel guards to settle into place, his guest had reached between the inner bars with a screwdriver and pried his ancestral Mezuzah free from its doorjamb. He was holding it in his hand and studying it, a distressed look on his face.

"Vincent, what-what are you *doing*?"

Tears started streaming down the American's cheeks, and his face was layered with guilt. Beneath that, however, Olek detected a mountain of dread.

"I'm so sorry!" Vincent cried. He dropping the screwdriver and started backing up while holding the Mezuzah in trembling hands. "He *made* me do it! He *made* me!" Then he turned and ran like the Devil himself was chasing him.

He wasn't, Olek realized.

He was across the street.

The antique dealer's heart took a bungee jump into his bowels as a shadowy form emerged from the blackness of a nearby alley. Even from sixty feet away, he could see the figure's eyes, twin embers, glittering within its cowl. For a moment, it stood there, studying him. Then it started mechanically forward. It seemed unhurried, yet its hooved legs quickly devoured the yards separating them.

As it drew closer, Olek was suddenly reminded of the big brown bear he'd encountered in his youth. He'd accidentally startled it while on patrol with his unit. It reared up out of a nearby snow drift and, before turning to flee, bellowed so loudly at him and his friends that several of them were forced to change their drawers when they got back to base. Later that night, while commiserating over their ration of beer, they'd estimated the bruin had stood over two meters in height and weighed a good three hundred kilos.

What was coming at him now was bigger.

Much bigger.

It was the snow demon. After all these years, it had finally found them.

The worthless piece of paper he held twirled to the ground like a discarded leaf. Then he was in motion. Slamming the heavy inside door closed and bolting it, he smacked the lever back up to reactivate the outer guards.

Fear-borne adrenaline shot through him and he started to run. It was coming faster now. He could hear the thuds of its impossibly heavy footfalls right behind him. He knew without looking that the outermost barrier would never close in time.

He had to get to the phone. Had to call—

Behind him, there was a thunderous crash, followed by a deafening bellow. The ground under him seemed to vibrate, and he heard the horrific sound of steel beginning to succumb to indescribable pressure.

Ahead of him, he heard the clatter of what sounded like a teapot crashing to the floor.

"Elena, run!"

* * *

It hadn't even been two hours, yet Andy Alvilda was already climbing the walls of his apartment. Not literally, of course; he was no high-rise-climbing ogre with grapnels for fingers. But he *was* starting to fantasize about making a rope out of his king-size bedsheets, tying it to a radiator, and using it to go out a window Rapunzel-style, in the hopes of making it to the street below.

Being under his captain's version of house arrest did not sit well with the hyperactive Californian. He could only pace back and forth within the confines of his modest, one-bedroom flat so many times before he started getting antsy.

He'd attempted to distract himself by turning on the television, but that lasted all of thirty seconds. Under normal circumstances, being able to binge-watch an entire season of *Family Feud* would have been a gift from the gods.

But not when there was a man-eating monster running around.

Steve Harvey's entertaining improvs would have to wait.

As he tiptoed to the window, Andy realized his partner had been right when it came to Janus; honesty was definitely *not* the best policy. Still, what was done was done.

He had more immediate problems.

A pair of them, in fact.

Two stories below and directly across the street, Detectives Ramirez and Tokaido kept watch from a handicapped spot.

In full ninja mode now, Andy rested the palm heel of one hand against his window's side jamb and craned his neck sideways, exposing just enough of his face to take a peek. He figured that, between his place's lights being off and all the lit-up stores lining the avenue below, no one would be able to see him.

He was mistaken.

Tokaido's hawkish eyes never missed a trick, and before Andy had time to react, he tapped his email-reading partner on the shoulder and pointed.

Ramirez's squinty eyes narrowed even further as he glared up at him. Then he raised one hand to his face, his index and ring fingers forming a V. The obscene tongue movements that followed required no elaboration.

Refusing to be baited by the vulgar display, Andy mouthed a kiss at him in response. Then he lowered the window's blinds.

His brow furrowed up and he started ruminating. He needed to get out of there. But how? Leaving the apartment wasn't an issue. He could certainly slip out the building's back entrance without any problem. There were no uniforms standing guard.

The big issue was transportation. "Laverne and Shirley" had their stereotypical Crown Victoria parked just a few yards from the subway entrance. Smart of them. And with his own car sitting in a parking garage, literally around the corner, the odds of him getting past the pair without being noticed were slim.

Unless . . .

Andy's eyes danced with merriment as he grabbed his cell phone. He scrolled through his contacts list, found the number he needed, and hit dial. As he waited for the expected pickup, he decided to check on "Thelma and Louise". Circumspection was called for, and instead of raising the blinds, he used his middle and index fingers to splay two of its slats apart so he could peer between them.

"Hello?"

"Hey, it's Andy," he said, turning away from the blinds. "I'm sorry to bother you, but I'm in a tight spot and I could use a hand."

"No problem," the voice on the other end of the line replied. "What's up?"

Andy hesitated. Something was wrong with his fingers. They felt wet . . . sticky.

He held them up to the light and did a doubletake. His fingertips were dripping with partly-coagulated blood.

What the ...

He prized open the blinds again, expecting to find them coated with the stuff, only to utter a gasp and recoil. The window slats snapped together loudly as he sprang back.

The demon was right outside his window!

He'd stared into its hideous face from a yard away. It was just standing there, as big as life and twice as ugly.

Andy drew his gun and waited for it to come crashing through the glass.

Nothing happened.

He started blinking furiously. This was impossible, right? He was on the third floor and there was nothing out there for it to stand on. No ledge, no fire escape – nothing. The thing couldn't float, could it?

He drew a breath and held it, then, weapon ready, grabbed the blinds' lift cord and pulled sharply down. The window was clear. No monster, no anything. Just the street outside, the building facing his, and Tokaido leaning forward, smiling and waving as he looked up.

Andy let the cord go and stood there shaking his head. A quick inspection of his digits brought on another headshake. Clean as a whistle. What the *hell* was going on? He decided either his imagination was getting the better of him or the stress of the last forty-eight hours had finally taken its toll. He glanced at a nearby wall calendar and gave a rueful headshake. In the bigger scheme of things, he supposed it didn't really matter.

Time was running out.

The irate voice emanating from the phone at his feet forced Andy to focus, and he bent to retrieve it.

"Uh, hey, sorry. I dropped my phone," he said. He cleared his throat, then paused and peeked through the blinds once more. Still nothing. His eyes lidded contentedly. "Here's what I need..."

* * *

Still cruising around midtown, Ilsa paused to check her look in her visor's mirror. She didn't like what she saw and slapped it closed. To an outsider, her countenance might have been unreadable. But she knew better. Any perceived ambivalence on her part was a paper-thin veneer. Beneath it, sorrow, fear, and fury waged a three-way tug-o-war that made her feel like she was being ripped apart.

The sorrow was for Kareema. She blamed herself for the adolescent's death, to the point her stomach felt like it was twisted up in knots. Although she may not have been directly responsible, there was no denying that, if she hadn't taken the pretty teen under her wing, she'd still be alive.

The fear she felt was more encompassing. It was for herself, for Andy, and in the bigger scheme of things, the entire human race. Short of hitting it with an anti-tank gun, the demon had proven itself unkillable. And now it had her in its sights. It was just a matter of time before it found her.

After repeatedly trying and failing to get LA on the phone, she found herself in a quandary. Her gut told her to run to him for help, but she summarily rejected the notion. At an instinctive level, she railed against the idea of playing the "damsel in distress". But there was more to it than that. She remembered seeing something on TV about creatures like Loptr. Supposedly, they were incapable of tracking victims that crossed moving bodies of water. As murky and sluggish as it appeared, she was pretty sure the Hudson qualified. She was also sure that Andy was on the thing's hit list; how could he not be? Which meant that if she went to Brooklyn, there was a good chance she'd lead it right to his door.

Then she'd have another death on her conscience.

Her rage, of course, was for the demon itself. The fire that burned in her breast when she pictured it outshone even her fear. All those poor families: women and children, slaughtered for what? Because they celebrated something it despised? And on top of everything else, there was her family's home, reduced to ash.

The muscles of Ilsa's face finally entered the fray and a look of determination flooded her features. She was tired of being afraid and she refused to continue running. She needed to figure out a way to destroy the damn thing. But how?

She snapped her fingers – a habit she realized with some annoyance she'd picked up from Andy. Perhaps daylight would do it. It always struck at night and disappeared before dawn. Was it vulnerable to sunlight like a vampire was?

A tingle of excitement shot up her spine. It might well be. Hell, as old as it was, it could well be the originator of the vampire myths and legends.

An all-too-familiar chime put her ponderings on hold. She reached for her phone and tabbed its notification key. There was a text. Stopping at the next light, she raised the screen to eye level.

So sorry about your home. Fire marshal says it started in the fireplace. Looks like a gas line ruptured. -Sheriff Jake B.

Ilsa's scoff was a derisive snort. "Yeah, I'll *bet* it did..."

She shook her head as she flipped on the radio, then resumed driving, her inner compass still searching for guidance. Things she might not have otherwise caught began to jump out at her. Across the street to her left, a mother rushed her two kids back inside their hotel, glancing back over her shoulder as they went. The trepidation on her face was palpable. A block further and to her right, a couple of punks sitting outside a bodega started grabbing their crotches and shouting slurs at an attractive Asian woman walking by. Thankfully, she walked hurriedly away from them and rejoined her friends.

When she stopped at the next light, Ilsa tried distracting herself by doing some station hopping. They were playing all the biggies: Perry Cuomo, Bing Crosby, Elvis . . . She exhaled hard and stopped pushing buttons. It was useless; there was no escaping Christmas. Then, as Johnny Mathis's version of *Silver Bells* – one of her parents' favorites – drew to a close, a feeling of acute sadness welled up within her. She remembered her last conversation with Olek Apostol, and how she'd taken umbrage with him referring to her beloved Manhattan as *Sin City*.

"So, you're saying, what, that we deserve this? That we've brought it on ourselves?"

Was he right? *Had* they?

A honk from the car behind her prompted Ilsa to get moving. She cleared her throat as she passed the green light and looked around to get her bearings.

For whatever reason, she'd somehow ended up back in the Diamond District. In fact, she realized, she was around the corner from the eccentric antique dealer's store.

The wry look she wore was discarded as she spotted a firetruck, two ambulances, and an entire squad of police cars arrayed outside *Apostol's Antiquities*.

"Oh, Jesus. Now what?"

Pulling over as quickly as possible, Ilsa jumped out and jogged across the icy asphalt, toward the waiting mayhem.

The three-deep throng of onlookers standing around blocked her view, and it wasn't until she was within a stone's throw of the store that she espied the damage.

The mesh-like steel guards that warded *Apostol's Antiquities'* ornate entrance had been peeled away like a sheet of aluminum foil – she could see traces of them protruding from their former tracks – before being crammed together and hurled through the windshield of a parked limousine like a spear. The thick bars directly behind the guards hadn't fared much better. They'd been bent and pulled apart like soft pretzels, leaving behind an oval-shaped opening that was big enough for a small elephant to pass.

The store's reinforced doorway and plate glass windows had suffered a similar fate. The former had been annihilated, the sturdy beams making up its frame lying Lord-knows-where, and all that remained of the latter were a few thousand shards of glass, sprinkled like rock salt atop the surrounding rubble.

Ilsa gasped aloud as she spotted a bloodied Olek Apostol, belted to a gurney and being wheeled toward the back of an ambulance. She made for him, shielding her eyes with one hand against the collective brightness of the assorted vehicles' strobes. A tired-looking beat cop stepped forward to intercept her, but she showed him her badge and her teeth and he gave way.

Olek didn't appear to notice her as she looped around a pair of picture-taking forensicologists and materialized by his side. Obviously in shock, he was soaked to the skin, bedraggled, and obviously terrorized. In his trembling hands he held a cross that, from the look of things, had been hastily assembled by lashing together two broken pieces of wood. There was blood oozing from his left ear and nostril, and he had a nasty scalp wound that was rapidly outclassing the quick-clotting gauze the EMTs had applied.

"Omigod, Mister Apostol. What happened?" Ilsa blurted out. She looked around hurriedly. "Where's your--"

She turned pale as she caught sight of a body being pushed toward a refrigerated coroner's van. There was a sudden creaking sound as one of the gurney's wheels dipped into a pie-sized pothole. The resultant jolt caused a blood-streaked arm to flop down from beneath the privacy covering. It remained there, dangling.

It was Elena's.

"It was me!" Olek wailed. "I did this! I killed her! I killed them all!" He gripped the jagged pieces of wood he held so tightly his hands bled. "It's my fault! I'm responsible!"

Ilsa's peripherals detected a hint of movement. Six paces to her right, a uniformed officer interviewing a witness looked up. Even from twenty feet away, she could see the suspicion in his eyes. The cop tried making it seem like he was jotting down notes on his interviewee's statement, but she'd have bet the farm he was logging Olek's "confession", word for word.

She scowled, then turned to the ambulance's driver, a short fellow with a distinctively Roman nose. "Where are you bringing him?"

"Theologist. By request."

Ilsa's lips vibrated as she clamped them together and blew out a breath. "Take good care of him, please. I'll meet you there." Without waiting for a reply and ignoring everyone else, she turned and entered Apostol's.

The store was pitch-black inside and she had her Surefire out before she'd taken two steps. She took a moment to sweep the area with its broad beam, trying to familiarize herself with her surroundings.

Then it hit her. The darkness. The fetid air . . .

It was like entering a tomb.

The interior of what had been a museum-quality exhibition of antiquities now looked like a London market after the blitz. Two-thirds of the plexiglass display cases either on shelves or lining the walls were smashed, and free-standing art lay trampled. Priceless paintings had been slashed in two, marble statues shattered, and the two suits of armor she'd been so impressed with pulled limb from limb. She spotted a Crusader-style great helm lying on the ground, a few yards away. It looked like it had been through a machine press, it was stomped so flat.

Not far from the knight's helmet lay what had once been a gorgeous Scottish basket-hilt sword. The tip of its ancient blade was missing – snapped off – and much of what remained was coated with a viscous green ichor.

Ilsa's lips tightened, but she afforded Olek a nod of admiration. The old man had put up one hell of a fight.

She looked around, one hand on the butt of her pistol, and the other swinging her torch back and forth in slow sweeps, searching for signs of life. There were none. Just a never-ending supply of creepy shadows and the unbelievably loud sound of water dripping from damaged sprinklers.

Just then, a loud clatter from behind caused her to jump.

It was nothing. Just a chunk of plexiglass, slipping from its frame and collapsing onto a mound of debris. She sighed heavily. From the look of things, the only artifact that had escaped unscathed was the big gold cross Andy had fixated upon during their initial visit. The ornately sculpted and bejeweled one that was worth a fortune.

She eyed the ancient crucifix's protective case from ten feet away. It was still illuminated by a lone accent light, situated directly above it. She noticed a big scuff mark on the bullet-proof glass, like something heavy had bounced off it. She wondered if that was what had set off the alarm.

Was that why Olek was still alive?

She'd have to ask him herself. Speaking of which, she realized there was something she needed to do . . .

Adjusting her flashlight's beam to full brightness, Ilsa made her way toward the old man's office. His office door was ajar but intact. Eyes tight and pistol primed, she kicked it the rest of the way open and shined her light inside.

Then she swallowed her fear and walked in.

CHAPTER 15

Ilsa had a brooding look on her face and a canvas-wrapped parcel pressed against one hip as she swept through Theologist Hospital's well-worn emergency room doors. She stopped when she reached the waiting area and took a moment to survey her surroundings. The last time she'd been there, the place had looked like an overrun field hospital. There'd been at least sixty people jammed together, with injuries ranging from minor to, *Oh, my God! Why haven't they admitted you yet?*

Perhaps the most memorable of these had been four perps, easily identified as such by their matching sets of handcuffs. Three of them were gang members, a rowdy group of Italian males. From what she'd gleaned, they'd decided to jump a short Korean man three times their age.

And had their asses handed to them.

Two had suffered broken noses and had eyes swollen shut from the blows they'd received. The third – based on his innate mouthiness, no doubt the fracas's instigator – had gotten his leg snapped at the knee. The bloated area encapsulating the broken bones was the size of a cantaloupe and she'd cringed when she'd seen it.

Their "victim", on the other hand, although a tad frayed around the edges, seemed in remarkably good spirits. Especially, for an old man who'd just endured a gang-assault. In Ilsa's eyes, the bullies were the gangbangers' equivalent of the "Three Stooges". One look at their chosen victim's steely eyes, scarred face, and cauliflower ears should have dissuaded them, but they'd ignored the signs. By the time they'd found out they were in over their collective heads, it was too late.

Ilsa could still picture the sardonic eyeroll one of the cops babysitting them had given her when she'd thrown him an inquisitive look.

As she walked through those same doors today, she'd anticipated a similar scenario. She ended up being pleasantly surprised. More than surprised, in fact; it was a Christmas Eve miracle. The waiting room was empty and she was able to walk right up to the alert-looking nurse at the reception desk without feeling guilty about bypassing someone.

Ilsa eked out a smile as she showed the woman her badge. "Hi, I'm looking for Olek Apostol's room?"

The nurse – an overweight blonde who appeared to be sweating just from the effort of sorting papers – gave a start. She eyed her athletic visitor up and down, then placed her hands on her desk and, with a grunt and a grimace, pushed herself upright. "Sure thing, officer." She waved her candy striper over and asked her to fill in, then gestured for Ilsa to follow. "C'mon, I'll walk you. Are you family?"

"A friend. How is he?"

The woman shrugged as she waddled along. "He's been out since they brought him in."

Ilsa followed her past a pair of hydraulic doors and along a series of corridors. Her nostrils began to twitch, and she soon resorted to breathing through her mouth. There may have been fewer patients, but the air still burned with the combined stink of betadine, bleach, and blood, with a sprinkling of eau de *toilet* thrown in for good measure.

She shook her head. Like most cops, she thought the world of doctors and nurses; but how they did their jobs was beyond her.

During the lengthy drive, she'd wondered why Olek had requested this particular hospital. After all, there were far closer, not to mention much more pristine facilities in midtown. As she'd crossed the Brooklyn Bridge, however, and saw the full moon reflecting off the Hudson, she realized it was a sage move on his part. The old man had been keeping tabs on their mutual nemesis for decades. He was undoubtedly familiar with the legends that suggested moving bodies of water impeded its ability to hunt.

Come to think of it, if the stories were true, she might have given herself a temporary reprieve, as well. She chuckled through her nose, only to grimace and step aside for an orderly pushing a heavily-laden cart marked "medical waste". On a more pleasant note, it would be nice to take a break from looking over her shoulder every five minutes. Even if it was just for an hour or two.

The out-of-breath nurse finally came to a halt outside Olek's room. Ilsa studied the antique dealer through its narrow window. He was festooned with wires and tubes and had layers of bandages covering his forearms and the top of his head.

"Injuries?" she asked.

"Surprisingly minor, given his age." She paused to review a clipboard hanging on Olek's door. "Mostly cuts and scrapes. He's strong too," she said, indicating his hands. "Been holding those old pieces of wood they brought him in with in a death grip."

Ilsa looked her in the eye. "Can I see him?"

The nurse hesitated. "Uh, sure. Just try to keep it brief. He just lost his wife, so . . ."

"I know. I was there."

The nurse's face turned ashen. "Oh, my Lord . . . Is it true?" she whispered, looking to see if anyone else was within earshot. "Did he do it? Is that why you're--"

"No. I'm just here to try and cheer him up. I brought him something."

"What is it?" she asked, intently eyeing the bundle she carried.

Ilsa gave her burden a fond pat and smiled. "His most prized possession."

* * *

Ilsa waited for the nosey nurse to leave before she entered Olek's room. She left the lights dimmed and made as little noise as possible as she set her cumbersome parcel on a nearby chair.

From five feet away, she studied the battered old ex-Soviet scientist. His badly scraped hands were atop his chest, his gnarled fingers white-knuckling the makeshift crucifix she'd seen earlier. He seemed to be experiencing REM, and every so often mumbled in his sleep.

She was glad to see an indication of brain activity. The old man was so pale that, if he'd been completely catatonic, she'd have thought him a reposing corpse, destined for the morgue.

Ilsa exhaled and ran her tongue across her teeth. She had to admit, she was impressed. At Olek's age, it was a miracle he'd survived. How he'd managed it, she had no idea. The ripped-open storefront left little to the imagination, but she needed details. Fear that it was her fault – that the creature had followed Andy and her to *Apostol's Antiquities* – loomed large. She had so much guilt bearing down on her already. She didn't think she could bear any more.

The minutes ticked by and Ilsa's eyes flitted to the nearby clock on the wall. It had been past midnight – technically Christmas Eve – when the couple was attacked.

She gave a sorrowful headshake. "I guess the rules no longer apply, eh, old man?"

As if he'd heard her, Olek stirred. His head turned back and forth upon his pillow and his lips began to tremble, like he was trying to communicate. Tamping down her apprehension, she drew closer, until she was at his bedside. "Mister Apostol? Mister Apostol?"

Not wanting to speak too loudly, she leaned over him. "Olek? Olek?"

His eyes opened a sliver, then he muttered, "Damn it, Elena! I told you not to get that boob job!"

Ilsa's jaw literally touched her chest. She hadn't realized how close her "big dumbbells", as Ramirez called them, were to the old man's face. Her own countenance turned a bright scarlet and she pulled back, shaking her head in a combination of discomfiture and amusement.

"Mister Apostol, it's me, Detective Dunbar. Can you hear me?"

Olek uttered a pain-filled groan, then his eyelids parted a bit more. "Dunbar..." he wheezed. "From the Gaelic...meaning fort or summit."

He blinked a few times, then his weary eyes took in her smile. "I'm sorry, detective...for a moment I thought you were..." Then reality came rushing back and a huge sob wracked his frail frame. "Oh, God!"

Ilsa's vision blurred and she focused on the door, in an effort to keep from tearing up. "I'm *so* sorry. Was it the . . . thing?"

Olek started shaking with grief and rage. "It was Vincent. *He* let it in . . . I tried to stop it. Tried to save her. So old!" He squeezed the cross like it was a lifeline. Then his head drooped and he said resignedly, "It will come for me next. You'll see."

Ilsa felt her throat tighten. "Maybe not." She reached for the bundle she'd brought and unwrapped it.

The old man's eyes lit up. "My history of Ded Moroz . . . thank you!"

Conscious of his assorted injuries, Ilsa handed him the book as gingerly as possible. He put aside his jury-rigged crucifix and accepted it with trembling hands, then wrapped his arms around it. He reminded her of a forlorn child who'd been reunited with his long-lost teddy bear.

Olek caught her staring and, despite all he'd been through, gave her an analytical look. "After everything you've seen, you still don't believe?"

All of a sudden, Ilsa felt dog-tired. She let herself drop down into the now-vacant chair. "Look, if you're asking me if I believe that some powerful, inhuman thing is slaughtering people, then yes. I've seen it." Her hazel eyes downshifted from his to the ancient tome, then back up again. "If you're asking me to believe in a fat, jolly, old elf who sneaks toys to kids while they're asleep, that's something else altogether."

The old man studied her face intently. His expression was hard to interpret, but it made her feel uncomfortable.

Is that pity?

She shrugged it off and attempted to steer the conversation in a more positive direction.

"You said you saw Ded Moroz's sleigh fall from the sky. Does that mean you saw *him*?"

Olek looked away and shook his head.

"Have you *ever* seen him?" she pressed.

"No, but my father did."

"Your father?"

"Back in the Ukraine. The year was 1933." A wistful look crept over him. "I was a baby. It was the year of the *Holodomor*."

Ilsa gasped. "Stalin's imposed famine..."

Olek gave her a nod. "I'm impressed, detective. You know your history. And history was what the 'Red Tsar' tried to make of us..."

He shook his head ruefully. "To annihilate the Ukrainian people, everything was taken from us: food, grain, livestock. Outside aid was rejected and travel was prohibited. The people were starving, and with starvation insanity follows. And the worst of this is--"

"Cannibalism..."

The old man's head lowered and his face lapsed into shadow. "Many resorted to this horrific practice. They preferred children. They were easier prey, softer..." He shuddered and held the book tight. "Many parents could not bear to eat their own, so they traded theirs for what food they could get."

"And your father?"

"A good man. A policeman, like you." He smiled sadly. "He risked being shot to catch fish from the stream, shared them with other men, other families."

"And?"

"It wasn't enough. They wanted meat and he knew it was simply a matter of time before they came for me." His eyes sought and found hers. "That night, Christmas Eve, in fact, my father stayed awake, waiting for the nightmare he knew would come."

Ilsa felt her breath shallow as she leaned forward in her seat.

The emotion leached from Olek's voice as he continued. "As babies, we tend to remember little, just vestigial images. Some of my earliest memories are of my father, sitting with his shotgun. I remember seeing torches move past our window, followed by menacing shadows under our front door. There were whispers, followed by startled cries. Then all became quiet."

He paused to lick his lips. "Suddenly, our cottage door flew open in a blast of wind and snow. From my crib, I saw the boots of an unseen figure enter our home. My father stared in astonishment."

"Did he shoot?"

Olek shook his grizzled head. "It was a miracle. Ded Moroz had come to our village. And with him be brought the gift of life."

Ilsa touched the base of her neck. "I'm confused."

"I saw my father standing outside our front door and looking up at the sky. And beyond him, piled on our front yard, there was food: huge baskets of bread and vegetables and sacks of grain."

"So, you're saying Santa Claus saved your life."

"Not just my life, but the lives of hundreds. Their souls, too." He closed his eyes and gave the big book a fond pat. "The next day, my father began assembling this tome as a tribute. And he kept at it until the day he died."

"And now it's yours."

"Not for much longer, I'm afraid . . ."

Ilsa studied him from beneath lowered eyebrows. "When they were loading you into the ambulance you were screaming it was 'your fault'. What did you mean by that?"

Olek tried and failed to maintain eye contact, then sighed. "As I told you, I was a mechanical engineer with the Soviet military. I designed . . . weapons. Specifically, the tracking systems for mobile missile systems, what you call SAMs."

He fidgeted, then pulled his brows together. "I am ashamed to say my improvements killed many of your brave pilots in war over Vietnam."

Ilsa pressed her index finger to her cheek and propped her chin on the rest of her clenched fingers. "That's how you were able to defect."

"Yes. But before that, in December of 1968, I was stationed at far outpost in Siberia, watching for American spy planes."

She nodded, noting how his slight Russian accent was becoming noticeably heavier, the longer he spoke.

"It was so cold and desolate . . ." He shivered at the memory and, beneath the blankets, his feet stamped up and down in invisible snow. "If not for Elena, I'd have lost my mind."

Olek's voice trailed off for a moment.

"On Christmas Eve morning, over a bottle of wine, the base commander told me about a phenomenon that always happened that night. Meteors would burn through the sky at incredible speed, coming from the pole and zipping by overhead."

When he turned to her his eyes were wide and unblinking, and she could swear she saw shooting stars reflected in his irises.

"They would repeat this, their trajectory changing each time, at least a dozen times each night. He said they'd tried shooting one down many times, but never came close."

His voice turned hoarse and Ilsa could see him struggling to clear his throat. She got up and looked around, then grabbed a bottle of spring water off a nearby counter and opened it for him.

"Spasiba," he said, sipping it then looking up confusedly. "Uh, where was I?"

"They were shooting at something," she replied, grinning.

"Da, da... They'd had a pool going for 6 years. It was huge, nearly five thousand rubles. A small fortune at the time," he emphasized. "I'd never seen so much silver. Of course, being a married man, I wanted to win the money, so I bought into the pool to shoot down one of these mysterious meteors." A conspiratorial look came over him and he lowered his voice. "You see, I could see the passings weren't random; there was a pattern. Of course, the base commander laughed as he took my money, but I knew something he didn't."

"Which was?"

"I had the thermal tracking systems for the new Dvina system."

Olek relaxed his grip on the big book and, with Ilsa's assistance, managed to sit up. Using his hands, he imitated something high up, moving laterally, and something else arcing up from below and slamming into it. "That night, I, Olek Apostol, won the pool. The money was *mine*."

Ilsa sat up straight. "Is that where you got the meteorite?"

Olek stared at the floor, his face a pain-filled grimace. "No. What I destroyed was no meteor. It-it was..." He touched the ancient book, then his eyes welled with tears. "Don't you see? It's *my* fault. Loptr broke free because of *me!* Because of what *I* stupidly did! All those deaths, they are all my doing. The parents, the children, my poor Elena..."

"Did... did you *see* him? Are you *sure*?"

"Everything crumbled to dust before our eyes. Only pieces of the sleigh remained." He held up the hastily-made cross. "Only *this* . . ."

Ilsa felt a flush creep up her face. "Wow. Is that what saved you from-from *it*?"

Olek nodded.

"Can I touch it?"

"Take it," he said, offering it to her. You need it more than me."

"Oh, no. I couldn't. It--"

"I insist. It's okay," he said, hugging the big book. "I'll be fine."

Ilsa accepted the cross with borderline reverence. It was formed of two fragments of rune-carved wood, gray in color, with the larger piece being about eighteen inches long. The sections had been lashed tightly together with a dark leather thong, and the terminus of the vertical portion ended in a ragged point, as if it was intended to be staked into the ground. The wood was surprisingly cool to the touch, yet her fingertips began to warm whenever they came in contact with it.

"Wow, it feels *old*," she said softly.

"Oh, it is. It is."

"So, what happens now. What do I do?"

Olek scratched at his cheek. "It may protect you. But if cold iron can't stop him, what can?" He shook his head. "Next year he will feed unchecked, and with each new life he takes his strength will increase. Eventually, he'll be invincible."

"So, that's it, we just run and hide? Live out our lives as prey, waiting to be hunted?" A storm settled on Ilsa's brow and she stood up. "I'm sorry, but I can't do that. That thing killed my friend, murdered your wife, and burned down my fucking house. And *now* it's not going away. Why?"

"You disrupted his plans, even managed to hurt him. I would imagine you, as you say, 'pissed him off'."

"So, he's not going to leave?"

Olek grew noticeably tired and, with her help, lay back down. "He will leave tonight," he said, nodding gratefully as she covered him with a blanket. "Before the stroke of midnight."

"So, there's still a chance to stop him. To *end* this."

His gloomy headshake filled her with desperation.

"Please, there has got to be a way. *Something. Anything.* We can't just sit this one out."

"I'm sorry, detective. Iron and silver are all I know." Olek drew his lower lip between his teeth. "Unless . . ."

"Unless what? *What?*"

He blinked sleepily. "It was a blood sacrifice that drew him here. Perhaps a blood sacrifice could send him back . . ."

Ilsa tensed as she realized he was fading on her. She touched him gently on the forearm. "Whose blood sacrifice? Olek, *whose* blood? *My* blood?"

The old man adjusted his grip on his history of Ded Moroz and closed his eyes. "It must be . . . willing."

"Willing how?" Ilsa pressed. "Where do I find him? Tell me how to find him!"

With an effort, Olek cranked back open his eyes. He contemplated her for a moment, then raised a weathered hand and drew a sideways figure eight in the fine dust coating the book's leather cover. His exhaustion was becoming more and more evident and he was forced to take a series of shallow breaths. Then he lifted a trembling finger and pressed it to the center of the figure eight. "It ends . . . where it began."

Then his eyes closed, his hand fell away, and he sank into his pillow.

"What does that mean? Olek? *Olek?*"

Behind her, Ilsa heard the sound of the hospital room door sliding open. A diminutive Filipina nurse appeared and made her way to the old man's bed, where she checked his chart and vitals and adjusted his IV drip.

Ilsa stood there, her ribs straining from the breaths she took as she tried and failed to process the situation. It was to no avail. All of it. Whatever hidden meaning may or may not have lain behind Olek's cryptic words was lost on her. She needed him to elucidate, but that was impossible. Any attempt to wake him now could prove disastrous. She'd seen enough people at Death's door to know he was reaching for the doorbell.

The room started spinning and she grabbed onto the top of a nearby chair for support. She was on her own, and that reality only surmounted her growing panic. A moment later, she found herself backing out of the room. She had to get out of there. She needed to clear her head, and she needed to put some distance between her and this never-ending nightmare.

Behind her, the door to Olek's room opened with a hiss. She backed through it, took two steps, then turned to flee. Her retreat was cut short by a grunt of pain and surprise as she ran headlong into someone with bone-jarring force.

"Andy!" she cried as she staggered back. Then before she knew what she was doing, she sprang forward and threw her arms around him in a desperate hug. "Thank God!"

The tall Californian stiffened, then glanced down at her in surprise. "Wow, this is a nicer greeting than your usual kick-in-the-nuts." He gave her one of those lopsided grins that were his stock-in-trade. "Did you miss me?"

"I-I thought maybe your number was already up," she said, her cheek pressed tightly against his chest.

"Nah, I've still got time." His baby blues swung from a nearby wall clock to the crown of her head. Then he cocked his own to one side, trying to see her face. "You know, Dunbar, this spontaneous display of affection could ruin your reputation as a consummate badass."

"Listen, 'dead nerd walking', just hold me for a fucking minute. Okay?"

Andy chuckled as he hugged her back.

Ilsa tried not to sigh but there was no help for it. Given her lack of a sex life – or a social life, for that matter – under normal circumstances, just the feel of a pair of strong male arms wrapping around her would have made her heart flutter. But now, with everything she'd been through and everything still to come, not to mention the fact that the arms embracing her belonged to her incredible-smelling partner, it was all she could do to keep from swooning.

God, can you imagine the guys at the precinct hearing about this?

She settled for one more awkward nuzzle, then backed away with a sheepish look on her face.

"That's more like it," Andy comforted. "Better now?"

Dreading the pinkening she felt creeping into her cheeks, Ilsa stared at the floor and nodded.

"I heard about Kareema and Olek's wife. I'm really sorry."

"Me too," Ilsa breathed.

"How is he?"

"Not good, he--" She stopped and stared at him. "Hey, how are you even *here*? I thought Janus had you under house arrest."

"Yeah, right. With those two nimrods standing guard?" Andy scoffed. "I had a few of the girls from the dance school pull up and fake car trouble. You should've seen Ramirez and Tokaido, arguing over who'd gotten better grades back in auto shop!" He made a serpentine hand gesture. "Meanwhile, I just slipped out the back."

One of Ilsa's canines dug into her lower lip. "But Janus took your badge..."

Andy unzipped the front of his black MA-1 flight jacket and held it open, displaying his custom .45 in a leather shoulder holster. Beneath it shone an ornate, bronze-colored shield with eagle's wings. It had the number 424 on it.

"Ah, I still got my old LA one," he said, winking at her. "We'll just say I'm a visiting dignitary." He noted her approving look, then added, "So, where we at?"

"Up shit's creek without a canoe, the way I see it," she said with a brittle smile. She indicated Olek through the nearby glass. "He was going on about blood and sacrifices and everything finishing where it started, or something like that."

"That mean anything to you?"

"Not a clue. The thing's already made its kill for the day. Olek thinks it's going to go into hibernation until next year. Then, all bets are off."

"Do we know where it hibernates?"

Ilsa shrugged. "No idea. I assume in a . . . volcano somewhere?"

Andy frowned. Well, it must have a door to get there, right? Like the fireplaces?"

"If it does, we have no way of finding it. After its final attack on Christmas Eve, it vanishes without a trace." Her eyes fell on Olek's book. "At least, that's what its pattern has always been." She scrutinized the faint figure eight the old man had drawn, then her pupils abruptly dilated. "Its pattern – *holy shit!*"

"What?"

"It ends where it begins!" Ilsa palm-heeled herself on the forehead. "Something Olek said before he passed out," she said, catching Andy's confused look. Then she spun on her heel and started jogging down the corridor. "I think I know how to find it. Come on!"

"Where are we going?" Andy said as he caught up to her.

"We need data, but with Janus gunning for you, nowhere near the office." She hesitated as they reached a side exit door, her brow creasing up. "I have a friend at central records who can help us."

Ilsa reached for the door's push bar release, only to freeze as their hands touched. She vacillated, gauging his intent, then thought, *whatever – let him play boy scout*. Withdrawing her hand, she looked up at him and did the Vulcan thing with one eyebrow.

Obviously pleased, Andy gave a cavalier-like bow, then pushed the door open and held it for her. He looked more than a little satisfied as she walked by, then followed her and said, "Cool, I'll drive."

Ilsa's feet stopped moving, but her jaw took an elevator straight down to disbelief town. "Wait . . . you actually *drove* here?"

Andy's reply was a sardonic smirk.

"Seriously," she pressed. "You gave up your sacred spot in Bay Ridge and *drove* here?"

Her partner said nothing, but his fast-growing grin had reached Cheshire cat proportions by the time he extracted a key fob from his pocket and pointed it at the vehicle parked directly outside.

Ilsa stood there gaping as the lights from the most gorgeous 1950 Cadillac Series 62 she'd ever seen flashed in response. It was a gleaming ivory marvel, with seventeen-inch custom whitewalls and so much chrome dripping from it, it was almost painful to look at.

For some reason, a vision of Andy as a sword-wielding knight, riding to her rescue atop a white charger, wafted before her eyes as she walked numbly to the car. When she got there, he was waiting, flashing that insufferable smile of his as he once again held her door for her.

"Anything for you, doll," he said in his mock Brooklyn accent.

Ilsa climbed in and sank back into a leather seat so sumptuously soft, she thought she'd died and gone to heaven. Her disbelieving eyes scanned the car's immaculate interior, while her nasal passages reveled in an impossible-to-believe new car smell.

"Wow, nice ride," she said as Andy got in and reached for his seatbelt. She studied the Cadillac's array of modern instrument panels. "Full resto-mod?"

He winked at her, then slid the key into the ignition and brought what sounded suspiciously like an iron-blocked LQ9 with a set of GM LSA supercharged heads to life.

"Hell, yeah. Classic 50's style with modern power, creature comforts, and reliability. You can't beat it!"

Then he smiled and threw her in gear.

CHAPTER 16

Ilsa winced at the insanely loud clicking sounds her boots made as they impacted on Central Records' polished marble lobby floor. Even with Andy Williams' *It's the Most Wonderful Time of the Year* playing in the background, she felt like she was walking through an echo chamber and forced herself to stare straight ahead. Why her partner's footsteps were so quiet by comparison made no sense whatsoever; the big galoot was wearing cowboy boots, for crying out loud!

It must be those ballet – I mean 'ballroom dance' classes he mentioned. I bet he's lying about it and he really wears a tutu. A frilly pink one. Imagine that?

Stifling a chuckle, Ilsa slowed her roll and took a moment to survey the surrounding space. The building's expansive foyer was a blend of Italian marble and granite with a touch of mahogany, yet was surprisingly warm. It was a welcome change from the late-night frigidity she'd grown accustomed to and she relished unzipping her jacket.

Her eyes finished their fifty-cent tour, and she gave a nod of appreciation. With its "we spared no expense" art-deco design, including soaring columns and vaulted, twenty-five-foot ceilings, the former bank was an undeniably impressive place. In her eyes, its only possible "flaw" was the series of giant, metal-framed windows that lined its entrance, like a battalion of towering tin soldiers. In many ways, they reminded her of the lobbies of the Financial District's long-gone World Trade Center towers.

She'd never seen them in person; she hadn't even been born when a gang of religious psychopaths brought the iconic buildings down. But she'd seen the video her parents had filmed, back when they'd celebrated their first wedding anniversary at *Windows on the World*.

Ilsa sighed. Better days. Better times.

She paused to flash her badge at the two uniforms standing guard, then made for the facility's trio of security checkpoints with Andy in tow.

When it came to her suspended partner, she figured a direct approach was the way to go. Judging by the barrage of calls she'd ignored from both Ramirez and Tokaido, the pair had figured out Andy's deception.

Ilsa glanced down at her phone and sniggered.

Yep. Ramirez's last text confirmed things; they were furious.

She couldn't have cared less.

Officially, she was off shift and uninvolved. Moreover, the odds of "Ernie and Bert" thinking to call CR looking for them were a thousand to one. And it's not like they could put out an APB on Andy. Hell, she doubted they'd even reported his disappearance.

They'd be fools if they had. That would mean admitting to Janus that they'd been outsmarted. Which they had, of course, but they wouldn't want the boss finding out. Or anyone, for that matter. That was the kind of thing that could turn a cop into a laughingstock. You'd be ribbed about it for years, maybe decades.

No. Their plan would be to either stake out Andy's place or show up at hers.

She was betting on the latter. Of course, the cordoned off, charred ruins they found when they got there would undoubtedly throw them for a loop – assuming they hadn't been watching the news, that is. But, either way, from that point forward, they'd be stuck and spinning their wheels. They couldn't track her and Andy electronically; they'd turned off their phones. That meant they'd have to resort to good-old-fashioned police work in order to find them.

Good luck with that.

Feeling a bit more buoyant now, Ilsa bypassed the first two checkpoints and made for the one on the far right. From forty feet out, she spotted her friend Tamara. She had her head lowered and was chowing down on a donut. A chocolate-frosted one, from the look of things.

Ilsa couldn't not crack a smile. The two had been besties since they'd shared a room at the Academy. And, despite the inevitable roadblocks life threw their way, they still managed to hang out several times a year.

She waved as they drew near and got beamed back at in response. She loved her former roommate dearly. A self-proclaimed "big, beautiful, black woman", Tamara was a blast to party with. She was *far* from shy. A mutual friend had once called her a 'randy she-bear on the prowl'.

There was some truth to that. Tamara went through men like they came on an assembly line. *I just can't seem to find Mister Right*, she'd lament. *I always end up with Mister 'Right Now!'*

Ilsa figured her problem was she set her sights too high. She was never satisfied. She wanted it all: looks, personality, sexual prowess, and most of all, money.

Humph, I should talk. At least she has a life. The last date I had came with D batteries . . .

"What up, girlfriend?" Tamara said, instantly perking up. "What brings you down to my lonely neck of the woods?" She dropped her donut and wiped her hands on a napkin as she rose.

The two women embraced, then her friend's eyes turned to teacups as she caught sight of Andy.

"Whoa! And *who* is *this* tall drink of I-don't-know-what? You brought me a bottle of champagne, girl?"

Ilsa studied her partner, her amused eyes searching for any signs of discomfiture. Nope, nada. Cool as a cucumber, as usual.

"This is Detective Alvilda, from LA," she said. "He's helping me with an investigation."

Andy clicked his tongue and winked at Tamara as he sauntered past, his jacket open and badge showing.

"LA, huh? Mmm-mmm . . . you go, Hollywood," she said, shamelessly admiring his backside. "Hey, y'all let me know if you need anything, a'right?"

Ilsa grinned and nodded. As she hit the nearby elevator button, she could hear her friend mumble.

"Oh, I need me a man, *bad* . . ."

Just then, a tall, simply-dressed Jamaican fellow wandered inside. He had a timid smile and a piece of paper in his hand as he approached Tamara.

"What you doing back here? I told you once, the shelter's next door!" She shook her head at the speechless look on his face. "And, don't look at me like that. I will bitch slap the dreads right off your head, fool!"

Ilsa grimaced.

As she watched, Tamara sat back down, muttering to herself and refocusing on her donut and a fresh can of Coke. Back by the entrance, the obviously intimidated Jamaican retreated and showed the piece of paper to one of the officers, who promptly pointed him in the direction of the luxury hotel across the street.

Homeless guy my ass. Ilsa thought. *C'mon, wake up, Tamara!*

She opened her mouth to say something, but the sound of the elevator doors opening cut her off.

* * *

After removing a toolbox some cretin left atop the research room's primary work station, Andy let his eyes wander. There was little else to do while he waited for Dunbar to do her thing. Under normal circumstances, he'd have gone online and done updates on his assorted social media accounts, but circumstances were far from normal. He didn't know if Janus had gotten around to filing his suspension's official paperwork yet, but he wasn't about to chance logging in and getting red-flagged.

That would have put both of them in a bind. So, for the time being, he was persona non grata – a ghost. The corners of his eyes crinkled up at the thought.

Eerily apropos.

Despite him being introduced as a "visiting dignitary", they'd been lucky to get their hands on a private room, away from potential eavesdroppers. He imagined such a setup normally required a reservation, like small law firms did when forced to share consulting space. Luckily, at this hour, there wasn't a cop in sight; they had the place to themselves.

Although Dunbar had yet to reveal the details of her eureka moment, Andy was patient. He was happy just being out of his apartment. Having a chance to throw a wrench in the works of their diabolical adversary was more than he could hope for. And it really *was* up to them. They couldn't relay their experiences to anyone. Nobody would believe them.

He understood completely. With the possible exception of select members of the clergy, accepting the existence of a real-life "snow demon" was a hard pill to swallow. Like, fist-sized. You had to see it in order to believe it.

Then again, he *had* seen it, and he was *still* finding it difficult to accept.

Or maybe his subconscious didn't want him to. He didn't know.

An impromptu loud burst of electronic interference, followed by a flash of light, drew Andy's eye. Dunbar had activated the record system's seven-foot wall monitor and was typing so fast it looked like she had ten fingers on each hand. As he watched her work, he took a moment to surreptitiously study her profile. The narrowed eyes, the taut jaw, the drawn-in lips . . . she had great features, but she sucked at hiding her emotions.

"So, what exactly are we looking for?" he ventured.

Dunbar finished typing and gave the enter key a whack. Almost instantly, an HD Google map of Manhattan appeared across the big flatscreen. Overlaying it, was a series of brightly colored dots.

She gave a push with her hands that caused her chair to slide smoothly back, then sprang to her feet.

"We've been looking for a pattern to all the killings, right?" she said as she advanced on the monitor.

"Yes . . ."

"And, until we found out about the fireplaces, there wasn't one, correct?"

"Except for the Christmas theme," Andy said off a nod.

"Exactly." Using a fingertip and the monitor's touchscreen paint program, she drew circles around a handful of locations. "Then you noticed an arced shape to the killings. The Stansons, the McKinleys, and so forth . . ." She drew a bright red curve, connecting those points. "Something Olek showed me made me realize there was a deeper, more hidden pattern all along."

She resumed playing connect-the-dots. When she stopped, a huge figure eight lay across a good portion of Manhattan, stretching from the East River, almost to the West Side Highway.

Andy's eyes widened. "Holy shit, the symbol . . ."

Dunbar held up a finger. "Wait, it's gets better." Returning to her keyboard, she brought the system's voice command function online. "System: overlay crime scene locations, 'Christmas Cannibals', for last year."

A second series of illuminated dots appeared on the map.

"System: draw linear connection between locations, as before."

A second figure eight appeared, overlapping the first, but offset.

Dunbar licked her lips. "System: overlay crime scene locations "Christmas Cannibals" for the year before last with the same linear connections."

A third figure eight appeared. This one was further offset.

Her eyes narrowed. "System, repeat for all previous years."

Andy watched in astonishment as the conjoined oval shapes stacked up on top of one another. All shared the same central point and, when combined, looked like the petals of some gigantic flower.

Dunbar swore under her breath. "It was there all along, right under our noses."

"Like spokes on a wheel," Andy said, eyeing the monitor as he took up position beside her. "Each year radiating outward from the same central point."

"And overlapped different precincts each year, which threw us off."

"Crafty bastard . . ." he muttered. "So, how does this help us find him?"

Dunbar lowered her eyebrows. "That was the other thing Olek said that got me thinking."

"'It ends where it begins'?"

"Right. Each year this thing emerges from hibernation, right?"

Andy nodded.

"And then it starts killing. So, if we go by dates, its first victims over the last ten years were here, here, here, and so forth," she said, touching the corresponding dots on the screen." She angled her head as she studied the pattern. "And its final kills each year – on Christmas Eve – ended here, here, and here . . ." She highlighted the dots, then stepped back. "And then it's gone. So, where does it go?"

Andy folded his arms across his chest. "Back into the fire, right? So maybe 'it ends where it started' just means that's how the pattern ends."

Dunbar frowned. "I don't think so. I think Olek was trying to tell me something." She mumbled, "It ends where it begins . . ." as she studied the screen. Seconds later, an alert look came over her and her hazel eyes began darting around the map. "System, store data. Now, show all felonies committed over the last decade for grid 27-B, sub-grid C."

The monitor shimmered and the overlapping figure-eights vanished. Replacing them was a swarm of dots – each one corresponding to a violent crime. There were hundreds of them, complete with dates, times, and the names of both the perpetrators and their victims. Aggravated assault, armed robberies, burglaries, rapes, murders . . . Soon, that portion of the screen became so congested, it was impossible to decipher details.

Dunbar snorted irritably. "System: cancel. Show just homicides, and for ten years ago *only*."

Like dry leaves, whisked away by the wind, the convoluted listings cleared. Replacing them was a single, glowing dot, and with it, its crime.

A triple homicide.

"Gotcha, you son of a bitch," Dunbar breathed.

"What is it?"

She rushed back to her station. "You were in LA when this happened. I remember it because I helped write the report." She paused her typing, clicked her mouse twice, then hit a key. "Not that any New Yorker living here then would forget . . ."

A barrage of images appeared on the monitor. Front and center was a mug shot of a bug-eyed teenager named Cranston R. McCauley. Haloing his photo was a collection of files, including official reports, crime scene photos, and a series of tabloid headlines that screamed things like, *"Billionaire's Son Slaughters Entire Family!"*

"Holy shit."

"*Un*holy is more like it. Cranston McCauley, the nineteen-year-old son of a billionaire real estate magnate." Dunbar moved back to the wall monitor and, using both hands, opened the teen's arrest report. "Kid was obsessed with demonology and the legend of 'Krampus'."

Andy grimaced as she opened a file marked 'crime scene photos.' The images were jarring, even for him.

Dunbar's nose wrinkled and she continued. "One night, he slits both his parents' throats while they sleep, then roasts his girlfriend alive in their mansion's fireplace."

She brought up the video log next. The initial footage was of a bloodsoaked and bedraggled McCauley being dragged, headbutting and biting, into a police interrogation. Following that, was file footage of him during his preliminary hearing. He was chained hand and foot, and alternated ignoring the judge, mumbling to himself, and smirking at the cameras.

Next came a series of clips of McCauley, pacing back and forth inside his padded cell. Over the years, he'd deteriorated into a gaunt, Renfield-like character. He had a series of winding snake tattoos on his forearms and the backs of his hands, and the walls of his cell were covered with disturbing drawings, including pastel sketches of Santa Claus being dismembered, and groups of people being burned alive.

Last but not least, was a recording made by the psychiatrist assigned to assess him. He was chained and seated in her office, when he unexpectedly sprang up onto her desk like a cat and started laughing hysterically.

"She wanted it!" he shouted as he tried to break free of his bonds. "She begged for it!"

McCauley hissed and spat at the orderlies rushing in to restrain him.

A struggle ensued and, soon, foam started running down his chin. He began to giggle. "You'll see, you'll beg too! You *all* will! Come on, let's join hands!" The last few seconds of the clip were of him singing, *Joy to the World* at the top of his lungs as he was carried out, kicking and cackling.

The video ended in a freeze-frame, and Andy stared wide-eyed at McCauley's frightening face. His tongue was lolling from his mouth and his bloodshot eyes brimmed with madness.

"Now *there's* a sick fuck. So, you think he started all this?"

Dunbar sighed. "System, combined saved overlay with current one."

There was a quick cross-dissolve as the spoke-like pattern of figure eights returned and overlapped the current one. In the exact center of the combined images, the McCauley murder scene glittered like the North star.

"Well, I'll be damned," Andy said, then brought his Brooklyn accent online. "Dunbar, you're a fricking genius."

She half-smiled. "Ground zero. The murders started there, that night."

"With a blood sacrifice?"

"A *willing* blood sacrifice."

Andy frowned. "I don't know about that. I hardly think his parents died willingly."

"I'm not referring to them." Dunbar swiped the screen and brought up another rap sheet. Atop it was the mug shot of a feral-eyed woman. She might have been attractive, if it weren't for the cluster of nose rings and all the tribal tattoos. "Hillary Hocker. Sadomasochist, drug addict, and McCauley's long-term girlfriend. She was as fucked-up as he was." She turned to her partner. "If she somehow *agreed* to it . . ."

Andy ground his molars. "Fine. Where is the crazy cockroach? Let's go squeeze him."

Dunbar returned to her keyboard. "Dead. This time last year."

"Let me guess. Torn apart in his padded cell?"

She hit a key. "Even better."

On the monitor, a link to a ghoulish website specializing in celebrity death images materialized. She clicked a tab marked, "Cranston McCauley, body and autopsy". There was a good sixty-seconds of black-and-white security footage, recorded by orderlies as they nervously entered his cell. McCauley's body was crumpled up in a corner in a fetal position. There were no obvious wounds, but his hair and skin were the color of cream, and he had a look of abject terror on his face.

There was a sudden cut to color footage then, this time from the mental hospital's morgue. McCauley lay naked atop a mortician's table, his arms folded like the letter X across his bony chest.

Andy's eyes slitted as the camera switched to a God's eye view. Posed as the dead man was, from that angle the serpentine tattoos adorning his forearms, biceps, anterior deltoids, and pectorals all combined to form a sideways number eight.

The symbol of Loptr.

"Wow, just like the doctor. Any signs of forced entry, like at the holding station?"

Dunbar's lips pursed as her fingers tabbed their way along. She opened a fresh window, then scrolled down until she found what she needed. It was classified footage from the official forensics investigation into McCauley's unexpected death.

Andy's eyelids drooped as he contemplated the now-barren cell. The demonic drawings that adorned the walls were gone, replaced by a collection of hastily-drawn religious images of crucifixes and angels. The final few seconds of the footage was of the far end of the twenty-foot-space. High up in the frame stood the lone window to the outside. Without a ladder, it was out of reach, not to mention extremely narrow; little more than an arrow slit.

"No." Dunbar gave a headshake. "The door, floor, ceiling, and walls were all undamaged, and a well-fed squirrel would have a tough time fitting through that window."

"True. But something outside of it would have no problem looking in." He hesitated. "Do you, um . . . Do you think this thing has the ability to actually scare people to death?"

Andy cleared his throat as she turned to look at him. "I mean, I don't mean scare, per se. You don't believe it can actually eat your, your . . ."

"Your soul?" Dunbar grinned disarmingly. "Come on, LA. What are you worried about? You live an enchanted life, right? Dodging bullets and what not? That's why you promised that waitress that—Wait a minute . . ."

He held her gaze, but only for a moment.

"Oh, Andy . . . tonight?"

"By midnight. Bummer, right?"

His partner's lips compressed and her forehead puckered. "Look, that doesn't mean anything, okay? Your mom could've been wrong."

Andy smiled sadly. "She was never wrong. Plus, with everything we've seen? C'mon . . ."

"No. No way." Dunbar shook her head stubbornly. "Look, I'll go and you sit this one out."

"Yeah, right," he chuckled. "What are you going to do, MMA that thing to death?"

"Oh, please, and you'll do what, waltz with it?" She scoffed, then began to fumble in her bag. She extracted a makeshift cross. "I have this. Olek gave it to me. It's made from pieces of the sleigh. You know . . . *his* sleigh."

Andy's eyes went wide. "May I?"

He swallowed nervously as Dunbar handed him the lashed-together pieces of wood. "Wow, it sounds nuts but it's like you can *feel* something when you hold it."

"Yeah, it's called really old wood," she said, taking it back. She hit the system's shutdown button and grabbed her bag. "C'mon, let's go."

CHAPTER 17

Andy grinned as he turned over his Caddy's rugged VortecMAX engine and checked his mirrors. His mood faltered, however, as he caught the morose expression on his partner's face. She had unzipped her backpack and was peeking at a framed photograph she had stashed inside.

The antique silver frame looked familiar. A moment later, Andy's brows contracted and he shifted back into park.

"Wait, that's the photo from your mantle," he said. He waited for her nod. "You got it out in time?"

Dunbar shook her head sadly. "Kareema ran in to save it. It . . . it cost her her life." Her eyes welled with tears. "I didn't want to leave it in my car. You know how it is."

"Sure. Some lowlife would've broken your window for sure." He hesitated. "Can I see?"

She gnawed her lower lip for a moment, then wiped her cheeks with the backs of her hands. Her hazel eyes sought his as she extracted the photo and held it up for him to see.

Andy's eyes flickered as he clocked the man in the Santa suit. "Your dad?"

"Yes."

"I see a doting father and a wide-eyed little girl in love with the holidays. So, what happened?"

Dunbar sighed. "The city happened. Christmas Eve, we were headed into St. Patrick's for midnight mass . . ." She turned toward the window and started running the tip of a gloved finger down the frosted glass. "We got caught in a dealer turf war. My mom died instantly. My dad shielded me with his body." Her head swiveled mechanically back toward the photo and her eyes became huge. "There was so much blood . . . I remember screaming and praying to God, to Jesus, even to Santa. No one helped us. There was a big crowd and nobody lifted a finger."

"Wow, I-I'm really sorry."

Her gaze lifted to find his. "I want you to promise me something."

"Name it."

"Don't die tonight. It's Christmas Eve and I-I already hate the holidays. If I lose you too . . ."

"Lose me?" Andy snorted derisively. "Are you kidding? With my moves, he'll never lay a claw on me." He grinned hugely and put the Cadillac back in gear, "Besides, didn't I tell you? I've always wanted to 'dance with the devil' . . ."

"'. . . in the pale moonlight'?"

"*Exactly.*" With a wink and a smile, he pulled out.

* * *

In my wildest dreams, I never imagined I'd cash in my chips trying to save the world from some Christmas-hating demon. What a crazy couple of days! A shame I can't stick around to see how things turn out.

Andy shook his head ruefully, then glared back at the waxing gibbous moon, gazing down at him from high overhead. His chest expanded as he drew in a cold lungful, then he sighed. Despite the noxious fumes exuded by the city's omnipresent automobiles, the New York wind still carried with it the scent of pine trees and snow. There was even a faint trace of wood burning in someone's fireplace, thrown in for good measure. It smelled of Christmas, he realized, and a faint smile broke through his mask of indifference.

He had his arms folded across his chest as he and his partner continued to lean back against his Caddy's passenger-side front fender. Their shoulders brushed unexpectedly and he tensed.

It was odd, her being so close. Nice, just . . . odd.

He threw Dunbar a surreptitious glance. She had her thick hair tied back, angular jaw set, and gloved hands jammed deep inside her jacket pockets. Like himself, she seemed in no hurry to separate her rear end from the warmth his car engine continued to give off.

He couldn't blame her.

It wasn't the weather slowing her roll, nor his, for that matter. Granted, the numbing wind and cold were far from desirable companions. But it was their imposing destination that was giving the pair pause.

Andy's eyes creased at the corners and he wracked his brain, trying to remember a horror movie with a house as creepy as the one they were about to investigate. His head shook as he mentally checked himself.

Make that *break into*.

He finally gave up. The best he'd come up with wasn't a movie; it was that old television series, *The Munsters*. Yeah, this was definitely the kind of home loveable ol' Herman and his family would've had.

That is, if they'd been a pack of preening billionaires.

The gray-hued McCauley mansion was enormous: a 62,000 square foot, limestone-covered monstrosity with soaring towers and turrets that reminded him of a medieval castle. He'd seen the stats and, in its day, the place had had it all. There was an inground pool, bowling alley, movie theater, and three elevators, just for starters. It had privacy, too. The wooded acres surrounding it were ensconced by jagged stone walls over nine feet high, and topped by the rusted remnants of once-imposing wrought iron fencing.

Andy whistled under his breath as he looked left and right. As vertically-inclined as New York City properties were, just the place's footprint was enough to make your jaw drop. It took up an entire city block. Its continued existence bore mute testimony to the vast sums of money the McCauley's heirs had inherited. Without it, there was little doubt the abandoned, century-old manor-turned-crime-scene would've fallen to the wrecking ball, as so many of Manhattan's other mega-mansions had, back in the 1930s and 40s.

Of course, he surmised, much of that probably hinged on the fact that the aforementioned relatives were still battling it out in court, to determine who got what. Come to think of it, a few Christmases back, he recalled seeing something on the news about this specific property. A particularly intrepid realtor had been on the cusp of closing the deal of a lifetime with a group of avaricious developers. The deal fell through, however. Or, rather, *he* did, when he took an unexpected header off one of its forty-foot towers.

His death had been ruled a suicide.

Andy shrugged. A moment later, he felt as much as saw Dunbar push herself upright. She had her backpack slung over one shoulder and a hardened look on her face. She gave the place a long-distance once-over, her gaze lingering on the main entrance's deep-set foyer windows. It wasn't hard to imagine why. The paired portals gave the once proud home an unmistakably menacing look, like dark eyes watching them.

Andy started forward, his chest rising and falling as he contemplated the heavy chains securing the main gate. Not good, but hardly unexpected. He shook his head and scoffed. "Well, *this* looks inviting."

"They say it's haunted," Dunbar said matter-of-factly. She caught the look he gave her, then added, "What? I'm just saying..."

He arched an eyebrow, then turned his attention to the rust-streaked walls, crowned with tetanus-laden spikes. *Nope.*

"Guess we better look for a way in." His calculating expression became one of befuddlement as he turned to find her missing.

"Dunbar?"

Andy's head whipped back around in the direction of the car. She wasn't there either.

"Dunbar!"

Panic began to set in then, and he spun in a circle; his hands cupped around his mouth.

"Ilsa!"

"Over here!" she whispered, her head poking out from behind a nearby stone post as thick as a phone booth. "And keep your voice down, you big chicken!"

Andy shook his head as he loped over to her. She was standing in front of a massive cleft in the mansion's fortified perimeter walls. An eight-foot section had collapsed outward, causing huge hunks of stone and foot-long strips of crumbly hundred-year-old mortar to pile up atop the frozen ground.

"I found our way in," she pointed out.

His lips made a smacking sound as he studied the debris field's pattern. "And, from the look of things, how something got *out*..."

They drew and checked their weapons, then produced matching flashlights.

"Okay, let's do this."

Eyes alert, they started forward. Their training had taught them to avoid bunching up and they made it a point to remain several yards apart.

It was slow going. The footing between the trees bordering the property was treacherous and their booted feet made loud crunching sounds as they broke through the slippery crust, often sinking to mid-calf. Bereft of the plowing, salting, and shoveling that had cleared the streets and sidewalks outside the mansion's walls, the grounds surrounding the abandoned oasis were covered with a good eighteen inches of compacted snow and ice.

As they worked their way along, Andy realized there was an eerie pall about the place, a stillness like that which usually precedes the presence of death. The sensation turned out to be eerily apropos; as they passed through a grove of ice-glazed elms that would have done Ansel Adams proud, the first thing they encountered was a graveyard.

Well, that figures . . .

He glanced down, then shifted several feet to his left, skirting the outer row of tombstones. They were old and blackened, he noticed, some dating back to the Civil War. Ancestors, no doubt. He glanced right and sighed. Unlike Dunbar, who appeared to have no problem traipsing over the dead, he took the term, "Don't tread on me" to heart.

Upon closer inspection, however, it became obvious that others had treated the aged graves with a lot less deference.

There was no graffiti. Instead, it looked like someone had taken a stroll through the center of the little cemetery, swinging a Paul-Bunyan-sized sledgehammer left and right as they went. Many of the grave markers had been knocked clean over, with some even shattered at their bases. They lay where they had fallen, face-down atop the unyielding soil.

Fucking vandals. Some people just have no respect for—

Behind them, a loud noise suddenly split the silence encapsulating the wintry landscape. Inhaling sharply, the partners spun as one with their weapons raised, only to exude matching sighs of relief. It was nothing, just a chunk of fractured tombstone that had separated from the rest of its crumbling marker and tumbled to the ground.

Andy cleared his throat, then pretended he was puffing on an invisible cigarette. He blew out a frozen cloud of "smoke" as he surveyed the ground around them.

"I don't see any hoofprints," he pointed out.

"There . . ." Dunbar said, shining her light. In its beam, an unmistakable discus-shaped track could be seen, pressed into the ice that coated a toppled headstone. "It uses the stones to mask its movements."

The two exchanged looks, then made their way past the last of the graves, until they reached the steps leading to the manor's main doors. Unlike the surrounding terrain, the elevated landing was frost-free, its windswept granite surface standing out in stark relief to its glacier-like surroundings.

Andy eyed the imposing doors warily. A full ten feet in height, they were made of some ancient, dark-colored wood – thick timbers, held together with iron frames and spikes. The kid in him couldn't resist an admiring nod. It really was like the gates of some feudal fortress.

He rested the palm heel of his flashlight hand against the closer of the twin doors and pushed. To his surprise, it creaked open easily. He winced at the crepitus-like noise, then took a step inside and studied the shattered lock.

"Deadbolt's been pushed out."

Dunbar nodded, then followed him in.

Andy stifled a chuckle as his eyes fell on a nearby wall switch, then he adjusted his flashlight's beam to maximum width and swept it back and forth across the surrounding space. If they hadn't been hunting the world's most dangerous prey, he'd have whistled aloud. The marble floors of the foyer may have been filthy and littered with dead leaves, and any furniture remaining covered with dust-caked shrouds, but much of the mansion's former magnificence still shone through.

The vaulted ceiling overhead stretched a good twenty feet above their heads and was covered with gilded wooden panels, as were the walls rushing up to meet it. The enormous, *Gone-With-The-Wind*-style grand staircase in the room's center was made of polished Italian marble, bracketed by ornate mahogany bannisters that were supported by web-like railings – custom-forged bronze latticework – with floral designs so intricate that staring at them made you dizzy. The once sumptuous rug that ran down the center of the steps was moth-eaten and rotten, but the ferocious-looking pair of Medici-style marble lions that stood guard on either side of the staircase's six-yard-wide base could've been carved yesterday. They were as tall as he was, and far more imposing.

He was willing to bet either of them cost more than his car.

Andy nodded his appreciation. If anything, the place seemed more befitting an eighteenth-century French king than some Manhattan construction mogul. But such was the way of things, he mused. If you gave people unlimited money, they usually found ways to spend it.

To his right, Dunbar looked around, her eyes tensing as she absorbed the sheer size of the place. It would take hours to explore. She made a hand signal, suggesting they split up to cover more ground

Andy stared at her like she'd lost her mind, then shook his head vehemently.

Hell, no.

He'd seen way too many horror movies to make *that* mistake.

Taking point, he guided them down a long, musty corridor that, judging by the absence of windows and the regularly-spaced, dust-free sections of wall, must have been an art gallery. He assumed the estate's executor had arranged for all the paintings and sculptures to be removed and stored away, long before potential looters had a chance to get their hands on them.

At least, he hoped so.

All of a sudden, his mind flickered back to Olek Apostol, and a tower of sympathy loomed over him. He liked that old couple; he really did. Elena's murder had been a terrible blow. He just hoped that, some way, somehow, the aged antique dealer would find the strength to bounce back.

A sudden creaking sound distracted Andy from his broodings and he glanced at the hardwood beneath his feet. It felt like it had flexed a bit, and he heard a distinctive crackling as he shifted his weight back and forth. He ran his tongue over his teeth as he peered around. All about him, large sections of the once priceless parquet had popped up or split and he swore he could hear water dripping inside the walls. Just then, a cold trickle struck the crown of his head and he looked up, aiming his light at the moldered ceiling.

Andy shook his head. As a boy, he'd spent more than one summer helping his uncle patch his grandmother's roof. The McCauley's aged, slate-tiled gambrels were definitely in need of repair. Leaks were running rampant and the season's inevitable freeze-thaw routine was only making matters worse. Left unchecked, it was just a matter of time before the legendary mansion rotted from the inside out.

What a shame that would be.

He turned to take a step, only to have Dunbar grab his arm and guide him away from a particularly porous-looking section of floor.

"The wood's all rotten," she whispered. "Tread easy, Sasquatch."

"Gargantua, Godzilla, Sasquatch . . . Pick a name and stick with it, will you?" he said with a chuckle.

She shot him a "good luck with that" grin, then her face inexplicably fell.

A moment later, Andy's nose crinkled up. A godawful stench had enveloped them both.

"Whoa, that was *not* me," he said, praying he was right.

"Sure, it wasn't," Dunbar chuckled. She cast about nervously, then her incisors clamped down on her lower lip. "Seriously, that's the same disgusting odor, right? What is that, brimstone?"

"Smells more like rotting devil's ass, if you ask me."

Her anticipated response was drowned out by an otherworldly groan that echoed throughout the mansion.

A muscle in Andy's jaw twitched as the noise's echoes slowly died. He waited a few more seconds then shrugged. He couldn't tell if it was the creature or the old house settling; it was tough to say. If he was being honest with himself, he was hoping for the latter.

Lips taut, he signaled Dunbar and continued toward a tall set of double doors. Based on location and design, he figured it was the entrance to a large parlor or sitting room. Just then, there was another eerie groan, this one shorter and lower than the last, and he pressed his ear against the cold wood, trying to determine if the source lay within.

He couldn't say for sure, but he had a feeling they were close.

Wrapping one hand around the ornate doorknob, Andy caught his partner's eye and mouthed a silent countdown.

Three . . . two . . . one . . .

With a loud whoosh, he yanked open one of the doors and they burst in, flashlights flaring and weapons raised. Andy felt a sudden rush of adrenaline. There was a figure by the far wall, perhaps thirty feet away. He couldn't tell if it was human or not, but it was tall and dark and had its legs braced apart, as if it were preparing to spring forward.

Both he and Dunbar swore silently as they took aim, only to freeze with their fingers literally on their triggers. The "figure" was nothing more than Andy's reflection in a massive, full-length, antique mirror.

A quick sweep of the room confirmed they were alone. Andy focused his attention on the ornate standalone. From the look of it, the mirror was centuries old. In fact, it reminded him of an Imperial French piece he'd seen recently in one of *Apostol's Antiquities'* display windows. As he drew closer, he noticed the furnishing's protective canvas dust cover had come undone. It lay like a discarded shroud, piled up around its base.

The corners of Andy's mouth curled up as he imagined their nemesis yanking the cover off and standing in front of it, striking bodybuilder poses as it admired itself. He stifled a nasally scoff.

Such egotism from a mindless, bloodthirsty hellspawn? Ridiculous...

He nodded glumly. On second thought, maybe it actually *had*. One thing he'd learned of late – *anything* was possible.

Andy's nose began to twitch. The smell of decay in the room was strong – mildewed plaster and rotting wood for the most part. On a positive note, the pungent odor had forced out the sulfurous reek from the previous chamber. It was the sound of trickling water, however, that drew his eye, and he swung his light in quick arcs until he pinpointed the source.

There was a thin stream coming down from a waterlogged crack in the moldy ceiling; it disappeared through a series of Swiss-cheese-like pockmarks in the wood. He turned toward Dunbar, only to squint as she shone her light in his face. Blinking in the impromptu spotlight, he holstered his weapon and began impulsively showing off for her by moonwalking around the leak, towards the antique mirror. He jabbed a thumb in its direction as he continued backpedaling and grinned.

"Man, that was *close*. We almost gave ourselves some serious bad--"

Luck?

Andy's words were overwhelmed as the unearthly groan again returned, only five times louder. Before he could even think about reacting, the floor beneath him dipped then collapsed altogether. There was a sound like seismic thunder and the next thing he knew he was falling through space.

A second later, he experienced a sudden cessation of movement, punctuated by a painfully loud crash as he came down hard on his back. He realized he'd lost his flashlight, but he could both feel and hear chunks of waterlogged debris falling both around and on top of him.

All of a sudden, there was a flash of red as something hit him between the eyes. He tried to move, but discovered he couldn't. Then the pain welled up and what little light there was did a quick fade to black. The last thing he remembered seeing was Ilsa's panic-stricken face, eerily underlit by her torch as she peered forlornly down into the gaping crevasse that had swallowed him.

"Andyyyyyyyyyyyy!"

* * *

Olek Apostol awoke with a wheeze and a jolt. He was sweat-soaked and breathing like he'd just finished a New York Marathon, but he managed a feeble smile and a thumbs-up sign for the nurse who responded to his sudden spike in heartrate. Her lips pruned up as she peered through the glass, studying her patient's pallor and his adjacent monitor's readings. After a minute or two of reassuring herself that he wasn't going to die on her watch, she nodded resignedly and returned to her station.

The aged soldier-turned-antiquities-dealer continued to lay there, his hand on his heart, waiting for his pulse to finish its return journey, down from the stratosphere. When his body finally recovered from the ordeal his nightmares had heaped upon it he glanced about the room, taking in the attempted sterility of the place. "Attempted" was the operative word. Despite the orderlies' best efforts, he could see several human hairs clinging to the bottom of one baseboard, and he was pretty sure the dull brownish splotch on the near side of a large receptacle marked "medical waste" was a blood splatter that someone had somehow missed.

Olek shifted a bit against the straps that crossed his chest and hips, holding him in place. As he reached over to loosen them, he felt a twinge of pain. He threw an unfriendly glance at the IV embedded in his forearm, then twitched his nose against the pinch of the nasal prongs he'd been outfitted with, to provide oxygen.

A downward glance at the set of handcuffs hanging, seemingly forgotten, from his hospital bed's side rail, brought images of Ilsa Dunbar to bear. He had a feeling that, were it not for the spunky detective's intervention, the other end of said shackle would have been around his wrist. And the uniformed police officer he saw standing outside his room would be stationed there to keep watch on a suspected "perp", instead of as a protector.

Olek inhaled deep, exhaled even deeper. His earlier, frantic and guilt-ridden spouting notwithstanding, anyone who'd paid a visit to the crime scene that had been his life's work would've crossed him off their suspects' list immediately. Just from a physical perspective, he was incapable of trashing *Apostol Antiquities'* showroom floor like their attacker had. And there wasn't a man in the history of the world with the strength to sunder stainless-steel bars.

Well, maybe Samson. Pre-haircut, of course...

Just then, a frightening vision of the demon showing up and smashing its way through the hospital, intent on finishing him off, wafted before the old man's eyes. He swallowed hard and reached for his *History of Sinterklaas*. As his fingers closed on the weighty tome, he breathed a sigh of relief, followed by a pain-filled grunt as he wrestled it to his chest.

Detective Dunbar to the rescue once again. Olek smiled. She was quite a prize, that one. Hopefully, her fleet-footed partner would realize it, before time clouded her judgment and she ended up settling for some *neudachnik*.

His eyes twinkled with ill-concealed mirth as he imagined what his beloved Elena would have said on the subject, then his vision clouded. He took a moment to wipe away the tears, then wrestled the big book onto his lap and opened it. By chance, the page he'd chosen was one of his favorites: an exquisite nineteenth-century color illustration of a Christmas hearth, late at night, with tiny sacks of treats suspended in front of a raging fire. He ran his fingers softly over the aged vellum.

Suddenly, Olek's weary eyes rounded and he shook his head in wonder. His ordeal must've taken more out of him than he thought. He swore he could feel actual warmth radiating from the inked flames.

CHAPTER 18

As she gazed down in disbelief, Ilsa's heart started pounding so hard she feared it would actually spew from her mouth. How surreal that would be, she thought, to watch it tumble after her partner, down into the life-sucking abyss that just opened beneath his feet.

Damn him and his oversized dancing shoes!

She got down on all fours to better distribute her weight and gripped the sinkhole's jagged edges. The smell of mildew was strong, and the broken boards and timbers beneath her were waterlogged and crumbly. More could go at any time. As if that weren't enough, there were rusty nails aplenty, starting with a headless one that punched through one of her pricey leather gloves and embedded itself in her palm. She drew it free with a grimace.

God, I hope my tetanus shots are up to date . . .

Despite the decaying mansion's moisture and near-freezing temperatures, the air above the collapse site was thick with a clinging cloud of silica dust. She could both smell and taste it, and blanched as she waved a hand back and forth in front of her face, trying to clear her vision.

When that failed, Ilsa adjusted her flashlight's cone into a tight beam. She aimed it at the center of the hole, only to curse as it reflected back off the billowing vapors. Frustration kicked in as she realized she didn't know what to do. She was afraid to move off, for fear Andy might call out. Instead, she stayed where she was, listening to the incessant sounds of particles of debris trickling down into the void, while waiting and praying for the grit-filled clouds to fade.

After several agonizing minutes, her prayers were answered. More so, in fact, when she saw Andy lying atop a series of broken joists, topped by a wavy blanket of collapsed floor and subfloor, some fifteen feet below her. She held her breath as she spotlighted his inert form with her torch, then inhaled sharply when she realized he was breathing.

From a distance, he appeared uninjured. She figured the main section that gave way must have taken the bulk of the impact, like when an elevator fails and its reinforced frame absorbs the kinetic energy generated when it hits bottom, sparing the people within.

To her relief, Andy uttered a surprisingly unmanly groan of discomfort. His eyes fluttered then opened and he began to move. A moment later, his face screwed up and he put a hand in front of his eyes, trying to shield them from her light.

"Andy? Oh, thank God!" she exclaimed, lowering her beam.

"Take it easy," he muttered as he sat up. "I've got enough of a headache without you shouting."

Despite the shifting pile of rubble beneath him, the tall Californian managed to make it to his feet. As she watched, he touched his fingertips to a bruised area on his forehead. He winced, then ran the same hand though his hair.

It came away bloody.

After a sorry attempt at discretely wiping the blood on the back of his pants, Andy grinned and squinted up at her. Then he halfheartedly shook his head.

"What was it you said earlier? We'll just, 'drop in'. . .?"

"There is something *really* wrong with you," Ilsa snickered. She leaned forward as far as she dared and scanned the visible space, hoping to espy a stairwell she might use as a guide. There were none.

"Hang on, I'll find a way down."

"No, no," Andy insisted, bending to retrieve his flashlight from beneath a small pile of lathing. Amazingly, it was still lit. "This whole place is one big collapse waiting to happen. Better if I come to--"

To Ilsa's horror, her partner's words were cut short by a termite-eaten chunk of debris as big as a shoebox, that clocked him over the back of the head before he could straighten up.

Andy dropped like he'd been tasered. He lay on his side, neither moving nor speaking, his tactical light still gripped in one hand. In its beam, she spotted his antique religious medal. It was a yard away, its chain broken, lying atop a warped slab of parquet.

"Andy?" Ilsa shook her head helplessly. "Andy?!?"

She tried again and again, even shouted his name despite the risk, but then stopped. She might as well have been yelling at one of the marble lions, back by the home's main entrance. Andy was down for the count – maybe worse, judging by all that blood – and she'd once again stood there and watched it happen.

She chafed at how powerless she felt. But what could she have done?

What should she do now? What *could* she do?

A feeling of desperation came over her, tailgated by a wintry dose of reality. She was alone, her partner was incapacitated, and she had no backup.

She had no one.

And, for the second time in her life, the cavalry wasn't coming.

Ilsa's throat constricted from the mix of emotions and her fingertips dug deeply into the rotted wood beneath her. She began to shake, but then, out of nowhere, a fierce determination shot through her and she pushed herself upright.

Enough is enough.

"Pension be damned," she snarled as she reached for her radio. "I'm calling for backup. I . . ."

Her voice trailed off as she saw the glow.

It was coming from a towering pair of open doors at the far end of the room.

She hesitated, her radio pressed to dry lips.

"I-I have to . . . I should . . ."

The eerie glow intensified. Accompanying it was a pulsing effect, infused patterns of red, yellow, and orange. It had an almost hypnotic quality and she felt herself drawn. She pulled her pistol, checked its mag and safety, then started to step. The floor crackled beneath her feet, but between her flashlight and the beckoning luminescence it was easy to discern the more dangerous parts; she skirted them with no ill effect.

As she reached the arch-shaped doorway, she hesitated.

God, what am I doing? What if Andy's already dead? Could this be what his mother foresaw?

She wallowed in a quagmire of hesitancy, torn between trying to find a way down to him and giving in to her burgeoning desire to see what mystery waited up ahead. The pull grew stronger – borderline intoxicating – until she finally gave in.

Beretta in hand, she entered the room.

And what a room it was.

It was the biggest non-commercial space she'd ever seen, a colossal ballroom of some kind, designed to astound and intimidate anyone in attendance. Off to her left, a few dozen yards away, the nearest wall was dotted with a series of tall French doors that opened to verandas unseen. The room itself had high walls and was circular, with a dome-shaped ceiling supported by a ring of blood-red marble columns, their bases nearly as thick as a man was tall. In between a series of gold-plated, sliver-like skylights, the dome was decorated with a montage of DaVinci-style religious paintings – now sadly faded and peeling – that reminded her of those in the Sistine Chapel.

In the center of the ballroom hung a ridiculously ornate waterfall chandelier that measured over fifteen feet in height. It must've weighed three or four tons. She gaped in disbelief as her flashlight's beam struck the glittering Bohemian crystals, creating a prismatic effect that caused motes of light to ripple along the walls, ceiling, and floor like a river of diamonds. She imagined that, when lit, the mineral monstrosity must have burned so brightly, it could've served as a homing beacon for Apollo astronauts passing overhead.

She stifled a snigger.

Or Santa, for that matter . . .

It must've also cost more than many luxury homes. Which wasn't surprising, Ilsa thought; her whole house could fit inside this insane space.

That is, if she still *had* a house, she conceded bitterly.

As a far more impressive light source became apparent, Ilsa clicked off her tac-light. The illumination that had drawn her hence was there, by the far side of the ballroom, not fifty feet from where she stood.

Her jaw dropped like a stone.

If the McKinley's fireplace had been impressive, this one was impossible. Seamlessly chiseled from a cottage-sized slab of black moonstone, it was shaped like a guffawing, Notre-Dame-style gargoyle's head, complete with skin folds, fangs, horns, and enormous pointed ears, not to mention an inset pair of glittering star ruby eyes the size of footballs.

Jesus, Mary and Joseph! How much money did these people have?

Pocketing her flashlight, Ilsa walked dumbly toward the towering hearth and the raging fire that burned inside its gigantean mouth. She shook her head as she drew cautiously closer, picking her way past a seemingly endless array of sheet-covered tables and chairs – a battalion of dusty ghosts. Many of the expensive antiques, especially those adjacent to the fireplace, had been overturned or upended. A few were even shattered – some so badly, they could've been used as kindling.

The hotness of the flames inundated her, and she stopped thirty feet away. A whistle escaped her lips as she unzipped her jacket and looked up. The inside of the firepit looked to be as high as Andy could reach – close to eight feet – and had to be fifteen feet wide. Her head swiveled mechanically on her shoulders as she studied the nearby walls. Soot-stained and in dire need of repair, they were plastered with hand-painted runes, including several impressively detailed versions of that all-too-familiar serpentine figure eight.

Ilsa half-shrugged and half-scoffed. For all his flaws, the McKinley boy had possessed some actual artistic talent. In addition to the snakes' remarkably realistic scales, he'd given them some scary-looking eyes.

Their eyes . . .

She'd have bet good money all the horrors she'd experienced the last few days were reflected in hers.

Ilsa's toned shoulders rose and fell and she remained where she was, her comparatively tiny form silhouetted against the colossal fireplace. She had to admit, the heat it gave off felt good; it'd been years since she'd experienced this kind of warmth. Too career-minded to do the stereotypical snowbird thing and jet off to Orlando for the holidays, she'd stayed home and kept her nose pressed to the precinct's grindstone.

The effect was predictable. Over time, you got used to that New York chill. It crept into your bones and brain and, eventually, your soul.

Ilsa's mind began to wander. She found herself distracted by the smells coming from the fire and the occasional crackling as some immolated beam or board shifted or split. Her eyes slitted up. Was that firewood some of the mansion's irreplaceable antiquitous furniture?

It certainly looked like it. God, what a shame.

Who would've done such a thing?

A sigh slipped from her lips, then her head twitched spasmodically and she began to blink. What the *hell* was she doing? Why was she standing there like some damn lizard, basking in the midday sun after an uncomfortably cool morning? She was a cop, a decorated veteran with responsibilities. She needed to find a way down to Andy and she needed to call for backup – FDNY, paramedics, emergency services – maybe even an elite Seal team.

She—

Her fragmented thoughts were waylaid as the wind outside suddenly kicked up. One of the tall French doors leading outside began to shiver, then it flew inward, slamming violently against the adjacent wall. There were the sounds of splintered and falling glass, followed by the unrelenting gust continuing inward. Penetrating the firelit ballroom, it threw itself against her. Its chilly touch was almost provocative, like a giant hand pressed against her back and buttocks.

Its blustering increased, and she felt herself being shoved toward the waiting fire. Spurred by the influx of oxygen, the flames rose in anticipation, but she leaned back and dug her heels in.

The inundating cold air was a much-needed pick-me-up, and Ilsa took the opportunity to clear her head. She inhaled deeply through her nose, then blinked. Along with the estate's usual mustiness, she smelled soot and snow.

And something else.

Something ... foul?

There was a low rumble, so deep she felt it in her bones. Accompanying it was a series of heavy thuds. Alarmed, she spun toward the disturbance and her eyes turned to teacups.

"Fuck me!"

It was there. The demon had come home.

Impossibly huge and horrifying, it strode boldly into the decaying ballroom, then gave the open door behind it a violent shove. For long moments it stood there, seemingly unaware of her presence. It had a glazed look in its eye and it appeared to be ... *chewing?*

A feeling of dread permeated Ilsa's being and she found herself unable to move. She was in what she referred to as spectator mode, watching with a sort of detached fascination. In slow motion, the monster raised something to its mouth. It was a partly-eaten human leg: a boy's, judging by the overall size and hairlessness.

The thing's scarred lips peeled back like a shark's, its maw splitting into a grotesque Joker's grin. Then its fangs buried themselves in the hamstring portion of the severed limb, like forks digging into cheese. There was a stomach-churning crunch as it bit down, then it yanked its head back and tore out a mouthful.

Assured of its own invincibility, it remained where it was, savoring its late-night snack. Its bulbous mandibular muscles knotted up in waves, then its mouth began to open. At first, Ilsa thought it was yawning, then she found herself cupping a hand over her mouth to keep from vomiting. She could see it's vile, lamprey-like tongue – an extension of its throat - contributing to the feeding process. After the initial chewing, it latched onto the bloody bolus and systematically gulped it down, like a python swallowing a rabbit.

As the demon's foul stench saturated the room it functioned as an ammonia capsule, freeing Ilsa from the horror that gripped her. Fighting to keep from panicking, she glanced back over one shoulder, then began her retreat. Her goal was to tiptoe back the way she'd come, hopefully without notice.

She had no such luck.

Although it was initially oblivious, as soon as she began to move the hellspawn's misshapen head snapped in her direction. Its gleaming red eyes targeted her like laser beams, then a shuddering snarl erupted from its thick-corded throat. Tossing the half-eaten leg aside, it made straight for her, uttering tigerish growls and backhanding sheet-covered chairs and tables out of its way.

Ilsa's heart sank as it stopped thirty feet away and jammed its knuckles against the floor. Its shoulder muscles bunched up and she could see it shifting its weight back and forth.

It was preparing to do one of its silverback-style charges.

She knew she'd never make it to the door before it was on top of her. Teeth bared, she ripped her pistol from its holster.

"Eat this, child killer!"

From thirty feet away she opened fire, mercilessly targeting the thing's face. Bellowing in pain, it staggered back under the hail of cold iron rounds. Before she knew it, it was directly in front of the fireplace. The possibility that forcing it into the flames might do something dawned on her and she advanced, tossing her spent magazine and reloading before taking aim again.

She could see her well-aimed 9mm rounds were taking their toll. The demon had resorted to covering up, protecting its vulnerable mouth and eyes with its massive forearms. Bereft of her primary target, she went for center mass instead, ten-ringing it right where she figured its black heart was – if it had one.

The eardrum-damaging barrage of bullets continued. All at once, the thing staggered drunkenly to one side, then dropped to its knees. Flames of exhilaration danced in Ilsa's eyes.

It was about to collapse! She'd done it!

Then she heard that awful *click* and her heart plummeted into her bowels.

She was empty.

With its bloodied head lowered and one huge hand resting on the cracked marble floor, the demon touched its free hand to the bubbling wounds that decorated its chest. It rubbed the sticky green ichor between its gnarled fingers, its ruby eyes narrowing. Ilsa felt a lump of fear coalesce inside her throat. Then it looked up and shook its head reproachfully. Its powerful frame tensed and, as it prepared to push itself upright, she gasped.

It was going to charge again. And this time she was defenseless.

Just then, a nearby set of veranda doors flew inward.

Ilsa gaped in astonishment as detectives Ramirez and Tokaido burst into the ballroom, flashlights in hand and guns drawn.

"Feliz Navidad, bitches!" Ramirez shouted gleefully. "Jailbreak's over, so you can stop celebrating!"

"Yeah, where you hiding, Alvilda?" Tokaido bellowed. He had a disdainful sneer on his face as he scanned the firelit furniture. "How long did you think it would take us to track down a snow-white, 1950s Cadillac?"

Ilsa's expression was a study in disbelief. The assistance she'd been praying for had arrived, but "Dumb and Dumber" were oblivious to the living nightmare hunkered down less than five yards to their right. Backlit by the flames, and with its enormous cloak wrapped about it, it must've appeared as just another piece of furniture.

You gotta be kidding me. Wake up, you idiots!

Her mind raced and she tried to utter a warning, but there was no time. With a toothy smirk, the demon rose to its full height.

Ramirez and Tokaido turned as one toward the unexpected movement. Judging by their puffed-out chests and swagger, they'd obviously been expecting Andy. It took them several seconds to realize how ridiculously wrong they were. As Ilsa watched, their indignant expressions were sidelined first by shock, then incredulity. Then the hellish horror started stomping toward them and their eyes turned to serving trays.

"Madre de Dios!"

To his credit, Ramirez managed to cap off two well-aimed rounds before it had him. There was a muffled scream as one clawed hand enveloped his whole head, followed by a horrific wrenching sound as it was ripped clean off his shoulders.

A gout of arterial blood shot six feet skyward. The demon smiled an awful smile, then tossed the avulsed head into its mouth like a piece of popcorn and started chewing. Ignoring both Tokaido's curses and the fusillade he unleashed, it drew

Ramirez's body close, took a sniff, then tossed it disdainfully back over one shoulder.

The still-twitching corpse landed in the middle of the fireplace, one leg snap-kicking a few times before the whole body was consumed by the flames.

Just then, one of Tokaido's .40 caliber rounds hit a sensitive spot – inside one of the creature's open nares. It recoiled, then wheeled on him. Choking down an awful mouthful of bone and brains, it sprang forward, uttering a deep rumble of annoyance.

The big Japanese was either too scared or too stupid to get out of its way and stood his ground, methodically pulling the trigger. He'd have been better off facing down a rogue bull elephant with a pellet gun. Too fast to follow, a huge hand shot out and seized him by the crotch, then lifted him right off the floor.

"My balls!"

Tokaido uttered a high-pitched shriek as he became a 300-pound fastball. A full fifteen yards later, he crashed down atop a ragged pile of broken furniture. He lay there: a twisted-up rag doll, bloodied and unmoving.

Now in full attack mode, the demon started toward Ilsa. One glance at the sadistic look on its face snapped her out of her remaining funk.

Playtime was over. The son of a bitch meant business.

With no more cold iron ammo or any other options, her only choice was to make a run for it. Head down, she sprinted toward the nearest column, hoping to put it between her and the wrathful monstrosity that was hard on her heels.

She was halfway there when its claws sank into her right shoulder and she ended up bouncing off a nearby wall. She smelled gypsum as she hit the floor and stared through a sea of stars, up at the barrel-sized dent her hip and thigh had left in the shattered laths.

Pain shot through her like red-hot wires as she tried to stand. She feared the worst, but there was no time to assess injuries. Heart pounding, she began crawling for it. Around her, stood a veritable forest of furniture, a field of phantoms spread across the ballroom floor. With any luck, if she moved fast enough, she could conceal herself long enough to—

Damn.

Ilsa winced as her left leg was seized by what felt like a vice with teeth. Then there was that uncomfortably familiar sensation of being tossed like a beanbag. As the wind whistled past her ears, she had an odd thought.

Why am I still alive? Why does it keep using me to play wallball? Why not just do me like it did Ramirez?

The realization hit her right between the eyes. The thing was toying with her, like a cat does a mouse. Only after it ran out of ways to torture her would the end finally come.

Bastard.

Ilsa's burgeoning pugnaciousness pancaked as she struck the ground hard and did an out-of-control roll. When the spinning finally stopped, she found herself flat on her back and struggling to stay conscious. The air around her felt incredibly hot, like she'd entered a blast furnace.

A heartbeat later, she got a taste of what real heat felt like. A shrill scream burst from her mouth and she threw herself desperately to her right, rolling and patting before gazing downward through a pain-filled haze.

Her left forearm had ended up in the fire.

As she fanned away the smoke, she realized she'd been lucky. Her now-ruined leather jacket and glove had borne the brunt of it. Even so, judging by the pain, not to mention that godawful smell, she'd suffered some bad burns.

How bad was difficult to say. But as her salivating nemesis stomped purposefully toward her, she realized she'd probably never know.

* * *

The searing pain caught Olek completely off guard. His whole body stiffened and an anguished wail escaped his lips. Then the soldier in him kicked in and he remembered who he was. Teeth gritted, he pressed the switch that raised him to a more propped-up position, then glanced apprehensively around. He was relieved to see no one had noticed his unexpected bawl, including the cop stationed outside his room and the rather buxom nurse he was shamelessly flirting with.

After a few controlled inhalations to bring things into focus, Olek slid the weighty leather-bound volume on his lap off to one side, undid his straps, and then leaned forward. Stroking his chin contemplatively, he studied the gauze bandages covering the myriad cuts and scrapes that decorated his left forearm.

There was no blood. But something was definitely not right.

Olek's face flushed as he began gingerly pulling the meshy material to one side. A grimace creased his already seamed features.

Kakogo cherta?

The exposed skin on the back of his hand and forearm was an angry red color with blisters popping up.

Blisters?

It was bad – like that time he'd been helping Elena cook and had spilled an entire pot of borscht on himself. Except, of course, there was no Elena here, nor was there any boiling beet soup.

A terrible realization came to him then and he swallowed fearfully. His breath started coming in pants, like an aging greyhound that's run its last race, and he hugged the big *Sinterklaas* book hard. A yard away, the fluctuating readings on his LCD monitor tracked the erratic beating of his heart.

Something terrible was happening. Something horrible.

It was the end, the endgame.

He didn't know how he knew; he just knew.

Olek's eyes closed so tightly they hurt, and his lips trembled as he started fervently praying in Yiddish. Deep down, he didn't believe it would help. But he did it anyway. It wasn't like he had any other options. After all, what else could a beaten and broken man who's lost the love of his life, and who now lies waiting for an unstoppable foe to come and tear him to pieces, do?

CHAPTER 19

Trapped in a bottomless pit of pain, Ilsa gazed powerlessly up at the form of her pending demise. The demon hovered deathlike, mere yards away. The seconds ticked by and it remained where it was. Its eyes were cold and hard, but its expression was otherwise bland. There was no hastening on its part, no hurry. It knew full well that its prey was too battered to escape; it was simply taking a moment to savor the fear that oozed from her, like the sweat dripping from her pores.

"Sweat" was an understatement. The heat radiating from the nearby hearth was unbelievable. Ilsa could barely breathe.

Predictably, the firestorm appeared to have no effect on the chimney-traveling monster. If anything, it seemed to be enjoying it. Its scaled lips split into a fearsome smile and it moved closer; so close, in fact, that one of its massive hooves shattered the thick marble tile a foot from her face.

With deceptive mildness, it leaned down, wrapped a knotted paw the size of a goalie's mitt around Ilsa's neck, and hoisted her up until it held her at arm's length. It stared dispassionately into her eyes, watching as she gasped and wheezed, her booted feet doing an impromptu Irish jig, a yard above the debris-speckled floor.

Aided by her desperate need for oxygen, cold fear settled in the pit of Ilsa's stomach. She was powerless. The hand gripping her felt like steel-reinforced concrete, the strength backing it irresistible.

She was going to die.

The only question in her mind was: how long would her death take, and how unbearable would it be?

As if reading her thoughts, the demon pulled her close – so close their noses practically touched. Its red-cored eyes burned like lava pits, and the stomach-churning stench wafting from its mouth smelled like a neglected slaughterhouse floor; it would've made a hyena vomit. If she hadn't been in the midst of being throttled, Ilsa would've puked her guts up. She'd never been so terrified in her life and it was all she could do to keep from pissing herself.

Then, just when she thought things couldn't get any worse, they did.

The demon cocked its head and started turning her from side to side, like it was studying her. A clip from that old '80s movie *Predator* started playing inside her head - the one where the industrial-sized alien pins a buff Arnold Schwarzenegger to a tree as it sizes him up.

The scene did an abrupt dissolve, however, as the demon leaned in and started sniffing. She felt its hot breath on her neck, followed by its batlike nostrils pressing against her exposed collarbones. Its inhalations became throaty and a mucousy string of drool overflowed its mouth and began dribbling down its anvil-like chin.

A beacon of revulsion-fueled anger ignited within her. As frightening as it was being this close, knowing that she was on the menu and being snuffled like a slab of fresh pot roast made things infinitely worse.

Still, Ilsa wasn't going down like wet biscuits.

Reaching up, she latched onto the thing's index finger and thumb with her gloved hands, trying her best to break its grip or at least reduce how much of her bodyweight was hanging from her neck.

It was useless. She'd have had a better chance at bending a tank gun.

"Screw you, you bastard . . ." she rasped as their eyes met. "I know who you are. You hear me . . . *Loptr?*"

The demon blinked in obvious surprise. Then it leaned forward, a crocodile's smile dividing its disfigured face. Its hooked teeth separated, and its lamprey-like tongue lolled from its mouth. In the firelight, it looked like some gigantic, salivating hellhound.

As she got a good look at it, Ilsa couldn't help but shudder. Its translucent proboscis was even grosser up close. Ringing the recurved teeth that lined its tube-like opening was an array of oily, three-inch-long projections. They reminded her of the one or two flexible fingers at the tip of an elephant's trunk, except there were many of them.

The cilia – for want of a better word – began to undulate as the entire tongue emerged. The phlegm-coated monstrosity curled sinuously back like a yard-long cobra preparing to strike, then it reached out and began exploring the exposed portions of her chest.

Ilsa quaked with the realization: *Loptr was tasting her.*

Her mind reeled as it was unwillingly hauled yet another rung up the ladder of ultimate horrors. She uttered a squeal of disgust and strove once more to free herself. Then, through squinted eyes, she saw the demon's vile tongue retreat back inside its mouth. Only the slime-coated tip remained, and that began to lick its indigo-colored lips.

Just as those lips peeled back to reveal rows of flesh-rending fangs, Ilsa's head snapped in its direction. Her own teeth were bared, her eyes sunlit peridots. She no longer feared what came next; she'd have spat in her enemy's face if she could've mustered the saliva.

"You think you're so big and bad," she hissed. "But you're *not*."

She twisted against its steely grip, battling to draw in what she knew would be her last breath.

"You're *nothing*. You're just Santa's little *bitch!*"

As the words hit home, the demon's head jerked back on its shoulders. Its eyes scanned the ceiling above it and it emitted an eardrum-damaging scream.

Taking advantage of its distracted state, Ilsa hauled back with one of her steel-toed combat boots and kicked it as hard as she could. Right where its balls should have been.

The impact made her wince. She didn't know if Loptr had testicles or not, but her instep felt like she just played crotch shot with a statue.

Her captor glanced down at its nether regions, then back up at her. Its cantaloupe-sized jaw muscles bunched, then she saw something unpleasant flicker in its eyes. A moment later, its lips snarled slowly back, exposing bloodstained fangs, and a deep snarl penetrated her to her core.

Ilsa shook her head. She refused to be cowed. If she was going to die, she would do it like a man. Except, she was a woman.

"Bite me, you fucking asshole!"

The demon angled its head to one side, its expression unreadable. Then it started lowering her. For the fleetest of moments, she thought it was going to let her go, or at least release its grip.

She was wrong.

The moment her feet touched the floor, it seized her left leg by the ankle with its left hand. Releasing its chokehold, it lifted her back up by the one leg. Inverted, she felt the blood rush to her head. Before she could figure out what the bastard was up to, it latched onto her other ankle with its right hand and hoisted her even higher.

Their faces were almost level and she saw that same, sadistic smirk crease its face. Then it lowered her until her pelvis was level with its chin. She felt her legs being prized apart until they were at a forty-five-degree angle, and a viscous stream of saliva dripped down, splashing her face en route to the floor.

One look at the thing's gnashing teeth and leering expression told her more than she wanted to know. It had understood her words and was going to take her up on them.

Literally.

It planned on eating her alive, starting with what lay between her legs.

The ultimate aghastness was more than Ilsa could take. Her courage finally failed her and she started screaming hysterically. Her legs were locked up, but she thrashed and flailed and threw her body forward, throwing punch after punch at the thing's stony abdomen.

She was a fly attacking a rhinoceros.

The demon's nightmarish mouth slowly opened and she closed her eyes, bracing herself for the agony of that first, artery-severing bite.

Then she heard a voice. It was hauntingly familiar, a ghost calling out.

A ghost with a . . . Brooklyn accent?

"Hey, tough guy! Over here!"

The monster's cowled head whipped toward the sound, and Ilsa's heart started doing cartwheels in her chest.

It was Andy.

The magnificent bastard wasn't just alive, he was striking a pose, barely ten paces away. She could see him clearly in the fire's simmering light. He was bloodied but determined-looking and had a feral gleam in his eye. His .45 was tucked in his belt, urban gunfighter style, and a cocky grin decorated his face.

"Sorry I'm late," he drawled, then made a show of brushing the dust off one of his bedraggled flight jacket's shoulders. "This place is 'holier' than we thought..."

Even with the depravity of her situation, Ilsa couldn't help but groan.

The demon, visibly annoyed at the interruption, adjusted its grip so it had both Ilsa's ankles in one hand. As it turned toward Andy, it uttered a deep barking sound that sounded suspiciously like a scoff. Its deep-set orbs blinked as they wandered from his pistol to his clawed-up chest. It realized his religious medal was missing and chuckled. Then it held its free hand up and showed off its talons.

They gleamed in the firelight like black butcher's knives.

Andy pretended to be unimpressed as he contemplated the thing's murderous weapons. Then he stuck his tongue out and tasted the trickle of blood that ran down his face. His bored expression faded and his eyes became as hard as agates. Then he cricked his neck to one side and brought one of his favorite Clint Eastwood impersonations online.

"Well, are ya gonna pull those pistols or whistle Dixie?"

The smirk on Loptr's face was replaced by a frightful grimace. Tossing its pending meal aside, it uttered a bearlike bellow and charged.

Ilsa landed hard, and as she tried to rise the pain of her assorted injuries did a dogpile on her. Even if she could've gotten up there was no time to react, nor was there anything she could've done. In truth, it was all she could do to keep from passing out.

Andy remained frighteningly calm as the demon thundered toward him. His quickdraw was too fast to follow, and from five paces out he emptied his pistol into its chest. To his dismay, the bludgeoning impacts of the big cold-iron rounds barely slowed it. A split-second later, it closed the distance and threw itself at the tall Californian.

With impressively agility, Andy managed to slip his oversized adversary's initial strikes, including one designed to disembowel him and another that would've opened his throat. Bobbing and weaving, he bided his time. Then, the moment it was off-balance, he coiled his muscular body up like a viper's and retaliated, nailing its nose with a stiff left jab, followed by an impressive left hook to the jaw.

Ilsa's own jaw went into freefall as the behemoth's head snapped hard to one side. The look of incredulity-mixed-with-pain gracing its hateful features was unmistakable.

Omigod, he actually hurt it!

The demon stumbled back, shook its head to clear it, then touched a hand the size of a Thanksgiving turkey to its face. A pair of swollen burn marks graced its upper lip and chin.

A look of ill-contained fury came over it, then its odious eyes zeroed Andy's left hand. He had his leather cowboy belt wound in tight layers around his fingers, boxing-wrap-style, with its big silver belt buckle on the outside, like a set of brass knuckles.

He brandished his fist and winked. "How's *that* for a season's greeting?" he asked from beneath raised brows.

Ilsa clamped her hands over her ears to protect them from the demon's bloodcurdling bellow. A berserker rage had come over it and it flew at Andy, jagged claws slashing and toothy jaws snapping. He stepped gamely forward to meet it, but from Ilsa's worm's-eye-view, her partner looked like a 6th grader trying to take on a professional wrestler.

She gritted her teeth as she prepared for the worst.

The wait was not a long one.

For a few more seconds, Andy's hit-and-run tactics continued to frustrate the creature. But then it stepped back, lowered its head and charged, its gorilla-like arms spread wide. Absorbing the punishment that he dished out, it scooped him up like a blowup doll. He was trapped, wrapped up in an inescapable bear hug.

Ilsa winced as she heard what sounded like ribs cracking.

Andy's pain-filled eyes flew open wide. Instantly realizing the futility of trying to break free, he twisted toward her.

"Get the hell outta here!"

Try as she might, she couldn't make it to her feet. Desperation welled up and her heart sank as she continued to watch the uneven struggle.

The demon had been calculating. It had Andy's dangerous left arm pinned against his side. Only his right was free. Eyes alight, it drew him toward its salivating jaws.

Teeth clenched, Andy jammed his free forearm against its throat and braced himself, tenaciously trying to keep it at bay.

"You know..." he grunted. "I don't think... you're practicing... safe social *distancing!*"

Eyes alight with anticipation, the demon continued to press forward.

Ilsa quailed at the sight. The thing obviously knew its soon-to-be-victim's strength was but a fraction of its own. There was no escape. It could overpower Andy whenever it wanted to. It was simply taking its time.

Her frustration at her own powerlessness got the better of her. She felt fear and despair bloom in the pit of her stomach. Desperate, she cast around, searching for something to use as a weapon.

Something. *Anything.*

She knew she still had a few rounds in her pockets, but her pistol was gone. Other than broken pieces of furniture, the only thing she could see was her backpack, lying seven or eight yards away. She clenched her teeth and blew out a ragged breath. She was a bloody mess, but she screwed up what remained of her courage and started crawling.

Halfway there, a burst of adrenaline kicked in. Her injuries were momentarily minimized and, with a Herculean effort, she rose, seized the knapsack, and tore it open. There was nothing. Nothing except the aged wooden cross Olek had given her and the vintage mantle photo Kareema sacrificed her life for.

Ilsa stared, wide-eyed, as her father and six-year-old-self smiled up at her from their antique silver window. She swallowed painfully, then reached down with trembling hands.

A moment later, the demon screamed in agony.

Rearing back, it managed to keep Andy restrained with one clawed hand while swiveling at the hip. Its malevolent eyes fell on Ilsa, then it peered back over its shoulder at the lashed-together fragments of sleigh.

She'd buried the pointed end of the makeshift cross like a dagger in its back.

"Merry Christmas, you mother--"

POW!

The backhand felt like getting hit by a truck. It sent her twenty feet through the air and she slid another ten before careening to a halt. Barely conscious, she lay on her side. The cough that followed was almost as painful as the strike. She tasted blood and reached up with numb fingers, feeling her chest. She'd been lucky. The splintered ceramic plate inside her bulletproof vest had absorbed the majority of the blunt force trauma – probably the reason she was alive.

Still, she'd have bet good money her sternum was cracked.

Ten paces away, the demon staggered drunkenly from side to side, hissing like the father of all snakes. With a squirming Andy still in tow, it twisted and writhed, trying to get at the source of its suffering.

Finally, it managed to reach Ilsa's makeshift weapon and claw it free. It glared malevolently at the bound pieces of wood, then its fingers and eyes splayed open wide and it emitted an ear-splitting shriek.

Ilsa did a doubletake. Despite its impressive fire resistance, the sleigh fragments had managed to burn the demon's thick-skinned palm like a cattle brand.

Screaming furiously, it flung the jury-rigged cross down the fireplace's beckoning throat. The effect was like throwing a drum of gasoline; there was a tremendous whooshing sound and the bonfire violently expanded, until the searing flames licked the very roof of the arc-shaped firebox.

THE SLEIGH

***

Olek Apostol sat up with a gasp. He could barely breathe, let alone speak, and hadn't the strength to reach for the nurse's call button. It took him a few minutes to close his eyes and mentally calm himself. Then, just as he was in the middle of drawing a breath, his body inexplicably spasmed. The pain was unbelievable; like he'd been zapped with an industrial-sized defibrillator. Every muscle locked up and his spine went board straight.

Worse, the sudden downward force his body generated derailed his elevated hospital bed. It crashed down into a supine position, taking him with it. He lay there discombobulated, eyes peeled wide, mouth doing the fish-out-of-water thing. Several long moments later, he finally managed to catch his breath.

And, with it, realization.

The battle was all but lost. Humanity's champions had failed and the darkness would soon emerge victorious. It was overwhelming the light. All his efforts had been for naught.

So many lives lost, so many dreams shattered . . .

Olek began to sob like a wounded child. His badly burned left hand continued to cradle his history of Ded Moroz, while his right clutched at his frantically pounding heart.

It felt like it was breaking. But, then, he realized he'd experienced that already.

"Elena . . . my beautiful Elena!"

* * *

Backlit by the fireplace's roaring flames, the demon stood stock-still. Its barrel-shaped chest expanded and contracted as it stared in annoyance at the singed flesh on its hand.

Then its eyes turned to slits and it focused its attention once more on Andy.

The Texan-turned-Californian was barely on his feet. Nonetheless, he managed an impressive arm punch as it seized him with both clawed hands.

Ilsa shook her head miserably. Andy was a powerful guy. But with the arm bearing his silver belt buckle still pinned, it was like throwing a marshmallow at a gorilla.

Before her despairing eyes, Loptr lifted him until his cowboy boots hung a foot above the floor. Fear crossed her face as it held him at eye level and she braced herself. She expected it to bury its fangs in his face, then something unforeseen happened.

The demon glanced her way, presumably gauging her condition and resolve, then it slapped a hand around Andy's neck. With both of its troublesome enemies immobilized, it reached up with its other hand and drew back its heavy cowl.

Exposing its face.

Ilsa went cold to the bone as she laid eyes on it. Its features were vaguely manlike, although its nose was more like a flattened pig's snout and its mouth was preternaturally wide. Its skin was leathery and bluish-black, with the sections around its mouth dotted with thumbnail-size protrusions that resembled black barnacles. Ochre-colored pus oozed from several, leading her to wonder if they had herpes in Hell. Its notched lips were thick and battle-scarred, and beneath them hung yellowed fangs with darkened tips – permanent bloodstains, acquired through centuries of use.

Its jaw was heavy, with rough skin made rougher by a peppering of short, wiry hairs. Its protruding cheekbones, on the other hand – reminiscent of some great ape – were surprisingly smooth. The hair adorning its globe-shaped head was shaggy and unkempt and hung down to its shoulders. That is, if it *was* hair. It was a glossy dark cyan in color, but the follicles looked more like strands of spaghetti. They appeared to have a life all their own; she swore she saw several of its locks undulate, like serpents on a gorgon's head.

Worst of all were the monster's fearsome eyes. Deep-set and concealed beneath a beetling brow, they were limpid pools of lava, glittering in the dark and eager to consume.

Andy blanched as he locked gazes with it.

Ilsa was still down for the count, but as she fought to clear her head, she realized something. This was the first time she'd ever seen her partner afraid.

As she watched, the monster adjusted its grip. Grasping Andy with both hands once more, it pinned his upper arms to his torso and drew him close enough to kiss.

Ilsa inhaled sharply as its horrid mouth yawned wide. But then, instead of avulsing half its victim's face, it began to . . . sing?

Actually, it was more like a protracted roar. It started off low, then rapidly rose in both pitch and volume. Louder and louder the demon bellowed, and wetly too, right in poor Andy's face.

Ilsa squinted then blinked. The twelve inches of space that separated the two adversaries had begun to waver, as if the very air between them was going in and out of focus.

A look of purest panic overcame Andy. He couldn't move, couldn't struggle, and no matter how much he wanted to he couldn't look away. His breathing had turned to rib-straining pants and the veins on his temples and the sides of his neck began to protrude.

Then his lips parted and he started to scream.

His baritone shriek blended with the demon's bellowing. It was a bizarre, offkey duet that rapidly increased in resonance. A moment later, the sound reached the point that it was physically painful.

Ilsa covered her ears and held her breath. It was impossible. Nothing on earth could utter a call that lasted that long.

All at once, Andy's voice began to falter and his eyes rolled up white. His already drawn skin became the color of cream and his tawny hair followed suit. The bizarre bleaching started at the tips, then worked its way down to the roots. It was as if the melanin in each and every follicle was being sucked out.

And all the while, the demon's foul phonations continued.

Unwilling to just stand there and on the verge of hyperventilating, Ilsa realized she had no choice. She drew in a lungful and added her own cries of anguish to the nightmarish mix.

CHAPTER 20

Ilsa's heart felt like it was being constricted by icy chains as she watched the nightmare unfold. Actually, calling it a nightmare was, appropriately, one *hell* of an understatement.

If her poor partner wasn't dead already, he soon would be.

Still in Loptr's clutches, Andy hung lifeless – a stringless marionette, beat up and bled-out. His eyes were closed and his skin and hair were milk-white. The only colors that remained were the red-and-rust-colored streaks that ran down his cheeks. Without them, he could've passed for an alabaster statue.

The demon cocked its shaggy head to one side, studying Andy's prostrate form. It shook him once. Twice. Apparently, content with whatever damage its vocalizations had done, it vacillated. An almost reflective look came over it. Then it glanced in her direction and made a show of stroking its chin.

Ilsa swallowed against the tightness in her throat as she watched it smile a diabolical smile. Expecting it to come thundering her way, she clenched her teeth and forced herself to her feet.

It didn't.

Instead, it refocused its attention on Andy. After wrapping one forearm around his waist to brace him, it ran the other up between his shoulder blades, until its shoebox-sized hand cupped the back of his head.

Ilsa recoiled. The pose had an odd, almost perverse look. Like a Classical Greek statue of embracing lovers.

The effect faded, however, as the demon yawned so wide its lower jaw disarticulated. It started making nasty retching sounds and its tongue erupted from its mouth in a flood of mucus. The appendage hovered snakelike for a moment, then its leech's maw made for Andy's bloodless lips.

Ilsa's stomach clenched so hard it hurt. It was going to regurgitate its most recent meal – the child it had just murdered – down Andy's throat. If he *was* still alive, the chunks of flesh would suffocate him for sure and, at the same time, frame him as a member of the supposed Christmas Cannibals.

Unless she missed her guess, she was slated for a similar fate.

The combination of pain and horror was too much. Her strength failed her and she dropped to one knee.

A lesser woman would've fainted on the spot.

Loptr's plan was the sickest thing she could think of, but utterly in character for the ageless monstrosity. It must've figured it was poetic justice that the first humans to ever successfully oppose it would end up taking the fall for its crimes.

And, of course, the bastard would return next year. Bigger and badder, with no one left to stand in his way.

No, it can't end like this! It can't!

Sheer stubbornness, combined with an innate unwillingness to lay down and die, kicked in, and Ilsa played the only card she had left. She cupped her hands around her mouth and began throwing a litany of curses at her enemy. She used every vile insult she could think of – insulting its appearance, its manhood – even mom jokes.

It was to no avail. The fiend would not be distracted from its kill and she had nothing left with which to fight it.

Futility finally won out. She was exhausted and her vocal cords too raw to scream any more. All she could do was hang her head and cry.

And wait for her turn.

* * *

If there'd been any strength left in his limbs, Olek would've thrown up his hands.

There wasn't. Yet even so, and despite his most fervent wishes, his withered body continued to resist. It knew what he was attempting and steadfastly opposed him.

The old man gritted his teeth. It was both confounding and frustrating, a man of his advanced years possessing such vitality. He could picture his beloved Elena peering down from the clouds, then smiling and rolling her eyes.

If only . . .

He lowered his eyelids and, using sheer willpower, attempted to rein in both his rapid breathing and the painful spasms that continued to wrack his aching muscles. It was working. Yes . . . yes, he could *do* this. His chest sank as he slowly released the breath he'd been holding.

As he did, he felt a familiar chill.

Despite all the decades, his military service continued to be of use. He didn't have to gaze at the pitch blackness outside to know what was happening. The sleep he'd invited was on its way.

It was the long sleep. The deep sleep. The kind you never woke up from.

Olek started to smile. But then the fear accompanying it welled up.

It was cold – colder than the numbness oozing icily through his veins. Finding no opposition, the fear began to explore. It skittered up his spine on little lizard's feet, spreading trepidation as it went.

He felt panic come a-calling. Soldier or no, scientist or no, the uncertainty of oblivion terrified him. But what choice did he have? He owed a debt and that debt must be paid. What other options remained?

There were none.

Atonement was the way. So, what was his problem? Could he not do it? Was he not man enough to take that final step?

His jaw muscles bunched like ball bearings and he shook his grizzled head. He'd failed. He knew that now, and what's more he accepted it. He'd failed at protecting the love of his life, just like he'd failed to derail the coming darkness.

The darkness.

Olek forced down what felt like an apple lodged in his throat. As it turned out, the darkness he dreaded was not the foreboding guest that pawed catlike at his hospital room door, hoping to gain admittance.

No.

His pending visitor was as nothing compared to the never-ending-night he'd unwittingly unleashed. And he had. Intentionally or no, the excruciating deaths of hundreds of men, women, and children rested squarely upon his shoulders.

Olek's aged frame shuddered and tears flooded his eyes. He railed at life's incongruities. An upstanding and respected member of the community? Hardly. He needed to stop fooling himself. When all was said and done, he was no hero or philanthropist; he was a genocidal monster, as bad as the Luciferians from decades earlier, who pushed their deadly pathogens on the deluded masses.

Or Josef Mengele, Hitler's very own "Angel of Death".

Or the Red Tsar, himself.

Actually, Olek realized, in the end he might actually prove worse. After all, the horror he'd let loose upon an unsuspecting world had barely begun. Those hundreds that had perished would become thousands, and those thousands, tens of thousands. On and on it would go, in a never-ending and ever-expanding spiral. Loptr could never be satiated. He would slaughter without mercy and, the more blood he spilt and the more flesh he consumed, the more his rapaciousness would grow.

And he along with it.

Olek's sniffles abruptly ceased and a dire thought occurred to him. What if the demon was eventually able to release others of its kind from Perdition? Was that possible? Could it open the infernal floodgates? And what about the souls of its victims? Were they forfeit? Would they be forever consigned to the same burning pit that spawned their killer?

Was that fair? Was there no justice in this world? Did they not have a choice?

Choice...

In his mind's eye, he pictured Elena's face. She was wearing that knowing look of hers, the one that always cut him to the quick. He thought he saw her lips move. Was she saying something? Yes, she was.

Moya lyubov, remember who you are.

Olek's shoulders pulled back in response and he felt flames of determination ignite within his chest. Ignoring the pain that lanced through his scorched arm, he bearhugged the old *Sinterklaas* book. Fresh tears ran down his cheeks as he looked heavenward.

He tried speaking, but only croaking sounds came out. His tongue was like aged parchment. A quick scan of his room showed no water within reach. Finally, thinking of the cannolis he'd served to those two valiant detectives – and poor, frightened Vincent – allowed him to summon some much-needed saliva. Then, without hesitation, he cleared his throat and spoke the words.

"Must . . . be . . . willing . . ."

Olek's already resigned face sank into serenity. Then his cracked lips parted and the air rushed out of his lungs.

There was no inhalation.

His bandaged arm fell away and the air was rent by an ear-splitting wail as his monitor began its high-pitched swan song. A cacophony of additional sounds – his hospital room door bursting open, stamping feet, and shouts of alarm – were lost on him.

He wasn't there to hear them.

* * *

Ilsa couldn't bear to watch as the demon's translucent feeding tube fastened itself onto Andy's face. The vile appendage was highly elastic and had the ability to shape itself as if it were an oxygen mask. It had enveloped her doomed partner's nose and mouth, ensuring a tight seal.

It was more than just the sheer gruesomeness, however, that caused her to avert her eyes. She simply couldn't take any more.

Who could?

She was forlorn, weaponless, and had been beaten within an inch of her life. She was done. All she could do now was close her eyes and try to drown out the gut-wrenching spewing sounds that were fated to commence. Her sanity and the contents of her own stomach teetered on the brink and she was moments away from losing both.

Ilsa covered her eyes with her hands and began to pray. For Andy, for herself, and for anyone else the thing got its claws on.

She didn't expect an answer. She knew prayers were useless.

She'd experienced horror like this before. Home-movie-like visions of her parent's bullet-riddled bodies drifted before her scrunched-shut eyes and she dug her palm heels into them, trying to blot out the awfulness.

It was a wasted effort. Her failing mind began to spin out just as a sudden disturbance gatecrashed its way into her thoughts.

It wasn't the sounds of pumping vomitus that she'd anticipated. This was more like a roar. And it wasn't coming from the demon. Though muffled, it was far more boisterous, like a distant avalanche; it filled the sprawling ballroom.

Hard on the thunder's heels came a powerful blast of heat. It slammed into her, stripping the air from her lungs and singeing them from the inside out. Her weary hazels snapped wide in alarm at the realization.

It was the fire.

The already intense flames filling the maw-shaped hearth were . . . *erupting*. Like a bevy of burning salamanders, they overflowed the firebox that sought to contain them. Slithering up and over its edges, they enveloped the entire length of the black opal lintel, turning several feet of it to charcoal. Above their lapping tongues, the flames reflected in the mantle's opaline eyes, causing them to blaze with a life of their own.

The effect the sudden conflagration had on the demon was odd. Its eyes bulged and its head recoiled on thick-muscled shoulders. A heartbeat later, its quivering tongue shot back inside its mouth like a released tape measure and Andy fell from its grasp. He hit the floor hard, his body twisted up like a disjointed action figure.

The demon tensed then took a step back. The dark skin of its face was awash in the orange glow of the flames and, on that face, Ilsa saw what looked like astonishment.

Before her eyes, its shocked expression faded. Then its crimson orbs turned to twin arrow slits and it zeroed the firebox. It was peering intently at the fire.

No, not at the fire.

At something *in* the fire.

A flush crept up Ilsa's disbelieving face as she saw what the demon saw.

A dark phalanx of spears was protruding from the flames.

Correction, not spears. It was more like a bristling wall of dark, bony spikes – spikes connected to what looked like enormous ... antlers?

Ilsa's fingers touched the base of her throat as she stared, flabbergasted. It was a *deer* of some kind. A gorgeous, majestic deer, like a red deer or an American elk, but immense – the size of a draft horse.

Head lowered and antlers pointed threateningly forward, the stag advanced. Its orange-brown eyes were locked on Loptr, and a column of whitish vapor spewed from its partly-open mouth. With a deep nicker, it emerged from the flames – flames that did nothing to it.

Ilsa marveled at the rock-hard muscles lining the hart's powerful neck and shoulders, as well as the length of its slow-heaving flanks. A glimmer of movement caused her to look down and she did a doubletake. She could see its long legs, terminating in elegant two-toed hooves. There were eight legs in total, and they moved in synch.

Wait, an eight-legged deer? What the hell am I looking at?

As the stag's yard-long head bobbed up and down, Ilsa caught a glimpse of a second furry muzzle, concealed behind it. She realized then that there were two of the giant creatures. Side by side, they continued forward, their gleaming gazes fixed on Loptr. Blasts of steam shot from their nares as they shook their great crowned heads.

Snorting angrily, they emerged fully from the fireplace and began to peer around. Ilsa wondered at the realization that they were harnessed. There were no reins that she could see, but they wore heavy leather breast collars, supported by forked neck and hip straps, and topped with jack saddles connected to sturdy traces, like the Clydesdales she'd seen around Central Park.

All of a sudden, and despite the painful glare from the flames, Ilsa felt her pupils spontaneously dilate. She realized the pair of huge deer were attached to something. They were pulling a--

What the f—

Partially protruding from the fire was the bow of what appeared to be a sleigh of some kind. It was enormous – on par with the Brobdingnagian beasts hauling it.

The sleigh was tall and sleek in design, with elegant runners reminiscent of the munitions-charred sections she'd seen in Olek's now defunct inner sanctum. They were long and rune covered, and curled up and back at the front, until they attached to the fore-section of the carriage. The carriage box proper was exquisitely carved and made of some sort of wood. In the flickering light, it was impossible to say what kind, but it had a rosewood hue and a rich patina. The polished runners, on the other hand, were as black as pitch – a far cry from the desiccated gray fragments she'd buried in the demon's back, moments earlier.

Speaking of which . . .

All of a sudden, the carriage box shifted with a groan. There was a heavy thud, as if something substantial had dropped to the ground. The demon's eyes widened in response and it uttered a frightful hiss. Teeth bared, it began to give ground.

Ilsa's eyes flew from it to her partner's prostrate form. She saw her opening and went for it, half-crawling, half-dragging herself across the ballroom's fractured marble floor. In a heartbeat, she was at Andy's side. Her maternal instincts kicked in and she wrapped her arms protectively around him.

She peered furtively about. Her senses told her that something strange was happening. But what?

Her fear-filled eyes flicked back and forth, from the demon to the sledge and back again. A moment later, she gave a start.

There was something moving on the far side of the sleigh. Whatever it was, it was sizable and standing in the center of the white-hot flames. Oblivious to the incredible temperatures, it advanced.

Ilsa cocked her head to the side, desperately striving to see. The shimmering waves of heat obscured her vision and she brushed an unwanted tear from her eye. Squinting hard, she was able to make out bits and pieces of the new arrival as it passed beneath the giant stags' bellies.

The first thing she spotted was a spearhead. It was sizable – close to a yard in length. The point was broad-based and triangular, and had sharp, recurved sides that suggested it was designed to not only pierce armor, but to be swung like a halberd in combat. The bladed part had an ornately embossed central ridge for added strength, and pointed lugs shaped like hawk's heads that protruded from either side, boar-spear-style.

The spearhead was affixed to a massive, gnarled shaft of some strangely decorated hardwood. Stranger still was the light its bladed portions gave off. She blinked repeatedly to see if it was a trick of the light – a reflection of the flames, playing along its edges – but she swore it was actually glowing.

A few yards behind the downward-pointed spear came a pair of big, booted feet. They strode purposefully forward, sure-footed and untroubled, extending from the depths of a billowing, fur-trimmed robe.

As the spear's owner moved past the two deer and afforded her a good look, Ilsa's breath caught in her throat. She did a doubletake, then her heart started beating like a hummingbird's as the realization hit home.

It *couldn't* be. And yet it was.

It was him.

He had many names: Ded Moroz, Grandfather Frost, Father Christmas, Sinterklaas...

But in the end, it was Santa Claus standing before her.

Any vestigial disbelief Ilsa still had literally went up in smoke. She felt awe transform her face and, for a brief moment, Loptr and all the horrors he represented were forgotten. Frozen in place, she gazed unblinkingly up at the powerful figure.

This was no fat, jolly elf.

Nor was he little.

He towered at least seven feet in height and had a hunter's build, with broad shoulders and powerful muscles that stood out through his heavy winter clothing. His fur-edged outfit wasn't red, but rather a mystical blue, so dark and glittery it seemed as if the very stars in the heavens were imprisoned within its satiny folds.

The voluminous robe he wore as an outermost layer hung almost to the floor and was secured around his waist by a thick crimson sash. A short cape of white fur was draped across his chest and shoulders, and a cap lined with the same material covered his head. His hair, mustache, and beard were thick and full, and were the color of arctic ice.

As he stepped forward, Ilsa was impressed by how gracefully Moroz – as Olek referred to him – moved. Despite his size and presumed age, his limbs had a distinctive ranginess about them. And with that suppleness, she suspected, came agility.

But there was more to him than the physical. This man, this . . . *being* literally exuded power. It was hard to explain; it came at you in waves that made your insides tingle. She'd never set foot inside a nuclear reactor, but she had a feeling the energy one gave off would have felt strikingly similar.

Ilsa lay there, cradling Andy like a baby and watching, dumbstruck, as Moroz assumed a relaxed pose some fifteen yards away. The ornate spear was in his left hand and he gripped what looked like a large sack in his right. His eyes swept the room, and her heart nearly jumped out of her chest as they fell on her. His brow knitted fiercely as he espied Andy's lifeless form, and he made a loud clicking sound with his tongue. The deer responded instantly, abandoning the fireplace and clopping further into the ballroom.

Ilsa's eyes turned to clam shells as she took in the remainder of the huge sleigh. Toward the back, lurked a pair of crouching creatures. At first, she thought they were demons, but upon closer inspection they seemed different. They were man-sized – that is if you considered an NFL offensive lineman man-sized – and heavily muscled. Their skin was lined with scars and similar to Loptr's in color, a cobalt blue. It was smoother, however, and lacked the reptilian scales, patches of fur, and overall knobbiness that disfigured his. The long blue-green hair on their heads was much the same, but was kept tied back, and they wore some sort of primeval clothing and armor – breastplates, vambraces, and greaves of a dark, chitinous metal.

It was their probing eyes, however, that reignited Ilsa's fear. They were the same gleaming red as the demon's and burned with that same, feral intensity. Then something dawned on her.

My God, are those . . . elves?

Her bewildered thoughts were waylaid by a sudden commotion that drew the intimidating pair's attention away from her and refocused it on their master.

Moroz had started toward the demon. His firelit face was bladed and cold, his features set in stone. He was still ten yards away when he muttered something. His voice was deep and whatever language he spoke was harsh and guttural. Try as she might, his words were lost on her.

All but one that is. She heard it distinctly.

Loptr.

He breathed it like a curse.

The demon's broad chest rose in response and its hateful gaze took a quick tour of the French doors leading outside. Ilsa got the distinct impression that it was torn between its unbridled hatred and a growing desire to flee. A heartbeat later, however, it made its decision. With a gnashing of fangs and murder in its eyes, it charged its ancient enemy.

Grim-faced, Moroz stepped forward to meet it. His left arm drew back and, faster than the eye could follow, he struck. The ten-foot spear slammed into the demon's solar plexus with what sounded like a thunderclap, lifting it off its feet and smashing it against the nearest column.

The three-story pillar shuddered from the impact but held, with Loptr pinned to it like some titanic scorpion, nailed to a wall. Greenish ichor and spittle sprayed from his gaping mouth as he tore at the spear shaft, trying and failing to free himself.

Moroz wasted no time. Tossing the sack to his minions, he stepped adroitly forward and grabbed hold of the spear's rune-coated haft with both hands. There was a low crackling sound as he twisted and torqued it from side to side, then he wrenched it free. With superhuman strength, he lifted his adversary into the air like a nine-hundred-pound shish kebab.

Ignoring the demon's frenzied flailing, Moroz held his weighty burden aloft and carried it toward the waiting "elves". As Ilsa gaped in disbelief, the pair stretched the sack's opening to impossible proportions. Then Moroz thrust Loptr inside. His already strained face contorted with contempt as he gave the spear's shaft a mighty shake, dislodging the demon and yanking the weapon free.

The waiting elves wasted no time and sprang into action. Cinching the end of the sack, they proceeded to wrap a stout leather thong around it, securely knotting it. The sides of the sack began to bulge as Loptr tore at it, trying to free himself by clawing his way through the thick material.

An annoyed look came over Moroz and he handed his gore-coated spear to the leaner of the two elves. Seizing the sack by the bound end, he hauled back and slammed it against a nearby column so hard the marble cracked. Once, twice, three times, the sack's imprisoned occupant struck solid stone with a force equivalent to a ten-story drop onto pavement. Finally satisfied, the big man handed the now inert sack back to the burlier elf, who stood there grinning.

Moroz exhaled heavily, then removed his soiled gloves and turned his attention to Ilsa. For some unknown reason, she felt strangely at peace as the imposing figure started toward her with a blue-skinned elf in tow.

As he stopped and dropped down on one knee, she felt the long-forgotten child in her rise to the fore. She smelled snow and pine forests and something she couldn't identify. Gooseflesh popped up all over her body and she stared blankly up at him. It was all so confusing. Her mind was a tornado of notions, all clamoring to be heard. There was so much she wanted to say, but as her lips parted she realized she'd somehow lost the ability to speak.

Moroz seemed to sense her predicament; his bearded face creased as he met and held her gaze. His sky-blue eyes were filled with more than just compassion; they held the wisdom of the ages. They--

Ilsa's gasp was a mouse-like squeak.

No, not eyes. *Eye.*

Moroz had a deep vertical scar on his right brow, starting an inch or two above the eyebrow. It ran through his ruined right eye and continued halfway down his cheek.

The great Northman was partially blind.

She couldn't believe it. For all his strength and power, and his ability to subdue a creature that could rend steel, he was not invulnerable. He could be hurt. Shame flooded her face, and her eyes fell to the floor.

Olek had proven that.

Ilsa's inhalation of surprise froze in her chest as Moroz reached out with one big hand. Gently gripping her chin with his thumb and forefinger, he carefully guided her gaze back up from the floor. His touch was soft and surprisingly warm and, as their eyes met, he smiled sadly.

A vision of her dying father doing that exact same thing began playing on the projection screen of her mind.

"Because that's what dads do . . ."

She started to tremble, and emotions she'd never thought she had filled her from the soles of her feet to the ends of her hair. The quaking stopped, however, as Moroz's one good eye bored into hers. An eerie calmness washed over her and she heard his voice inside her head.

Brave child of light, you will be alright.

The edges of his eyes tightened, however, as she realized she wouldn't. She stared mournfully down at Andy's lifeless body, then forlornly back up at her savior.

Moroz's brow furrowed up, then his gaze swung from her to the scary-looking elf loitering a few yards back. Something unspoken passed between them, causing it to drop down into a crouch. Without warning, it crept fluidly forward, its movements so hard to follow, it seemed to be made of quicksilver.

Ignoring her, the elf ran deft hands over Andy. Its fingertips shimmied as they passed over his wounds, then it lowered its pointy-eared head and started sniffing him, like a hound dog tracking its quarry. The seconds ticked by, then it looked up at Moroz and shook its maned countenance.

Ilsa felt fresh tears stream down her face as she fought to contain the grief that threatened to overwhelm her.

LA was right. His mom was always right.

Moroz wore an inscrutable look as he contemplated her. Then he sighed heavily and rested a callused palm atop Andy's bloodied chest. His head dipped, and a sorrowful look came over him. Then he rose and headed wordlessly back toward his sleigh with the elf in tow.

Ilsa felt a growing sense of numbness. She remained where she was, clutching Andy's body and watching sadly as the *real* Santa Claus prepared to walk out of her life.

He began making cooing sounds as he approached the giant stags, then reached out and started scratching them both under their furry chins. Meanwhile, the two elves picked up the demon-filled sack and made for the rear of the sleigh. They were almost there, when its enraged occupant sprang to life and started flailing so wildly, they dropped it.

A pissed-off look came over the pair. Then the more heavy-set of the two reached back over one shoulder and produced an ornate hammer of some kind. It was rune-carved and had a sizable metal head, like a maul or mallet. Rearing back, he inflicted a series of thunderous blows on the imprisoned fiend, some so powerful that bright sparks flew. He stopped only when any hint of movement had ceased.

Satisfied, the two seized the sack once more and tossed it and their unconscious prisoner aboard.

After a final look at the ruined ballroom, Santa climbed aboard. He took up position at the sledge's bow and quickly settled in. After a brief glance toward the back, he made a clicking noise and gave the sleigh's floorboards a thump from one booted foot. His chargers responded with a snort and a headshake, and immediately "put it in reverse".

Ilsa watched, mesmerized, as the sleigh and its occupants slowly retreated back into the fire. The deadly flames rose to welcome them, their brightness flaring to the point she had to hold a hand in front of her face to keep from going blind.

The muzzles of the deer were the last things to disappear from view. Then a dazzling flash followed that cast vertical shadows on the walls and, for the briefest of moments, turned night into day. Then the sleigh and all its occupants were gone, leaving Ilsa with nothing but colored motes dancing before her eyes.

The fire died down with surprising speed, and within seconds all that remained was a fast-fading collection of embers that hissed and crackled within the badly charred firebox.

Ilsa was alone.

CHAPTER 21

Ilsa sat there in a daze, trying and failing to come to terms with everything that had just happened. She could feel the "rational" portion of her mind hard at work in the background, determinedly trying to convince her she'd somehow imagined it all.

That was cute.

She would've laughed aloud if she'd had room for any more emotions.

The realization that the ordeal was over, that Loptr had been defeated and was no longer a threat, loomed large. But any relief she felt was overshadowed by the compiled tragedies of the last few days. She thought about all the families they'd tried and failed to save, including poor Olek, who'd lost both his wife and his livelihood.

Then there were the losses that affected her personally. Kareema was gone and so was her home. On top of that, she'd lost Andy.

For some reason, that last one hit her particularly hard. She hated to admit it, but the big lunkhead had really managed to get under her skin the last few days. Hell, there was more to it than that. After everything they'd been through, including the times he'd unhesitantly put himself in harm's way for her, he'd managed to worm his way into her heart.

And then, just like that, he was gone.

She glanced down at his bloodless face, so calm and still. He looked like a sleeping infant.

If only.

Just then, a brisk breeze passed through one of the mansion's shattered French doors and invaded the ballroom. She felt its icy claws dig into her, a chilling reminder of the warmth she'd come so close to having, but ultimately lost.

Was this her destiny? Was she to end up old and alone with no husband and no children of her own? How could that be? After all, there was magic in the world, *real* magic. She'd seen it with her own two eyes.

Was there none put aside for her?

Not even a *little*?

The wind continued to blow, forcing its way further into the chamber and ricocheting off its dome-shaped ceiling. Soon, the smoky haze that hovered above the now-charred fireplace dissipated.

Ilsa shined her tac-light at the defunct firebox. The flames were all gone, and the glittering embers it contained were fading fast. One by one, they winked out of existence, with hardly any ashes left behind. The stone was practically barren. The hillocks of antique furniture that had fueled the earlier blaze had been completely consumed, as had Ramirez's body, for that matter. She saw nothing to indicate he'd ever existed.

Wait.

No, not nothing.

Ilsa recoiled in surprise. There *was* something. Something small. She tightened her beam on the stone, just as the last of the embers disappeared.

Directly in front of the firebox was a cluster of some sort of blackish particles. Just ash, she surmised. As she espied the shape, however, she stared in wonder. It wasn't a numerical eight, as she'd expected. It was the shadowed remains of the lashed-together pieces of sleigh, the cross whose sharpened end she'd buried in Loptr's back.

She thought about getting up and collecting some of the ashes, or at least taking a photo of them with her phone. After all, it was proof of sorts. Proof that everything that had happened was real, no matter how her mind might try to convince her otherwise over the coming weeks, months, and years.

Before she had time to make up her mind, an even more powerful gust blew through. Swirling willy-nilly about the fireplace, it whisked the ashes into the air above her and scattered them.

Ilsa's heart sank as she watched the tiny particles shower down around her in slow motion, like glittering motes of dust. She reached up with her free hand in an attempt to touch one.

Only to jump and utter a squeal of unadulterated fright.

One of Andy's legs had . . . twitched?

A moment later, the dead man's eyes opened and he sucked in a tremendous breath, like a free diver who barely makes it to the surface.

"Oh, my aching head . . ." he groaned.

"Andy?!?" Ilsa felt her heart do a pole vault inside her chest. "Oh, my fucking God, you're alive?" She hugged him so hard it hurt them both. "I don't believe it; you're *alive!*"

The big man winced. "Yeah? Well, I *won't* be if you don't ease up on that sleeper hold, woman!"

"Oh, bite me, you big crybaby," she said as he grimaced and struggled to sit up. Her cheeks hurt from smiling so big, and she hurriedly wiped away a fresh batch of tears before he took note.

Andy blinked, then leaned forward at the waist and shook his head. "You know, you *really* need to stop saying that.

Someone could—" His neck and back went stud-straight and he looked alarmedly around. "Shit, the monster! Where's it—"

"Relax, big guy," Ilsa said, shushing him and resting a reassuring hand on his shoulder. "We're okay. It's gone."

"Gone? Are you sure?"

She nodded, her eyes brimming with hidden mirth. Teeth gritted, she pushed herself to her feet, her curvaceous form straightening as she paused to take stock of her condition. Her lower back and buttocks felt like the New York Yankees had used them for batting practice, and between the nail punctures, bruises, and second-degree burns, her left arm was pretty much shot. She shifted her weight cautiously from foot to foot, then nodded approvingly. At least her hip and leg seemed a bit better. She could stand, even move.

Praise the Lord, she thought. *Or someone* . . .

"Thank God, because I am totally dead." Andy exhaled long and low as he considered the mausoleum-like space surrounding them. One hand crept absentmindedly to his scalp and began exploring. A confused look crept over him and his lips quirked up. "Geez, how long was I out? Did I miss anything?"

Ilsa chuckled. "Quite a bit, actually." She reached down and offered him her good arm. "C'mon, I'll tell you about it over a cup of eggnog."

"Eggnog? You?"

"Sure, why not?" She uttered a grunt of discomfort as she wrestled him to his feet. "Okay, no eggnog for *you!* What did you have for dinner, an anvil?"

Andy grinned sheepishly. He started to step, but his legs buckled, forcing her to drape one of his arms across her shoulders. The increased load sent what felt like a jolt of electricity through her glutes and spinal erectors, but she set her jaw determinedly.

Her partner was definitely "worth the weight".

As they hobbled through the derelict ballroom, Ilsa found herself unexpectedly taken aback. She realized with more than a little discomfiture that she was starting to get turned on by Andy being pressed against her.

"So, how do you feel?" she asked, licking dry lips.

Andy pressed a fingertip against his lacerated pectorals and flinched. "I have a sore throat, and my chest feels like Mama June was twerking on it. How about you?"

Ilsa pursed her lips, then her brows went rock climbing. "Considering a thousand-pound demon with saw blades for teeth almost made a meal out of my vagina? I'm pretty good."

Andy smirked, then made a face as he checked his watch. "Shit, it's smashed. What time is it?"

"Past midnight."

"Are you sure?"

"Pretty sure."

He started patting himself with his free hand, as if to convince himself he was really there. "But, I, uh . . . I'm not dead."

"Not *yet*," she said, winking. A thought came to her, and she stopped and twisted around to look at him. He stared confusedly down at her as she reached up and pushed a stray lock away from his face. "By the way, uh, your hair. It's . . ."

"It's what?" Andy said, stiffening. A panicky look came over him and he began frantically exploring his coif, checking for loose hairs. "It's not falling out, is it? Please don't tell me I have to get a jar!"

Ilsa snickered. "No, silly. But it's turned white."

His forehead puckered. "Wait, when you say 'white', do you mean platinum-blonde, or are we talking actual--"

"Hold on," she said, digging for her cell. She snapped a quick photo and held the phone out. "Like the driven snow, babe."

Andy lifted an eyebrow. "Great . . . I'm twenty-nine-years-old and I look like fricking Santa Claus!"

Ilsa shook her head knowingly. "Nah, more like *Stripper Claus.*" She nudged him playfully with her hip. "Actually, I think it's very becoming. Sexy, even."

"Sexy, eh?" A calculating look replaced the dubious expression on his face. "Wait, does this mean you're experiencing an overwhelming desire to sit on my lap?"

His jaw dropped when she smirked, reached over, and gave one of his oh-so-firm butt cheeks an aggressive squeeze.

"You never know."

"Whoa! I hope you're not motivated by any *primal urges.*"

"Primal urges?" Ilsa's eyes lit up, then she did her best to imitate Andy's Brooklyn accent. "Fuhgeddaboudit!"

The two burst out laughing. Their guffaws ended abruptly, however, as an unearthly groan echoed throughout the ballroom. The unmistakable sound of debris shifting followed.

Ilsa's heart sprang into her throat.

There was something out there – something moving in the darkness.

Instinctively reaching for Andy's hand, she pointed her torch at the source of the disturbance. The sounds of movement continued, then a hulking form emerged from the blackness. It started toward them, heading for the light.

Was it possible? Had Loptr somehow returned?

Ilsa felt her flight-or-flight instinct kick in, along with a boat-load of adrenaline. She was about to yell to Andy to make a break for it, when a dust-covered form emerged and began staggering toward them. It was a man. A big one. Whoever he was, he was limping badly and cupping his crotch.

"Tokaido!" Andy exclaimed, beaming. "When did *you* get here?" He looked around and swept the area with his own flashlight. "Where's your partner?"

"He's gone," the big Japanese said, carefully skirting an upended piece of furniture. His right pants leg was torn and caked with dried blood, and his bloated left arm appeared to be sporting the mother of all compound fractures. His eyes tightened as he gazed fearfully around. "I guess you could say he, uh . . . he lost his head."

Andy shrugged and grinned affably. "Wouldn't be the first time. He's a bad penny, that one. No worries. I'm sure he'll turn up."

Ilsa's neck tensed as she and Tokaido exchanged doubtful glances. There was an awkward silence, then the three turned and began making their way out of the wreckage-strewn chamber. Both men tried walking on their own, but soon settled for resting one hand each on Ilsa's shoulders. Behind them, creepy, creaking sounds emanated from the now-darkened fireplace as it cooled.

Tokaido looked back worriedly, then he noticed Andy's hair. "Yo, 'Snow White'. What the hell happened here?"

A bittersweet smile twisted Ilsa's lips. "It's a very old, very long story."

"Yeah?" Well, who's gonna call it in?"

"You can do it."

Tokaido blanched. "Yeah, screw *that*. *I'm* not calling this in. Are you crazy?"

Ilsa's eyes danced with merriment as she indicated her partner. "No, but the captain thinks Andy is."

"Yeah, that's right," Tokaido nodded vigorously. "Alvilda, *you* should call it in."

"Not a chance," Andy remarked. "And speaking of 'crazy', Dunbar, you never told me what you said to our waitress, back at the diner."

As she felt her face pinken, Ilsa developed an instant affinity for the surrounding darkness. "I didn't? Oh, no problem." She pulled him a few yards away and pressed her lips hotly to his ear. "I told her that you . . ."

Tokaido's face screwed up and he turned his back in an effort to distance himself from whatever was being said.

All of a sudden, Andy went ramrod straight. "What?!? Are you out of your mind, woman?"

Ilsa smirked as she batted her eyelashes coquettishly. "That's what they tell me. Oh, and before I forget--" She grabbed Andy by the ears and kissed him on the mouth. "Merry Christmas!"

"Seriously?" Tokaido scoffed and shook his head, then gripped his injured testicles and resumed limping. "Great . . ." he drawled. "Not only have I been emasculated, now I'm gonna be sick!"

EPILOGUE

The sleigh glimmered in the pre-dawn darkness as it hung suspended, ten meters above the ice-strewn waters of the Arctic Ocean. Twilight had yet to raise its hoary head, and the skies above the dark-hued conveyance and its chargers were aglow with the splendor of the northern lights. It was a firework display beyond compare: shimmering waves of teal, green, and gold; they danced and dazzled as they lit up the dark and reflected off the surging seas below.

The entity known as the Wanderer stood by his vessel's helm. His gruff, bearded face was impassive, booted feet braced, and big hands clasped behind his back. A brisk wind kicked up, armed with tiny shards of ice, and he breathed it in. The cold and stinging crystals were as nothing to him, but the gusts were beginning to cause the sleigh to sway.

He made a dismissive gesture, calming the irksome turbulence.

As the wind died down, a sudden nickering caused his glacial eyes to drop. They ended up on Dvalinn and Duneyrr's broad backs, and he grinned as the pair shifted against their traces, locking antlers and playfully jostling one another.

The huge harts were happy to be back. They were all happy. And back.

All, that is, except Geri and Freki.

The Wanderer's granite expression softened. He missed his wolves terribly. Fortuitously absent when he and the others had been struck down, the unruly beasts had found themselves masterless. They'd been free to wander the globe. And wander they had. As far as he could tell, they were roaming Canada's largely unexplored Northwest Territories, where they spent their days hunting bear and moose and spreading panic among the poor Inuit.

They called them *Amarok*.

The Wanderer stroked his beard and took a moment to revel in the sounds of the roiling waves. All around them lay the foreboding vastness of the Eurasian Basin. But it was what lay below those waters that had brought them hence.

The Litke Deep.

The deepest water in the region, the oceanic trench plummeted to an astonishing 5,449 meters – deeper than his beloved Alps were tall. He nodded. With its unplumbed depths shrouded in eternal blackness and numbing cold, the submarine chasm was well-suited for his needs.

Behind him, he could hear Víðarr and Váli grunting and muttering as they struggled to finish their task. The preparations were almost complete.

The deed would soon be done.

Although not soon enough.

A sudden squeal curtailed the Wanderer's musings. The pungent smell of salmon washed over him as he stepped to the sled's port side, the floorboards creaking beneath his weight. A pod of killer whales had gathered below, a family of a full dozen animals. Curious by nature, the black and white creatures swam in wide circles, their sail-like dorsal fins slicing through the waves and tiny eyes peering upward.

He wore a pleased look. He'd always liked Orcas. The huge dolphins were surprisingly intelligent and communicative, not to mention fearsome predators. It was good to see them, even if these particular individuals had no memory of him.

The Wanderer's smile slipped as his head swiveled toward the rear of the sledge. He closed his eyes and sent a quick coda to the pod's battle-scarred matriarch. She responded with a snort-like blast of water vapor, then sent a series of clicks and whistles to her extended family. They responded instantly, gathering together in a wedge-shaped formation, their door-sized flukes propelling them forward. They began to move off and, within moments, were lost from view.

He pursed his lips. It was a relief to see that, unlike many species, the Orcas had not been eradicated in his absence. So much had changed. So many other creatures had been less fortunate.

The Wanderer's silvery brows knitted up and he focused his attention on the nighttime sky. Further and further, he scried, until his gaze pierced even the *aurora borealis*.

Above the sleigh's position, he spotted an assortment of winged craft. From horizon to horizon, there were nearly a score of them, soaring like great white birds. He was familiar with planes, but far above them were other mechanical contrivances, the likes of which he'd never before seen. As he watched, they raced through the void of space at speeds that rivaled his own, their trajectories suggesting they orbited the very Earth itself.

His eyes lidded and he concentrated, his myriad senses soaring as he took in the world around him. His brows crept slowly upward. It was no wonder things felt different.

There had been a noticeable shift in the planet's magnetic field. Despite his initial bemusement, he was unvexed by the discovery.

It was inevitable. Every few dozen millennia, the poles shifted. The last occurrence had coincided with his birth. This time, his rebirth.

The ice was being affected as well. It was melting in some regions, piling up in others. Such was the way of things. There was naught to do but adapt.

Nature is something to be tolerated, not tamed.

The Wanderer pressed further, and his nose crinkled up. Mankind had made impressive progress while he'd been gone. but it had all been technical. As a society they had deteriorated, and the earth was decaying along with them. Moral turpitude was now the norm, and the violence, greed, and corruption he detected rivaled that of the late Roman Empire.

Still, there was hope. His thoughts returned to the young couple he'd rescued from Loptr and the corners of his mouth cranked up. A rare breed, those two; they were reminiscent of a modern-day Askr and Embla. They put the needs of others before their own, and had showed admirable courage in the face of overwhelming adversity.

This world – *his* world – needed more like that.

Many more.

As the Wanderer fixed his eyes on the horizon, his expression turned stony once more. Dawn would soon be upon them, and the bands of ionized particles that concealed him from prying eyes would dissipate. Time was running out. They needed to--

"Wuotan, it is done."

He turned to find Váli's sweat-streaked face staring up at him. Behind him, his brother stood with his hands on his hips, overseeing the now trussed-up sack. Its sides were so bulged, it looked like it contained an ox.

Víðarr stepped proudly back and inclined his head as his master moved to inspect the pair's work.

The sack itself was made of a unique elastomeric material; it was incredibly tough and tear resistant. But now, in addition, it was encapsulated by a dense mesh of heavy chains and padlocks, many of which had links as thick as a child's forearm.

The Wanderer wore an inscrutable look as he crouched down and ran his fingers along the rune-inscribed fetters, gauging the power of their charms. Then, without warning, he seized a meter-long section and tore at it with all his prodigious strength. The seconds ticked by, then he uttered a grunt of satisfaction. The adamantine would hold. It had taken a great deal of energy to create so much of the numinous metal, so soon. Not to mention the mystical wards he'd bestowed upon the links and locks. But he'd had no choice.

The bloodthirsty demi-jötunn they'd bound had claimed too many lives.

His vendetta-fueled rampages must cease.

He turned to Váli and Víðarr and gestured at the water. He could see the disapproval in their eyes. They would rather see their former comrade disemboweled and decapitated – preferably, with them in the roles of executioners.

He faulted them not. If anything, he was likeminded.

But Loptr was no longer of the fae. He was a true demon: the embodiment of evil. Slaying him would release all of that darkness back into the ether. The effects would ripple outward, like a pebble tossed into a pond. He'd seen one Pandora's box opened. He didn't care to see another.

No. Loptr would pay for his crimes.

Harshly.

He would spend eternity imprisoned at the bottom of a lightless abyss. And as long as there was an ocean above him he would remain there, bereft of sight and sound and blanketed in suffocating cold. Unable to die, he would drown and revive, then drown and revive again – repeating the agonizing process over and over into perpetuity. But most of all, he would never again revel in the screams of his victims, nor glut himself on their bodies and souls.

His fell deeds were at an end.

The Wanderer folded his arms across his chest and watched as his jötnar effortlessly hoisted their still unconscious captive aloft.

Then they tossed the sack over the side.

There was no ceremony, no words spoken. It was like disposing of the contents of a chamber pot. Weighed down by its contents and five hundred kilos of adamant, the sack landed like a geyser and sank like a stone. He watched it for a time as it spiraled down into the darkness, but by the time it passed the thousand-meter mark he became bored. Pushing off the gunwales, he praised Váli and Víðarr in their primitive tongue, then headed back to the helm.

After settling in, the Wanderer signaled the sleigh's chargers. The great stags sprang eagerly to life and started smoothly forward, the multi-ton craft they drew following so silently, it seemed made of mist.

He relaxed back in his seat and watched as his team maneuvered. Per his commands, they arced smoothly about until the rays of the rising sun were at their backs. Then they began to accelerate.

Within moments, they were chasing night.

Faster and faster, they traveled, until nautical twilight became midnight, and everything around them a blur.

Eventually, their speed eclipsed even that of the artificial satellites, orbiting high above. The shimmering waters of the North Atlantic began to churn beneath their sharp-edged hooves. A few minutes more, and North America's Eastern seaboard hove into view.

Ahead, skyscrapers gleamed in the distance like giant, lit-up trees. As he espied them, his ageless eyes danced with merriment. It was still Christmas in this part of the world and he had gifts to deliver.

Oh, yes. Many, many gifts . . .

THE END

We hope you've enjoyed The Sleigh by Max Hawthorne. For updates on Max's next book and other exciting projects, go to www.maxhawthorne.com

Also, by Max Hawthorne

Kronos Rising
Kronos Rising: Kraken (Vol. 1)
Kronos Rising: Kraken (Vol. 2)
Kronos Rising: Kraken (Vol. 3)
Kronos Rising: Diablo
Kronos Rising: Plague
Memoirs of a Gym Rat
I Want a Tyrannosaurus for Christmas
Monsters & Marine Mysteries
Kronos Rising: Purgatory

ABOUT THE AUTHOR

Max Hawthorne is an American author and screenwriter. Referred to as the "Prince of Paleofiction", he is best known for his *Kronos Rising* series of sci-fi suspense thrillers which have garnered both *Book of the Year* and *People's Choice* awards. He is the Amazon #1 bestselling author of the cryptid research book, *Monsters & Marine Mysteries*, as well as *Memoirs of a Gym Rat*, an outrageous exposé of the health club industry, and the heartwarming children's book *I Want a Tyrannosaurus for Christmas*. His song, *A Tyrannosaurus for Christmas*, peaked at #2 on the *2021 World Indie Charts Top 100* and stayed there for three weeks. He has been interviewed by both *The Washington Post* and *Fangoria* magazine, and has appeared on QVC, *Coast-to-Coast AM*, *Spaced Out Radio*, and in *A Tribe Called Quest's* rap video, *I Left My Wallet in El Segundo*.

Max was born in Brooklyn and attended school in Philadelphia, where he graduated from the *University of the Arts*. In addition to being a bestselling novelist, he is a singer/songwriter, independent paleontologist, cryptid researcher, Blog Talk Radio host, IGFA world-record-holding angler, and a Voting Member of the Author's Guild. Max is an avid sportsman and conservationist. His hobbies include archery, fishing, boating, boxing, and collecting fossils and antiquities. He lives in the Greater Northeast with his wife, daughter, and a pair of enormous Siberian Forest Cats who, when they're not stalking Max's toes, sleep on his desk as he writes.

Printed in Great Britain
by Amazon